TO HAVE
or to hold

TO HAVE
or to hold

Josi S. Kilpack

Bonneville Books
Springville, Utah

ISBN: 1-55517-842-1
v.1

Published by Bonneville Books,
an imprint of Cedar Fort, Inc.
925 N. Main Springville, Utah, 84663
www.cedarfort.com

Distributed by:

Cover design by Nicole Williams
Cover design © 2005 by Lyle Mortimer

Printed in the United States of America
10 9 8 7 6 5 4 3 2 1

Printed on acid-free paper

DEDICATION

To Lee. Of all the finer things in life, you are by far the very best. Thank you for all the having and all the holding.

ACKNOWLEDGMENTS

Thanks to Julie Wright, Rachel Ann Nunes, Anne Bradshaw, and Carole Thayne for reading this manuscript. Their combined feedback helped me iron out the rough spots and make the story work. Thanks to BJ Rowley, who once again edited the final manuscript and kept me from sounding like the grammatical idiot I am at heart.

Thank you to my anonymous contact who explained to me what Hyperemesis Gravidarum is and how truly debilitating it can be. I can't thank you enough for answering my many questions, sharing your very personal heartbreak, and inspiring me with your strength. I hope that life gets better from here on out; you've earned it.

Thanks to the members of LDStorymakers for your continued friendship and answers to my endless questions—we are birds of a feather. I am grateful to you all for many reasons.

Thanks to the Cedar Fort staff for helping yet another novel see the light of day, and thank you to all the readers who gave them reason to do so.

Thank you to my family and friends who cheer me on, especially my sweetheart, Lee, and our wonderful kids. I couldn't write a word without their continual love, support, and enthusiasm. All of my books revolve around family—I can't imagine life without mine.

And as always, I thank my Father in Heaven for all of the above. When I take time to count my blessings, I am truly in awe of the One that gave them all to me.

CHAPTER 1

October

*E*mma pulled into the driveway at ten minutes to six. She could still smell the nursing home on her clothes—a nauseating mixture of Lysol, pork roast, and other old-people smells she preferred not to dwell on. Between eight hours of work and two hours of CPR training, it had been a long day. So long that all she wanted to do was shower, put a bag of popcorn in the microwave, and watch reruns of ER all night. The thought was deliciously tempting until a set of large, multi-colored, plastic keys sailed over her shoulder and rattled across the dashboard of her five-year-old Toyota. She looked into the back seat and reprioritized her evening.

Her daughter, Catherine, reached toward her, straining against the car seat.

"I guess you're ready to get out," Emma said with a weary smile. After undoing her own seat belt, she opened the car door and proceeded to release her fifteen-month-old daughter from the safety of restraining nylon straps.

On the way to her basement apartment, she picked up

the mail and tucked it under one arm. Inside, she turned on the TV for Catherine before thumbing through the mail, hoping there would be no bills today since the paycheck she'd received last Friday was already spent and the next one didn't come for ten days. When she encountered a cream-colored envelope with swirling gold ink across the front, her whole body was instantly washed with heat, and her stomach turned. With slow, careful movements, she tore open the envelope as she sank onto a kitchen chair. The photo landed in her lap as if Jake had somehow planned it that way.

There was her husband—ex-husband for the last four months actually—with his arms around a beautiful blonde—Emma's replacement. They had agreed that they would inform one another if and when either of them planned to remarry. *Couldn't he have just told his attorney?* Then his attorney could have called her attorney, who in turn could have called her with the news. But that wouldn't have hurt like this—Jake knew her well enough to know that. After taking a breath and lifting her glasses just enough to wipe at her still-dry eyes, in case a tear had escaped unnoticed, she flipped open the announcement. It was a sadistic thing to do, but she couldn't help it. After reading the first few lines, she removed her glasses and closed her eyes as the tears rushed through on a new wave of hurt and bitterness. The invitation fell from her hands. Careful not to draw her daughter's attention, she quickly shut herself in the bathroom.

Emma put down the toilet lid and sat down with a thud, dropping her face into her hands. The divorce had only been final for four months. Four months was all it took for Jake to get on with his life, as if she'd never been a part of it. Before she knew it, she was sobbing, reacting to the news at a degree that surprised her. Self-pity enveloped her like water around a drowning man, and she wondered how it was possible that anyone expected her to live a normal life again.

Every morning she woke up, took care of their daughter, went to work, paid the bills—all the normal things normal people did. *And what for?* All the dreams she'd had were gone. She had no husband, no home, and little hope for the future. Yet Jake, the beginning and end of all her happy plans, was getting married—again. *This cannot be my life!* Her brain was buzzing, her heart beating fast; even her stomach hurt in a physical reaction to her emotional state. It was one more blow, and she hadn't yet recovered from the first beating.

"Emma?" a voice called through the door.

Emma lifted her head and wondered how long she'd been in there.

"Emma, are you okay?"

She recognized Lacey's voice and wished she'd go away. Lacey was her sister-in-law, the wife of her brother Chris. When Emma had moved to Utah three months ago, she'd considered herself lucky to find this basement apartment just two houses away from Chris's family. But, right now all she wanted was privacy. "Yeah, I . . . I'm fine," she said as she stood and wiped the mascara smudges from her cheeks. When she opened the door several seconds later, Lacey was standing there with Catherine on her hip and a look of concern on her face. Lacey's two daughters were playing in the living room. As soon as Catherine saw her mother, she strained forward. Emma took her and held her against her chest, wishing she could lose her pain through the contact but knowing she couldn't.

"We came to see if you wanted to have dinner with us. I let myself in when you didn't answer the door." Lacey paused, looking a little guilty. "I found the announcement on the floor," she admitted after a moment. "I can't believe he sent one to you."

Emma's lip started quivering as she moved Catherine's head to one shoulder. She shook her head. She hated it when emotions got the best of her, especially in front of other people—especially when they were perfectly normal people with normal lives and regarded her with so much irritating sympathy.

"If you'd rather not have dinner with us, why don't I take

Cate for the evening?" Lacey offered. Emma shook her head again and pulled Catherine tighter, but Catherine pulled away, and Emma put her down, watching as she toddled back to the living room to join her cousins. She looked back up at Lacey.

Emma hadn't had much involvement with her siblings and their families before now—her life had been too different. She and Lacey still had almost nothing in common. Whereas Lacey was short, stocky, and blonde, Emma was dark-haired, five foot ten inches tall, and shaped like a broomstick. Lacey was also the epitome of the sweet Mormon wife. She stayed home with her two daughters and taught Primary every Sunday. Her biggest worry in life was whether or not her food storage was up to date—or so it seemed.

Emma, on the other hand, was only just coming back to the Church after several "prodigal" years in Babylon. She'd once said the S-word in front of Lacey, leaving her speechless.

"She's been gone all day," Emma finally said. "I need her with me."

"If you're sure."

Emma nodded. Besides, she didn't want to burden them any more than she already did. She wanted to sail through this with no one being the wiser to her pain. But the look on Lacey's face told her she'd failed at that already. *Great. One more failure to add to the list.*

Lacey put a hand on Emma's arm and looked at her with concern. "You don't have to pretend it doesn't hurt, Emma."

Emma looked at the floor and finally nodded, hating the spotlight she felt shining down on what was still a deeply private and personal pain.

"Thanks, Lacey. I'll let you know if I need anything."

Lacey nodded before gathering her girls and leaving. With her playmates gone, Catherine ran back to her mother. Together they made stroganoff for dinner. Catherine mostly played with Tupperware, but Emma was glad for the companionship. As she moved about the kitchen, she couldn't help but reflect on her life again. Or what was left of it.

When Jake left six months ago, she'd moved back home to Oklahoma to live with her parents. They were in the process of filling out their mission papers. Their excitement had been tempered by their youngest daughter's latest crisis, but she insisted they go on with it, that she could take care of herself. Emma's older sister, Camilla, and her family were going to stay in the house while their parents were gone, and although they offered Emma a room, she declined. Camilla was constantly advising Emma on her life, and Emma hated it. Instead, she asked her brothers for advice, and that had brought her to Utah. Two weeks ago her parents had left for Ontario, Canada, where they would stay for the next eighteen months.

In addition to Chris and Lacey and their two daughters, Emma's oldest brother, Tally, also lived in Utah, thirty miles north of Bountiful in a little town named Willard. Tally and his wife, Janet, had a daughter, Miranda, who was five months old, and Tally had adopted Janet's four-year-old son from her previous marriage. Emma hadn't known either of her sisters-in-law well before coming here; however, they had both been kind, accepting, and encouraging. Lacey was always offering to watch Catherine and inviting them to dinner. Emma shook her head as the scales of comparison showed all of her deficiencies. She wished her life was as well put together as Lacey's was. Sometimes she hated Lacey for being so perfect.

After dinner Emma gave Catherine a bath, momentarily free from the weight of her circumstances as she piled soap bubbles on her daughter's hair and made gurgling noises with the toys. Catherine giggled and splashed, and until Emma put her to bed a short time later she was feeling better. She finally showered, fully releasing herself from work for the day, and put on a pair of old, gray sweats she'd owned since high school. There was a yellowing stain on the left thigh and a cigarette burn on the front, but years of washing had made them soft and comfortable. She twisted her long dark brown hair into a bun and wrapped it up with a green scrunchie she found in the drawer. It had been three days since she'd had a cigarette, but she needed one now and grabbed the pack out of her dresser drawer. She never smoked in front of Catherine, and she was trying to quit, but a little nicotine right now would make her feel better, and it was all she had at the moment.

The announcement lying on the table mocked her when she entered the kitchen area on her way to the front door. She narrowed her eyes as she put down the cigarettes and picked it up. With one effective squeeze of her fist, she crumpled the photo and card stock in her hand as she walked to the kitchen sink. She turned on the water, flipped the switch that activated the disposal, and stuffed the invitation and photo through the black hole. The blades strained as they shredded the thick paper, and she smiled at the dramatic moment. The disposal returned to its original whirl, but she continued to stare into the sink. If only she could get over Jake so easily, just flip a switch and watch him disappear. It was so unfair that she couldn't discard him the way he had discarded her. She remembered his words that night when he left. "I just don't love you anymore, Emma. I haven't for a long time." The memory seared through her tonight as it had all those months ago. Had he any idea what it felt like to hear such a statement from the person you loved? Would he ever know? She hoped so. She hoped his new little wife broke his heart into teeny tiny pieces and then sent *him* the announcement when she got married to *her* next husband.

With a sigh she finally turned off the disposal and went outside. It was cold, so she huddled around herself and lit up, fully enjoying every breath. She would quit again tomorrow. After all the feelings of hurt over the last year, through the separation and divorce, it surprised her that she could feel even more empty and alone than she had thus far. She'd loved Jake so much, going against everything she'd been taught be with him; and now it was over, and she was left with nothing. All the grand dreams she'd had—every one of them—were gone, and she didn't know how to mold what she had left into any semblance of a future. Never in her life had she wondered how she would make it as a divorced single mother at the age of twenty-one. Not until now anyway. Now the thought consumed her every waking moment.

After snuffing out the butt a few minutes later and letting the wind blow the smoke from her clothes and hair, she went back inside and got ready for bed. Lying in the dark, she wondered when she would not feel like a boulder was sitting on her chest. How long would it take to feel like there was once again some point to her existence? Another tear slid down her cheek when she realized she had no answers.

CHAPTER 2

$\mathcal{T}$he next day dawned bright and clear. Catherine woke up earlier than usual and they made a breakfast of pancakes and scrambled eggs before taking a chilly, and therefore short, walk in the autumn sun. It was early October and rather than dwell on the dark evening, Emma focused on the beauties of the season and tried to ignore her strong desire for a cigarette. It was her day off, and she *lived* for her days off.

As soon as they walked in the door, Emma glanced at the clock. "Oh, we'd better hurry and get ready, girlfriend," she said to Catherine who was trying to pull off her gloves. Emma's hair was pulled up in a ponytail, and she had no makeup on—not that it mattered. She brushed her teeth and packed a diaper bag. Wednesday, her scheduled day off from the nursing home, was the day she ran her errands, went to appointments, and cleaned the house of the phantom Mr. Andrew Davidson.

She'd found the online ad for a housekeeper just before she moved to Utah. She'd called and spoken to his secretary, explaining her circumstances and almost begging for the job. Mr. Davidson had owned a condo in Salt Lake until last winter when he'd decided to sell it and buy a house instead. He was looking for someone to manage and clean the house for him, keeping it ready should he come to town. The job had sounded perfect to Emma, especially since Catherine could go with her most of the time. When the secretary had called her back the next day, she'd felt things were looking up.

Even after finding the full-time position at the nursing home, she'd continued to care for Mr. Davidson's house on her day off. She was paid almost five hundred dollars a month for her few hours a week, and the extra income was going into a savings account for school.

She arrived around eleven and marveled again, as she had each time for the last three months, at this incredible house.

Andrew Davidson owned some kind of construction company or something based out of Los Angeles. Besides this house in Salt Lake, he had an apartment in L.A. Emma thought his living arrangements were backwards. If it were her and she was determined to have a residence in Utah, she'd have the *house* in L.A. and the *apartment* in Utah. Mr. Davidson had a pool put in during the summer with a sun room built around it, attaching it to the house. The pool filled most of what used to be the back yard. A pool man had come to oversee it every other week since its completion, but Mr. Davidson had only come to town once since she'd started working for him. Since she came on Wednesdays, and he'd come on the weekend, she hadn't met him.

Emma's job was to clean the house and coordinate the other service companies and decorators that popped in from time to time. She basically kept the house running the way Mr. Davidson wanted it with the understanding that when the ski resorts opened, he would spend nearly every weekend in Utah. She'd never met nor spoken to Mr. Davidson, communicating with his secretary when necessary. Sometimes she wondered if he existed at all.

Over the months, furniture had been delivered, walls had been painted, and plants had been added throughout the house. It was beautiful but cold. Just as you'd expect of a house that stood empty all the time. Emma had insisted on double locks and an alarm on the pool room door—Mr. Davidson hadn't even questioned it, and his secretary had given her permission to have whatever security on the pool she thought was necessary. She'd gotten the best, so there was no risk in bringing Catherine to this palace.

There was a huge aquarium of beautiful tropical fish in the living room; this was where Catherine spent the first half hour of every visit, watching the fish, tapping the glass, and singing to them in toddler talk. A mechanical feeding system fed the fish every day. Emma refilled the food cartridge and snapped it back in place on the top of the aquarium. They would now live another week.

She shook her head at the excessive lifestyle, refused to dwell on how unfair life was, and went upstairs to set up the portable crib in one of the spare bedrooms. After returning to the main floor, she peeked at Cate, still happily immersed with her little fish friends. Emma took the baby monitor out of her diaper bag and plugged it in, clipping the beeper-sized receiver to the waistband of her jeans. Then she headed for the kitchen, easily her favorite room in the house.

To get to the kitchen, she had to go through the living room, past the solarium and study, and through the dining room with its massive cherrywood table and ten matching chairs. The kitchen almost wasn't a part of the rest of the house. Rather, it was its own separate world, complete with its own sitting room, fireplace, and television.

Emma pushed open the swinging door that separated it from the dining room and smiled. Sheer luxury. For just a second, she took in the marble floors, granite countertops, olive wood cabinets, double oven, and flat stove. She loved to cook, and each time she entered this room she fantasized about the wonderful creations she could make here.

Only a countertop separated the cooking area from the sitting room, keeping the room open and bright as sun filtered in the two six-foot windows on either side of the TV. There was a switch on the wall that pulled the shades—amazing. Her whole apartment could fit into this room. If given the choice, she'd gladly trade and sleep on the floor snuggled up next to a 9x13 baking dish.

From the closet in the sitting room she retrieved her cleaning supplies and reflected on how coming here was like living a double life. When she was here, she felt powerful, capable; the house and all its entailments relied on her to keep it going. She knew it was silly to feel that way since she was only a housekeeper, but for whatever reason it was a huge ego boost to be a part of this place. When she left, she'd be the bitter single mother again, struggling to get out of bed in the morning. Andrew Davidson's house was her own fantasy world. She loved Wednesdays, and yet the fact that she enjoyed it so much made her feel that much more pathetic—but she rarely let herself look at it that close.

Three hours later, Emma was packing up the crib while Cate watched a video in the sitting room. The monitor clipped to her pants transferred the muted sounds of the TV. Just as she finished zipping up the crib case there was a knock at the door. "The wayward plant man," she muttered under her breath as she went to open the door. Sure enough, the white polo shirt on the skinny teenager read *Plantitorium*.

"You're late," she said as she let him in.

"I am?" he said with feigned surprise as he passed by.

She rolled her eyes as she shut the door behind him and without a word returned to packing the crib. She'd called the company twice in the last month to confirm that they had a standing appointment for one o'clock every Wednesday afternoon. They always agreed that they did, and yet they were never on time.

Less than five minutes later, he announced that he was done.

"Done, as in finished?" she asked with surprise.

"Yep." He headed for the door.

Quickly she reviewed where she knew he had gone and

where she knew he hadn't. "Did you get the potted plants in the solarium?"

"Sure did."

Emma knew he hadn't because the solarium door had a little frog croak that sounded anytime someone opened it, and she hadn't heard it. You couldn't miss a croaking frog in an empty house. "And the master bath? There's a lot of ivy up there. Are you sure you got it?"

"Yep, I'll see you next week."

She let him go and then filled up a watering can and went through the house herself. Before she put Catherine in the car, she called the number by the phone for the *Plantitorium*. She told the receptionist that Mr. Davidson would no longer require their services since it was apparent that not only was it impossible for them to come at the appointed time, but their prepubescent help wasn't doing his job. Then she locked up the house for another week and pulled out of the driveway to return to her two-bedroom basement apartment, complete with mismatched furniture, a broken dishwasher, and one electrical outlet per room.

CHAPTER 3

*A*ndrew Davidson glanced at his watch and let out a breath as he pushed his chair back from the conference table. It was a mistake to have come. He stood up and proceeded to the door. He wasn't the kind of man that gave in to fanciful possibilities—he shouldn't have fallen prey to this one.

When he'd received the letter two weeks ago asking him to schedule an appointment with an attorney concerning a Davidson family trust, he'd been unable to resist. He'd set up the appointment, cleared his schedule for the day, and tried to remember everything he'd ever been told about the man whose name he'd inherited. There was little to recall.

Richard Davidson, Andrew's father, was born into a wealthy family but had been disowned after years of drug addiction and disappointment. When Andrew was two years old, his mother, Karen, had given up on Richard too. For five years, she'd endured her husband's depraved life of nothingness, and she was no longer willing to do so. She took her young son and moved to Las Vegas, Nevada, where she got a job as a cocktail waitress while the divorce was held up by one legal technicality after another.

Just two weeks after Andrew's third birthday, nearly a year after Karen had originally filed for divorce, Richard died of a heroin overdose, making all the legal difficulties moot. Richard had been thirty-five years old, only six years older than Andrew was now. Despite Richard's lavish lifestyle, he'd died a pauper and left Karen and Andrew with only a $10,000 insurance policy which Karen used to pay off her divorce lawyer. It hadn't been a happy marriage, and since it became a miserable divorce it wasn't a subject she cared to speak of often.

Andrew grew up in Las Vegas, surrounded by other children of single mothers. He never thought much about his paternal ancestry, other than when his mother demanded that he not turn out to be a bum like his father.

Andrew had worked very hard to do right by his mom in that way, but finding out there was some kind of trust fund connected to the family he knew nearly nothing about piqued his interest. This morning he'd flown from his apartment in Los Angeles to San Jose, where the attorney's office was located. Now, after cooling his heels for twenty minutes, he was ready to cut his losses and chalk up his insanity to depraved nostalgia over a man he barely remembered and a family he'd never met. When the Davidsons had turned their backs on their drug addict son, they had turned their backs on his little family too. Andrew had grown up a latchkey kid in the Vegas projects with never two coins in his pocket. But he wouldn't have had it any other way. He had gotten where he was now all by himself, and it made his success that much sweeter. He didn't need or want them or their money now.

His hand was inches away from the door knob when it turned, causing him to pause and quickly step back to avoid getting hit with the door as it opened. A short, round man with wire-rimmed glasses and a fringe of gray hair swirling his bald-spotted head looked up at Andrew and nodded.

"I'm sorry to keep you waiting, Mr. Davidson," the man said as he stuck out his hand. From the tone of his voice,

Andrew guessed he not only made a habit of making people wait, but he expected people to do so without complaint. "I'm Mr. Austin, a partner of this firm, and if you'd take a seat we can go over the stipulations of the trust."

Andrew wavered for a moment; he had a lot to do in L.A. and was offended to have been kept waiting so long. Yet, his curiosity was still getting the better of him. He finally nodded and headed back to the seat he'd just vacated moments before. Besides his curiosity, he'd always run his business by his gut, and his gut told him it was worth his time to stick around. Once seated, the other man smiled politely and passed Andrew a spiral-bound folder with his name on the cover. He kept an identical folder for himself.

"I'll get right to the point, Mr. Davidson," Mr. Austin said, opening his folder and clearing his throat twice. "The Davidson family has a trust account that you'll be eligible to receive on your thirtieth birthday. This meeting is to inform you of the stipulations and requirements associated with this trust, as well as its limitations and provisions."

Questions began swirling around like bees in Andrew's head, but Mr. Austin didn't give him time to ask anything before continuing. "Let me fill you in on the full spectrum, and then I'll answer any questions."

Andrew nodded and began thumbing through the folder as Mr. Austin found the page he wanted to start with. Andrew bit back his questions and forced himself to look comfortable.

Mr. Austin didn't waste any time. "This trust was established in 1918 by your great-grandfather. The trust was to continue for as long as there were sufficient funds and is available to all legitimate male descendants of the Edward Davidson line." His monotone voice droned on as if the details of this trust were of no interest to him whatsoever. He may as well have been a plumber fixing a sink. "The trust is payable only if all the following requirements are met.

"First, the heir's father must have received the trust payoff. Second, the heir must have completed at least two years of upper-level education. Third, the heir must be of sound mind. Fourth, the heir must be in a stable marriage for the duration of at least one year with the added—"

"Whoa, wait a minute," Andrew interrupted. "What—"

"Please let me finish, Mr. Davidson. Now where was I? . . . Oh, yes, there can be no current legal actions pertaining to the absolution of the marriage. Your wife must use Davidson as her legal name, and you must reside at the same address. The fifth and final stipulation mandates that no legal action can be instituted against the trust. If any one of these requirements are not fulfilled in whole, the trust is forfeited." Mr. Austin looked up, his face deadpan as he continued. Andrew's head was spinning. "I've learned enough about you, Mr. Davidson, to know that you fulfill the first three stipulations of the trust. Although you're not married, you don't turn thirty for almost eighteen months, which gives you time to complete the fourth requirement. The fifth requirement is up to you. However, to date there have been four disputations and four terminations of eligibility because of that requirement. Our meeting today is the official declaration of eligibility, which is to take place eighteen months before the payoff date."

Andrew waited several seconds to be sure Mr. Austin was finished. He couldn't help but chuckle as he spoke. "And this is for real?"

"Absolutely," Mr. Austin said with a nod as he laced his fingers together and rested them on the table.

"What's the point?" Andrew then asked. He knew enough about trusts and deeds and other legal contracts to know that few people went through the effort of creating such trusts as this without a very good reason.

"Edward Davidson struck it rich in steel and oil. He had two sons, both of whom took their father's lifestyle for granted. As the boys grew older, Edward became obsessed with preserving his family's name. He was an eccentric old man anyway and spent two years creating this trust in order to ensure that his sons changed their ways, settled down, and bore legitimate heirs before he died. It worked, for the most part, and, obviously, the trust has continued. You are one of the only two remaining heirs, however, since most of the David-son men seem to have an aversion to having children and often die young due to the lives they lead once they get the money." Mr. Austin shook his head as if disgusted but continued with the same monotone voice. "The payoff is determined by divid-ing the total trust amount by the number of heirs at the time the current heir turns thirty, which means you are entitled to fifty percent of the total trust amount."

"Okay, fine," Andrew said, still chuckling at the insanity of the whole thing. Edward Davidson had gone through a lot of trouble, and now, eighty years later, when he should have had hundreds of progeny, he had two. Andrew found it quite fitting. He didn't appreciate dictatorship. "So how much is left? Five thousand dollars?"

Mr. Austin's cheek twitched, but he only held Andrew's eyes for a moment before busying himself with the folder once more. "Well, it's an invested trust; therefore it fluctu-ates according to how well the investments are doing. Edward may have been eccentric and controlling, but he was a brilliant financier." Andrew watched as Mr. Austin moved his wrinkled finger down the page. When it stopped, he looked up, peer-ing over his glasses and watching Andrew intently. "It looks like your payoff will be somewhere in the neighborhood of two point four million dollars, give or take a couple hundred thou-sand."

Andrew's mouth went dry. He became completely still and stared at the older man. The sum of two point four million dollars implanted itself in his brain, but he didn't take a breath for nearly thirty seconds. "Two and a half million dollars," he repeated when he found his senses again. The words rolled off his tongue like butter.

"Yes," Mr. Austin said with a small smile—his first.

Andrew remained silent for a few moments as the feeling came back to his fingers and toes. The meeting, purely for the sake of curiosity a few minutes ago, had suddenly become interesting. *Two and a half million dollars*, he repeated in his mind.

"How much was my father's payoff?" he suddenly asked. His mother had mentioned Richard having family money but not in a way that had prepared him for this—especially since Richard was broke by the time he died.

Mr. Austin consulted the folder for a few moments. "Richard received just under one million."

One million dollars, Andrew repeated silently with disgust. And yet his mother had worked two jobs most of his life. He was intrigued, the "to do" list in his planner completely forgotten. He opened the folder to page one and began reading the legal description one word at a time. When he turned to page two, Mr. Austin cleared his throat, causing Andrew to look up at the older man.

"You're welcome to look this over as long as you like, but the information itself must remain in this office at all times— you'll read about that provision in a few pages. Edward didn't want any of the information made public. Anytime you want to review the trust, call my secretary, and we'll set it up." Andrew stood when Mr. Austin stood, and they shook hands again, although Andrew barely noticed. His head was spinning.

Mr. Austin continued, "You'll find a letter of intent in the back of your folder. If you intend to claim the trust in full, you must sign the form. It allows us to make the necessary stock adjustments for the payoff. This paper also gives your consent for us to hire an investigator who will verify, every few months, that you're fulfilling the requirements. If it ever becomes apparent that you do not, you will either be informed that the trust payoff has been canceled, or, if it is a circumstance you can change, you will receive a letter of warning to inform you of where you fall short."

"And if I don't sign?"

"If you don't sign this, we can't make the adjustments to get you a full payoff. If on your thirtieth birthday you happen to meet the requirements, you will be eligible for a lump sum of five hundred thousand dollars—the maximum available for immediate withdrawal. It really makes little sense not to sign this form, especially since marriage is the only requirement you lack. However, signing is in no way a guarantee. The requirements must still be met in full or you get nothing." He smiled once more as he withdrew his hand. "My secretary will help you with anything you need."

Andrew waited until the door shut behind Mr. Austin before pulling his cell phone from his pocket. He punched in the number, put one hand in the pocket of his Armani dress pants, and turned to stare out the window overlooking downtown San Jose.

"Davidson Development," his secretary said when she got on the line.

"It's me," he said in a tone that still betrayed his distraction. "I need you to cancel my afternoon. I won't be making it back to the office today."

CHAPTER 4

Catherine was in the middle of getting two molars, and subsequently mother and daughter suffered through a long week. Tuesday night was particularly infuriating, and since there was no need to be there for the plant man, and the pool man didn't come until next week, Emma skipped going to the house on Wednesday. She consistently had Wednesdays off, and it was easiest to go to the house on that specific day. But she also had one other day off that varied from week to week. Her other day off for this week happened to be Saturday. She got up that morning and made the necessary arrangements to go to the house and get things taken care of. Lacey offered to keep Catherine so that she'd be sure to get her full nap. Emma thanked Lacey profusely and stopped at 7–11 to indulge herself with a Snickers bar and a Coke. Nothing like a sugar-caffeine buzz to start the day, especially after being awake most of the night with a screaming toddler. She was tempted to buy a pack of cigarettes, but she'd been tar and nicotine free for four days and didn't want to spoil a good thing.

As always she entered the house, sighed adoringly at the kitchen, and got her cleaning supplies. *Where to start?* she thought a few minutes later as she tapped her chin and looked around the immaculately clean house. *I could clean the clean floors or dust the dusted shelving; what a choice.* One of these days she and Cate would go for a swim, but obviously not today. There had been a fly buzzing around the master bedroom last week. It was her job to find the now-deceased insect and deal with it accordingly.

The master bedroom was her second favorite room. Every detail was etched into her mind, a mental oasis to which she loved to escape when reality became too taxing, which was increasingly often. Even before she entered the room, she could see it in her mind, and it made her smile. The large four-poster bed, although rather masculine and angular in design, was, of course, gorgeous. It was placed at an angle in the far right hand corner, flanked by two large windows and facing a gas fireplace with a recessed television above it. The carpet was a thick, soft sage green that would suck her in with every step. The accompanying bathroom came complete with a jacuzzi tub, separate shower, two sinks, a skylight, and a huge walk-in closet. After last night, she'd have given about anything to snuggle up under the down comforter and sleep the afternoon away. She turned the door handle and walked in, looking at nothing in particular, and armed with a dust buster with which to suck up the dead fly before going about her other tasks.

She was four steps into the room before her eyes met those of the man lying on the bed.

He was already looking at her, and she froze. He was beautiful—tan and lean and dressed only in a pair of black boxer shorts. In those first dazed seconds, she couldn't figure out who this guy was and then realized it must be Mr. Davidson. But . . . this wasn't how she'd pictured him and certainly not how she planned to meet him for the first time. The scene before her looked like a magazine ad for men's underwear. He smiled slightly, and she felt her mouth drop open just a little, but no words would come.

"Good morning," he said after a few more seconds of

silence. She blinked twice, his voice reminding her that this was not a magazine ad, and she looked like an idiot. In the next instant, she turned and ran for the door, shutting it with a resounding thud. She'd never been very good with surprises.

Emma didn't move from the doorway after slamming the door behind her. She was already mortified about her immediate reaction—*what a great first impression!* However, an amused smile played at the corners of her mouth as she pictured him again. She shook her head. *That was Andrew Davidson!* She'd have never guessed.

Emma tried to recall how she had pictured him before now. The house had no photographs of him, and she really hadn't pondered on it. She'd assumed he was in his forties or fifties—he *did* own a very successful company in California. She imagined him as an eccentric, worn-out surfer with leathery skin and a toupee.

Mr. Davidson pulled open the door several seconds later, stopping immediately to avoid bumping into her. He had faded jeans on now and was just pulling his shirt over his head. She tried not to stare as he finished pulling it over his contoured stomach.

"Uh, sorry. I didn't expect you today," he said with a friendly smile.

"Oh . . . uh, I . . . I mean . . . that's . . . well," she stopped and took a deep breath; she sounded like a complete idiot. She stuck out her hand. "I'm Emma. I'll be sure to make more noise next time, Mr. Davidson."

He chuckled and shook her hand. "Nice to meet you, Emma, and please call me Andrew." He retracted his hand, and they both stood there awkwardly for a few seconds, looking anywhere but at each other. Finally, he pointed over his shoulder toward the room he'd just exited. "I'm just going to take a shower, and then we can go over some things. Sound all right?"

"Oh, yeah, just fine. I'll be . . . somewhere."

He smiled, nodded, and reentered the bedroom. Emma

shook her head and headed back downstairs, leaving the fly for later.

For the next twenty minutes, she tried to mesh her previous expectations with the reality of Mr. Davidson. In hindsight she realized that the home gym in the basement and his love of skiing should have given her some clue to his physical composition, but she just hadn't thought about it too much. The real Andrew Davidson looked like he was in his early thirties. He was just over six feet tall, not quite as tall as Jake. Jake was also a little broader and had more of a belly on him, Emma decided, and then she paused. *How did Jake get into this?*

She finished vacuuming and went upstairs to start watering the rest of the plants. Most of the plants in the solarium were watered with an automatic indoor sprinkler system, but there were a few pots that needed hand watering, and the plants throughout the rest of the house needed some attention too. She wondered if his teeth were capped. They seemed a little too straight and too white not to be.

"What happened to my plant man?"

His voice startled her, and she turned too fast, spilling water from the watering can all down the front of her T-shirt. Smiling with embarrassment, she tried to keep the cotton fabric from sticking to her skin by pulling it away from her body. He just smiled politely, awaiting her reply. "Um, I fired him," she said distractedly as she looked around for a dry rag while adjusting her glasses that had slid down her nose. There was nothing lying around to help dry her shirt so she walked past him to the kitchen to retrieve a dish towel.

Mr. Davidson raised his eyebrows. "You fired him?"

"Yeah," she said as she continued to the kitchen. He followed her. She let go of the shirt after toweling it off to see if it was still clinging. It wasn't too bad. "I called and talked to them several times, and they still weren't coming on time or watering everything. So I told them not to bother anymore."

"I see," he said slowly. "Any other changes in my help that I should be aware of?"

His help? Emma thought, looking up with her back still toward him, not liking the arrogant tone in his voice. "The gardener didn't show up for three weeks, so I fired him too."

He was silent for a moment, and when he spoke his voice sounded even, as if forced. "Really?"

"I understood it was my job to coordinate the care of this household," she said with slight irritation, finally turning to face him.

Mr. Davidson nodded. "Did you hire another gardener then?"

"I can plant flowers and pull weeds."

"You weeded my flower beds?"

Was it so hard for him to believe anything she said? Looking at the pitcher in her hand, he continued. "And you water the plants too?"

"Watering plants really isn't that difficult," she snapped

"I don't suppose it is, but do you plan to give them the adequate vitamins every month and rotate their sun exposure in order for them to grow to their optimum potential?"

Emma laughed, her ire growing by the second. "Is that what the '*Plantitorium*' said they were doing?" He was silenced by her insulting tone. The infamous Mr. Davidson obviously didn't get much cheek. "They'd show up an hour late, walk through the house, and leave. They weren't even here for five minutes. You should be thanking me for saving you some money—not to mention the lives of your *precious* plants."

"I don't care about the money," he said with clipped words. His mask of cocky condescension had disappeared, and annoyance had replaced it.

Emma walked past him to finish watering the plants being discussed. "And they don't care about your plants, so I guess you're even." Mr. Davidson had thoroughly destroyed her haven of fantasy. She couldn't wait to finish the day and leave. She heard him turn and follow her back to the solarium.

"Do I still have someone coming to take care of my pool?"

Emma took a breath and pushed some foliage out of the way so as not to splash any water on the edge of the ceramic pot. "Yes, and as long as he can keep to his scheduled appointment, he'll keep his job."

"But if he doesn't *keep to his scheduled appointment* you'll fire him too? And then I assume you'll take over the pool duties as well."

Emma turned and cocked her head to the side. Handsome or homely, she wasn't nearly as impressed with him as she'd been earlier. "Why don't you stop patronizing me with your petty investigation and get to the point? I was under the impression it was my job to run this household, and that's what I've done."

"Yet instead of replacing them you just do it all yourself. Have you thought what happens when you are no longer here? I lose my housekeeper, my plant man, *and* my gardener. And guess who then has to replace three positions instead of one? On top of that, I am assuming that you have not checked my sprinkler system to see if it's winterized, and you probably neglected to dig up and pot the seasonal plants that can't winter over. So, yes, it is a bit of a problem for you to turn everything upside down and not replace those that you disposed of."

Emma took a deep breath and pursed her lips as the irritation turned to full-blown anger. She was so tired of haughty, overbearing men. "Ya know, I hadn't considered any of those problems, but since you bring it up, I guess you're about to find out *just* how hard it is to replace all three. I apologize for the *devastating* inconvenience I've caused you." She handed her water pitcher to him and headed for the door. "Your housekeeper, gardener, and plant *woman* just quit. I recommend in the future letting your secretary deal with any problems you might have with *your help*—you suck at it." She slammed the front door and headed for her car. She had more important things to do than convince some spoiled, arrogant brat that people who don't do their jobs aren't worth paying. A pang of regret tempted her to turn around, to at least give her fare-well to the beloved kitchen, but she kept on walking. She had been so impressed with him at the beginning of their meeting. *What a shame to have a lousy personality ruin a perfectly good-looking man.*

She drove to the closest gas station and bought a pack of cigarettes.

CHAPTER 5

*H*ours later, Emma was still stewing when the phone rang. She looked at the caller ID and took a breath before picking it up. Why was Mr. Davidson calling her?

"Hello," she said dryly as she leaned against the wall.

"I want you to reconsider," he said.

Emma squinted up at the ceiling, feigning deep thought. "No."

"Oh, come on, Emma. I was just trying to understand your motives."

Emma opened her mouth but then shut it. Her brow furrowed as she looked at the situation from another angle.

He continued, "I *was* surprised that you had made so many changes. Not necessarily upset, just surprised. And I'm sorry for giving the wrong impression. I would really appreciate it if you would come back and let us start from scratch."

Emma sighed and clenched her teeth. It had been a beautifully dramatic moment, the kind of thing you tell to your friends for the rest of your life. How perfectly lousy to have to rethink it from this new perspective. When she spoke, her voice was streaked with humility. "Why on earth would you want me to come back? You could find another housekeeper without any trouble, and you could make sure she wasn't like me."

"Yes, I could do that," Mr. Davidson replied. "But I didn't get the chance to tell you how great the house looked, and how impressed I am with the grounds. I also really appreciate your independence. I know I offended you, but I would really like you to reconsider. I won't question your decisions in the future."

Emma said nothing, softening despite herself. It had been a long time since she had received a compliment.

When she didn't respond, Mr. Davidson continued. "I've got half a mind to hire you to follow me all over the country, keep both my houses clean, and tell off annoying salespeople."

A smile tugged at the corner of Emma's mouth. "I've always been a little . . . impulsive."

"So will you come back? I'll even give you a raise."

Well, nothing talked to Emma quite like money did. "Okay, but I'm not coming back until Wednesday."

"You didn't finish today."

"But I went, and it's too late tonight. I work all week, so if you want me back you'll have to wait until I can fit it in."

He chuckled. "Okay, have it your way this time. And thanks, Emma. I appreciate this."

"You're welcome." *I think.*

CHAPTER 6

The next Wednesday, Emma took a deep breath and entered the house holding Catherine's hand. She learned soon enough that Mr. Davidson wasn't there, which was a good thing since Cate immediately pulled all the pillows off the living room couch. He had left a note on the counter; next to it was a box of chocolates with a little white flag made of a plastic fork and a napkin taped to the side. Emma smiled and picked up the note.

> *Emma,*
>
> *Truce? I appreciate all you have done and hope that we can repair our relationship and continue on as we have been. A week from Saturday (the 22nd) I'll be arriving with some friends. We'll be staying until Wednesday, and I would appreciate it if you could have some food on hand. There will be eight of us. Please spare no expense.*

*Use whatever money you need out of the envelope, but keep
your receipts. And yes, this is a test.*

Andrew

A test! Emma snorted as she opened the envelope. *He is
such a snob.* Her eyes widened, however, as she counted out ten
one hundred dollar bills. *A thousand dollars for four days worth
of food?* With a shake of her head, she put the money back in
the envelope and popped one chocolate into her mouth before
putting Cate down for her nap and starting to clean.

As she cleaned, Emma started forming some ideas about
the food request. If she could spend one day doing whatever she
pleased, it would be cooking. It wasn't just meatloaf and chocolate chip cookies; she liked the fancy stuff. One Christmas she
had prepared roast duck—it was fabulous. Over the years, she
had discovered a pumpkin soup that was out of this world and
stuffed mushrooms that were to die for. She loved Indian foods,
rich desserts, and anything Italian. However, the problem with
this hobby was that gourmet cooking was expensive, she was
broke, and her kitchen was tiny. She didn't get the chance to
dabble in it very much. But she now had an envelope with a
thousand dollars in it and free reign to provide whatever food
she deemed necessary. She walked into the kitchen and looked
around, imagining the sheer joy of creating culinary perfec-
tion in this palace of a room. She could come over after work,
bring Catherine, and have a blast. Ideas swirled and formed
as she finished the laundry, cleaned the tub, and emptied the
dishwasher. This would be fun. Mr. Davidson had said it was
a test, and she was going to work her tail off to pass it with
flying colors. She left a note explaining that she would come
that Friday afternoon to put the finishing details on his weekend.

When she arrived after work that Friday, still in her
scrubs, she noted that the party hadn't arrived yet. *Good,* she
thought as she headed out to the car to get the few things she'd
done at home as well as several bags of groceries. She touched

up the house while burning some candles in hopes of setting just the right feel. On the dining room table, she left another note explaining to her boss what she had prepared, and how to eat or heat it, and included her phone number in case he had any questions. She left the envelope with the remaining money and all her receipts on the counter, explaining that she took an additional hundred dollars to pay herself for her time. She pulled out of the driveway with a smile of satisfaction. She couldn't remember the last time she'd had so much fun.

Sunday was her weekend day off this week, so she went to church with Chris and Lacey in the afternoon. Catherine was horrible and refused to stay on her lap. By the time church was over, Emma was wondering why she bothered to go at all. She definitely didn't get anything out of it, but she still clung to the belief that there was a purpose to it. Jake hadn't been a member, and it was easy not to go once they got married. She'd never had a burning testimony anyway, and although she was trying to find the "fire" that the rest of her family had, it was slow in coming. For her, church was just one more thing she felt guilty about not doing. But she had to admit that the people she knew who did the church thing were happier than she was. So she kept going when she could. But it didn't break her heart when she couldn't.

Upon getting home, she changed Catherine's clothes, and they read some books together. Eventually Cate ended up curled in Emma's lap. Emma ran her fingers through the baby's silken curls while finishing one last book. This was much more soothing to her spirit than church was. She eventually put Cate down for a nap and noticed by the blinking light on her phone that she had missed a call. She accessed her voice mail and listened to a message from Mr. Davidson asking that she call as soon as she could. A little tremor of anxiety ran down her spine as she wondered what he was calling about.

Was he going to tell her she had failed, or was he simply wondering how best to serve the individual quiches?

A giggly woman picked up the phone, making Emma feel strangely jealous that she didn't have a reason to be so amused.

"Hello, may I please speak to Mr. Davidson?"

The woman moved the phone from her mouth a little and hollered, "Mi-ster Daaavidson," in a very bad English accent, causing Emma to roll her eyes. Luckily Andrew got the phone before the woman repeated herself.

"Hello?"

"Hi, it's Emma. You left a message?"

"Oh, yes," Andrew said. She heard the background voices fade and then the shutting of a door, telling her he'd gone into another room. "Thank you for calling back. I hope I'm not bothering you."

"No, you're fine. Is everything okay?"

"Everything is wonderful," he said immediately, causing her to smile with relief that he wasn't upset about how much money she spent. "I can't believe the work you put into this. I thought you would get some bacon, eggs, maybe some ice cream and cocktail shrimp."

"I hope I didn't overdo it, then."

"Oh no, not at all. Everyone has been really impressed. Did you make all of that?"

"I like to cook."

Andrew was quiet for a minute. "Are you busy tomorrow?" Emma raised her eyebrows. "We had thought to go out for dinner downtown, but then Mark, one of my guests, has a conference call at seven thirty Utah time, and I thought if you're not busy maybe you could do a dinner for us? I'll make it well worth your time."

"Oh." Emma blinked, but her stomach quivered. *He must really be impressed.* Quickly she scanned through her day. *Drop Cate off at day care at 6:20, work by 6:30. Pick Cate up and be home about 3:00.* If she did some shopping during her lunch break, had Lacey watch Cate after work, and went immediately to Andrew's, she could probably pull it off. "It would have to be a late dinner, maybe eight o'clock?"

"That would be perfect; we're all on California time anyway."

Emma smiled. "Any suggestions?"

"Nope. I'll leave it in your court. Buy whatever you need, and I'll reimburse you for it . . . as well as pay you for your time, of course."

Emma agreed to be there around four and hung up before hurrying to her recipe file to find just the right thing.

After work the next day, she went straight to Lacey's house. She wanted to look nice but also needed to dress practically. She decided on khaki slacks, a white button up short-sleeved blouse, and black loafers. She wasn't going to stand out, but she didn't look like a bum either. Besides, her long figure was best shown by classic lines and color anyway; at least that's what her mother had always told her. Lacey did Emma's hair in a simple French twist that would keep it out of her face and loaned her a pristine white hostess apron she'd never worn. A little mascara, a touch of blush, and lip gloss were the final touches as she ran to the door, saying "thank you" on her way out. She arrived at Andrew's just after four o'clock. Perfect.

Andrew found her in the kitchen half an hour later. At first sight, she was glad not to feel the giddiness from their first meeting, but maybe that was because he was fully clothed this time. Yet even with a turtleneck sweater and jeans, he made quite an impression that she wished she didn't notice.

"I didn't know you were here," he said. After pausing a moment, he added, "You look nice."

She couldn't tell from his tone whether he wished she looked better or was surprised she looked so good. She just smiled and ignored his tone altogether. "I didn't want to disturb you and your guests."

"Come meet everyone," he said, nodding to the doorway.

She scrunched up her face and shook her head. "I'm just

the cook. I don't need to be introduced."

"Nonsense," he said, waving off her protests. He took hold of her forearm and tugged her toward the door.

She smiled as he introduced her to the guests, none of whose names she remembered. Afterwards she went immediately back to the kitchen. For the next three hours, she cooked like a mad woman. No one bothered her until just before eight when Andrew popped in to see if she was nearly ready. She was just removing the Harvest Berry Cobbler from the oven and told him it would be ten minutes. Exactly eleven minutes later, she brought out the homemade cream of mushroom soup in eight small bowls on a tray and put one down in front of each guest. Everyone was complimentary and polite except for one woman Emma deemed as "Minnie" because of her high-pitched voice. "Ohhh, I absolutely hate mushrooms," she said with a pinched look on her face. Then looking up at Emma, she added, "No offense."

None taken sweetheart, Emma wanted to say, even though she was very much offended. Instead she simply picked up the bowl and headed for the kitchen. "I'll take that one," a dark-haired man said, and she set it down with a smile. He thanked her, and she took his already empty first bowl back with her. Next she brought out the main course: raspberry chicken, wild rice, seasoned veggies, and fresh rolls, receiving another round of compliments as she did so. Once that was over, she brought out the harvest cobbler with cream cheese whipped topping and couldn't help but smile over all the gracious comments. *You'd think they had never eaten this good.*

Once that was done, she went back into the kitchen and began cleaning up. After a couple minutes, Minnie popped in. "Can we get some dessert wine? A nice red would go great with this."

Emma turned, taken off guard by the request. She'd noticed they had wine with dinner but figured Andrew had taken care of that since she certainly hadn't. "Oh, um. I don't know where Andrew keeps the, uh, wine," she said as she looked through cupboards, finding nothing.

"I thought you were in charge of dinner," Minnie said accusingly.

"Well, yes I was," Emma responded, trying hard to keep the irritation out of her voice. "But I don't do wine."

Minnie left the kitchen, and Emma heard her comment, "She says she doesn't *do* wine," as she went back to the dinning room. Irritated, Emma continued rinsing dishes and tried not to let the woman's comments take precedence over the praise. She was almost finished when Andrew came in. "Thank you, Emma. That was absolutely perfect."

Emma smiled, not completely satisfied, and pushed a few strands of hair off of her face with a soapy hand. One person out of eight shouldn't be that big a deal, but it still bothered her. "Minnie didn't seem to think so," she said after a moment, if only to get it off her chest.

"Minnie?" Andrew repeated with a furrowed brow as he took the platter she was drying and put it back in the cupboard—the wrong cupboard, she noted.

Emma's face reddened at the slip. "Oh, sorry," she said. "I have a problem with giving names when I can't remember the real ones."

"And so you chose Minnie?"

He was smiling, so she assumed it was okay to explain, "You know, like Minnie Mouse." Then raising her voice several levels shriller, she mimicked, "I don't like mushrooms. Where's my wine, Mi-ster Davidson!"

Andrew chuckled and put a stack of plates away—in the right cupboard this time. "She is a little . . . uh . . ."

"Simpering?"

Andrew chuckled again. "I guess that's a good word. She's a really nice gal though."

Emma blew a breath out her nose. "If you go for that totally-helpless-female-with-no-class crap."

Later that night, Andrew reviewed the evening and mentally scratched Veronica—Minnie—from his list of potential wives. He had always found her a little annoying, but not until tonight did he realize how obnoxious it would be to have to be with her on a somewhat regular basis. Emma's comments had definitely helped the decision along, but he didn't dwell on that. There were still three other women staying here, and they were all possibilities. So he was only one down.

By Tuesday night, Andrew was frustrated. He'd spent time with each of the women he'd invited to his home, and the only thing that was clear in his mind was that marriage was a prison. Long after the household retired, Andrew got out of bed, changed into his swimming trunks, and headed for the pool. Swimming had always been a relaxing experience for him. In high school he'd lettered in it and gladly practiced for hours each day to keep his muscles tight and his skill precise. Swimming had earned him a scholarship, and he'd used the college years well.

He dove into the water and could feel the tensions drain from his body as the cool water enveloped him. Breaking the surface a few seconds later, he drew a deep breath before slicing the water with his arms as he began strong, swift strokes toward the far side of the pool. As he swam, he continued to review the situation.

It was still rather amazing that he was going to follow through with this whole marriage thing. He'd spent hours and hours trying to talk himself out of it, but it was impossible to ignore what that kind of cash injection could do for his company. He'd started Davidson Development six years ago, with ten thousand dollars given to him by his mom, a cell phone, and a lot of ambition. Now it had become a lucrative company that allowed him the lifestyle he'd always dreamed of. The added luxury was that he spent his days doing his favorite thing in the world: finding deals and making them happen. Two and a half million dollars would take him from being a self-sufficient development company to a contender for major projects, with multiple offices, and greater financial leveraging. It was an offer he just couldn't refuse.

However, there was still the little problem of finding a wife, a lifestyle change he had never planned on.

As he had quite often lately, Andrew missed his mother. All his life it had been Mom and Andrew—just the two of them. She had been his best friend and biggest fan. What he wouldn't give to talk to her about this. But breast cancer had changed everything, and two years ago the disease won the battle. *She'd get a kick out of this whole thing if she were around though.* In fact she'd have probably found him a wife already. He wondered if she'd known about the trust. He couldn't imagine that she wouldn't have told him, but she had always made a point of telling him how family money had ruined his father. Had she kept the information from him on purpose, hoping he wouldn't qualify? Or did Richard keep the details of the trust to himself? He'd never know the answer.

After twelve laps, he hoisted himself out of the pool and shook the water from his hair. During the last three weeks, he'd taken any woman that was even slightly interesting out for drinks or dinner, and not one of them had given him any reason to take her on another date—at least not when his goal was putting a ring on her finger. In search of a tall glass of water, he diverted to the kitchen and opened the fridge, illuminating the darkened room only slightly. Miniature cheesecakes, stuffed mushrooms, and dill rolls stared back at him as a whole new thought struck him. He stood up a little straighter and stared at nothing in particular.

Maybe he was going about this the wrong way. A new idea—one he hadn't even considered before—began to dance in his head. He made himself a little plate of food, filled up his glass with cold, purified water, and headed back to his room, deep in thought. He was attempting to find a *marriage*. Maybe what he really needed was more of a merger—a business deal of sorts.

CHAPTER 7

$\mathcal{E}$mma put both hands flat against the small of her back and stretched, trying to ease the aching muscles. It was ten after three; work was over—life was sweet at ten after three. She pulled her time card out and swiped it through the time clock, officially ending her shift. When she exited the break room, Tina, another nursing assistant, was walking toward her. "I found a message for you at the front desk."

"Thanks," Emma said as she took the pink paper.

Tina waved as she turned back in the direction she'd come, her footsteps echoing across the linoleum floor. Emma looked at the paper and let out a breath before crumpling the message in her hand. Jake had been calling her at home for two days straight. She hadn't answered and deleted the messages he left without bothering to listen to them. Her attorney had already informed her that Jake wanted Catherine to come to his wedding in a couple of weeks. Emma had no intention of attending, and there was no way Catherine would be going without her. She hoped he wore out the buttons on his phone trying to reach her.

She dropped the crumpled message slip in the ashtray

outside the door and continued toward her car, feeling rather smug. Catherine's day care was just down the street. Emma pulled up within minutes of leaving work. Kids were everywhere, watching TV, playing house, and taking turns on the playground. She scanned the wiggling, giggling masses but didn't see Cate. She approached a day care worker whose name she didn't know, the woman having just started this week. "Hi, I'm here for Cate Tribol. Where's she hiding?"

"Your husband already picked her up," the woman replied with a smile.

Emma froze for just a moment and then realized the worker must have Cate confused with someone else. "You must have the wrong kid. Cate's only allowed to be picked up by me."

The worker's face paled, and she began darting her eyes around.

Emma's heart sank, and when the day care worker turned to find her supervisor, Emma was right on her heels. She grabbed her arm. "You let someone take my daughter?" Her brain started spinning. Surely there was some mistake.

The worker swallowed and motioned to someone from across the room. Emma swore just as the supervisor intervened.

"What's the matter?" she said, standing between her employee and Emma.

"This idiot let some man take Cate today." The panic was starting to rise now, and it was all Emma could do to keep from exploding.

"It was her dad, I swear." The worker wasn't talking to Emma; she was directing her comments to her supervisor. Emma wanted to strangle her.

"Her father lives in Texas!" Emma spat, but her thoughts were still churning. Jake *had* been trying to reach her, but why would he come all the way to Utah now?

The supervisor's eyes went wide, and she pulled her employee aside for a hasty conversation. Emma heard every word but waited for the supervisor to explain as her thoughts continued to run in wild circles.

"She checked his ID. She said his name was Jack or Jacob Tribol." Her eyes were pleading with Emma to be calm—as if!

"I put on the paperwork that she is never to leave with anyone but me!"

"I'm very sorry."

Emma couldn't even speak but turned on her heel and ran for her car. Being left by her husband had been devastating. The divorce had been brutal, and her whole life had seemed to slip through her fingers. The one thing Emma had held onto was Cate. Through all the proceedings, she'd worried that Jake would ask for joint custody, but he seemed too distracted by his new girlfriend to pay much attention. But ever since the wedding announcement had been pureed in the disposal, she'd worried that with a new wife he might change his mind. His would be the two-parent home, and although he had never asked for custody, she wouldn't put anything past him. That fear overpowered her right now. Why else would he show up unannounced? The thought made her sick to her stomach.

She drove furiously back to work. Without turning off the car, she ran to the ashtray and sifted through the cigarette butts until she found the crumpled message slip. She smoothed it out and ran inside, grabbing the first phone she could find and punching in the number she assumed was for a cell phone, since he obviously wasn't home. He answered after two rings.

"Hello?"

"Bring her back," she demanded. "Wherever you're going, turn around and come back."

"We're at a restaurant getting dinner," Jake said. "And I have every right to visit with my daughter. The settlement clearly states that I—"

"I don't care what it states! You don't just show up here and snatch her without my knowledge."

"I've left you a dozen messages," Jake countered with a little less calmness. "I have a work conference in Boise, and I chose to take time off and drive rather than fly so that I could see her and introduce her to Suzanne. I've called you at home, I've called you at work, and you've played your little power game by ignoring me. I'm the one that pays for day care anyway, so don't even try and tell me I had no right to pick her up. I haven't seen her for months, and I'm not going to give up my only chance. I got Chris's address from the phone book. I'll drop her off at eight! Neutral ground." The phone went dead, and Emma swore. Then she swore again, hung up the phone, and marched back to the car.

As soon as Jake pulled into the driveway that night, Emma ran for the door. Chris grabbed her arm and pulled her back. "Wait," he said strongly. "Don't make it worse." The two of them had been sitting in the living room waiting for nearly twenty minutes. Emma had chain smoked most of the afternoon, and she knew Chris could smell it on her. She didn't care—she was at the end of her rope and felt it was about to break.

"He's late," she snapped, ripping her arm from his grasp. However, she took his advice and let Jake come to the door. Seeing her little girl in his arms made her irrationally angry, and she could feel her face harden. Cate seemed comfortable with him too, and that only made her feel worse. He'd been very close to her in Texas, but Emma had hoped four months would have erased those memories from Cate's young mind. When Chris invited him in, she couldn't take it any longer and sprang forward, roughly pulling Cate from his arms. Jake let her go, and Emma held her daughter close. "If you ever do that again, I swear I'll—"

"You'll what, Emma?" Jake interrupted with a smirk, looking thoroughly bored with the dramatics. "I'm entitled to visitation."

"Like hell you are," Emma spat, not caring that Lacey and Chris were watching. "Go have your own kids, okay? Leave mine alone."

"Our kid, Emma!" Jake shouted. "She's my daughter too."

"And you *want* to see her Jake?" Emma screamed back at

him, turning and coming back into the room. Cate started to whimper, and Emma placed a protective hand on her head, smoothing her hair.

"You've moved over a thousand miles away from me—I'm trying to be a part of her life as much as I can."

"That must be why you let us move in the first place. You're just trying to play the happy daddy role for your little tramp—"

"WHAT!" Jake roared, taking a step toward her.

Chris quickly stepped between them. "That's enough," he said, putting his hands on Jake's shoulders and moving him toward the door.

"Get your hands off me," Jake spat as he hit Chris's hands away. Chris put his hands down but stayed in front of Jake. Looking around Chris's head, Jake yelled at Emma again, "You're the one making this hard, Emma." Emma gallantly cussed at him and his eyes flared. "I should never have let you move," he said with forced calmness. Instant heat nearly consumed her at the insinuation that he had any kind of control over her. "If I had said so, you would still be in Texas. But I decided to let you get on with your life the way you wanted to. You should be thanking me."

"Okay, Jake, we've heard enough. It's time to go," Chris said with forced calmness, trying to push him out the door.

"She has two parents, Emma. Don't forget it," was the last thing Jake said before Chris pulled the door shut.

"Oh, I hate him," Emma hissed, holding a confused Catherine even closer. The baby's silky brown hair stuck to Emma's still-wet cheeks, and Catherine's eyes were wide as she clung to her mother. Emma's chin trembled despite her rage, and she turned to leave. "I hate him so much."

"He is her dad though," Chris said quietly.

Emma turned and narrowed her eyes at him. "He left me and he left her too—that counts for something."

"But not everything."

Emma turned to leave. Chris grabbed her arm and stopped

her. "It's time to accept what is, Emma. Cate deserves a dad—why would you want to rob her of that?"

"Because she is all I have," she whispered angrily.

"But *she* has two parents, and if you deprive her of this now, it will haunt both of you."

Emma felt the tears overflow. There was truth in his words; she knew that. But it burned, and she didn't want to face it. Catherine was her everything, and she wanted to be Catherine's everything too. Was that really so wrong? Jake could have a dozen more kids if he wanted. Emma had almost given her life to create Cate's, and it wasn't fair that she should have to share that with the man who took his family so lightly.

She took Cate home, gave her a bath, and put her to bed. She tried to watch TV, but the feelings were so intense she couldn't sit still. After another cigarette that she hoped would calm her, she started to clean up from the day. At nine thirty the phone rang. She was going to ignore it but finally picked up the phone. "Hello," she said briskly. If she was lucky, it would be some telemarketer she could swear at and hang up on.

The voice was hesitant. "Emma?"

"Who is this?"

"Andrew."

It was Emma's turn to pause. "Andrew?" she said, looking at the caller ID for the first time. "Uh, hello."

"I just got into town," Andrew explained. "And I'd like to talk to you about something."

Emma furrowed her brow. "Talk to me about what?" Was he going to fire her? That's just what she needed to make this a perfect day.

"Uh, I'd like to wait until I can talk to you in person—tonight, if possible."

"I just put Cate to bed," she replied. "And I work at six thirty. I don't know—"

"Can I come there?" he broke in. "It's important and will only take a minute."

Emma finally agreed and gave him the address. Then

she ran into the bathroom to make herself presentable while wondering what on earth was so important that Andrew had to talk to her now. Her face was still puffy from crying, and she looked as tired and hopeless as she felt. She considered putting on makeup but decided against it. She wasn't out to impress anyone, and it was silly to pretend she was. Less than fifteen minutes passed before there was a knock at the door. She opened it and they exchanged polite, cautious greetings as she invited him in.

"Take a seat," she said, indicating her mismatched living room set while trying not to compare her home to his. "Can I get you anything?" All she had was milk, water, and pineapple Kool-Aid. She hoped he didn't want anything.

He shook his head as he sat on the living room sofa, surveying the apartment as he did so. She smiled and sat down on the love seat across from him, sure that he'd never been in such a dump in his life. An uneasy silence descended. She clasped her hands together and rested them on her knees, awaiting his explanation for this impromptu meeting.

"I have a business deal of sorts I wanted to discuss with you," he said. There was a trace of nervousness in his voice, but he covered it well, especially when he smiled. His smile helped her relax, despite all the tension of the day. "I'm not sure how to say this other than to just say it." He paused yet again and then looked up and began talking again. "I recently learned about a family trust that will pay me a substantial sum of money if I meet certain requirements." His speech had quickened but not overly so. He reminded her of a slick salesmen—the type that sell you a TV or VCR before you even know you want one. "One of those requirements is that I be married at least a year before my thirtieth birthday, which is seventeen months from now. I've been looking, and I can't find anyone I want to be my wife. But then I thought of you."

Emma's eyes went wide, and she was sure her heart stopped for just a moment.

"It would be purely a business arrangement," he added

quickly. "And I'd make it worth your while."

Emma was speechless for a moment. He wanted her to marry him? Was he insane? She laughed. "Very funny," she said cautiously as she stood. "I don't know what you're—"

"Emma, I'm serious," he said bluntly, standing to face her. "This is for real."

She pulled back and stared up at him. His auburn hair was ruffled, and the lines on the sides of his eyes showed that he was very tired. Even though she didn't know him well, she couldn't doubt that he *was* serious, and the realization stunned her. She opened her mouth, but it took a few moments for her to review what she'd just heard and form words. "You have to get married?" she repeated. It sounded like a plot from a pathetic romance novel—except there was no romance.

Andrew nodded and let out a breath. "I think we could work it out so it benefits us both."

"What do you mean?" she asked with caution. This was too weird. It couldn't be for real, but why else would he be saying this?

"Once I get paid, I'm prepared to pay you ten percent of the total trust—about two hundred and fifty thousand dollars."

"Uh-huh." She shuddered and then clamped her mouth shut. For almost a minute, she couldn't speak as she went over what he'd said again. Her heart rate quickened. Finally she returned to her seat, reclasped her hands, and told herself to pay attention. "Okay, start over, but talk slower."

When he finished his second explanation of the trust, things were clearer—but not much. She stood and let out a breath. "What would it be like?" *Am I really even considering this?* she asked herself.

"Well, in order to fulfill the trust, I'll need you to move into the house, and you'd have to take my name." She nodded. Davidson was better than Tribol any day. She caught him glancing around the room again. *He knows it won't be hard for me to leave.* "I'm a professional man, and I have no desire to let any of my associates know that I've got a business marriage. So there may be times I need you to help me keep up appearances—parties, weekends, that sort of thing."

"You don't expect me to . . . well . . . you know."

"No, no, no. There will be no intimacy. You'll have health insurance and plenty of financial support, if you'd like to go to school or anything like that. You'll still run the house, and I'll still spend most of my time in L.A. When the trust is paid, I'll give you your cut, and we'll go our separate ways. I think this could be just what you need to get a head start, and I want this to work for you in the best way."

She forced a laugh to cover her shock but couldn't help picturing herself living in that house. The thought made her giddy, and she had to force herself to think rationally. "I can't believe you're asking me to do this."

"No offense," he said carefully, "but I don't want or need a wife. And I don't want to be wanted or needed as a husband." He smiled coyly. "I think we're perfect for each other."

She shook her head at the insanity of even considering his offer. "I need to think about this," she said, still shaking her head—but already taking an inventory of what she would pack and what she would burn. *Stop it!* she told herself. As Chris had only recently reminded her, she was a grown-up now, and she had to handle this . . . grown-upishly.

"Believe me, I understand," Andrew said with a nod. "I'm in town for the weekend. Why don't you call me when you've taken the time you need to figure this out."

CHAPTER 8

*E*mma didn't sleep well that night. She knew she was crazy to even consider saying yes. Then again it seemed crazy to say no. She went back and forth all night long. Lacey had agreed to watch Cate until Emma could find a new day care, and when she dropped off her sleepy daughter at six-twenty the next morning it was all she could do not to tell Lacey what had happened. But she could only imagine the response and so she choked it down and tried to act normal. When she got to work ten minutes later, she learned that the other aide had called in sick, leaving Emma to run the floor alone.

By eight o'clock in the morning she'd had enough. She called Andrew after giving her twelfth bath of the day and made an appointment for them to meet later that afternoon. After work Emma called to tell Lacey that she'd be a little late, thanked her profusely, and drove to Andrew's house. He answered the door, and she walked past him before turning and getting right to the point.

"I've got some questions for you."

"Okay, shoot," Andrew said once they were settled on couches in the living room.

For the next ten minutes, she grilled him about domestic abuse, drug use, and any possible criminal record. He answered willingly. She weighed every answer, looking him in the eye to determine whether or not she could trust him. She made it clear that she would not accept any harmful behavior, that the first hint of such would send her straight to the police. He was in perfect agreement with her feelings and said that she had nothing to worry about. When she had completed her interrogation, she was silent for a moment and then looked up at him. "I've decided to do it." Andrew's eyebrows shot up, but she continued before he could speak. "However, I have some stipulations."

Andrew paused and then leaned forward, resting his elbows on his knees. "Okay," he said. "What are your stipulations?"

"First of all, I want a contract. Now, I'm not planning to go to court or anything, but I want to know that we both fully agree to the terms and know exactly where we stand. I don't want either of us trying to remember exactly what we agreed to later on."

"Okay, I had planned on that already."

"I assume you want a prenuptial agreement signed first?"

"Yes."

"I want to be sure you stipulate the ten percent in there. I don't want to get through this and then find out you skunked me."

Andrew laughed. "I promise not to *skunk* you, but that's a good idea to make the provision."

"I want my own bedroom, my own office with my own computer, and a room for Cate. I want these rooms designated as mine so that I don't need to infringe on your privacy, and you don't need to infringe on mine."

"Agreed," Andrew said with a nod. He seemed rather amused by her requests.

"And I want you to promise me that for the length of our marriage you will not date or be involved with anyone sexually."

This wiped the smile off his face. "Excuse me?"

"I realize this is a marriage of convenience for both of us. We are both getting what we need out of it. But it is still a marriage—a sacred thing that deserves a commitment. We will still be making vows, and I won't have you making a mockery of the whole situation."

Andrew was silent for a few moments. "You'll be here, and I will spend most of my time in L.A. There is no reason for either of us to babysit the other. Anything that takes place away from here won't involve you in the least."

Emma stood up from the couch. "I won't agree unless you can promise me this. I believe strongly in the sanctity of marriage. I realize we're already fudging on much of its intent, but I won't budge on this. Whether I'm in love with you or not, I demand that you be faithful to me. Otherwise this is *just* a game, and I'm not willing to play."

"If we aren't sleeping together, then being faithful isn't an issue," Andrew countered.

"It doesn't matter whether we're sleeping together or not. If you can't agree to wait until we're divorced to resume your bachelor lifestyle, then I won't agree to be your wife. This isn't just pretending. We are making promises to God, and I expect both of us to keep this one."

"But it *is* just pretending. We're not in love; we don't share anything intimate—so I don't see the conflict."

Emma took a breath and vacillated. He did have a point, but . . . so did she. For just a moment, she considered seeing it his way, but she just couldn't. "I don't know how to make you understand how I see it, but it's a big deal to me, okay? I've already shared a husband—my fractured ego can't do it again."

Andrew clenched his jaw and let out a breath. "Okay, if it's that big a deal to you, I'll agree not to date or become involved with anyone until we are no longer married."

Emma finally sat back down and put her hands in her lap. "That's all," she said with smile.

"Good," he said with feeling. "Since we're being so picky, I have a few stipulations of my own."

Emma repositioned herself on the couch and nodded.

"First of all, you need to get that hair fixed."

"Excuse me?" she said after a moment of shocked silence.

"Your country look of pulling it up in that braid thing all the time might be good enough for you, but it isn't going to cut it for me. Then get some new clothes and some contact lenses so you can get rid of those glasses. The night of the dinner was a good start with the hair, makeup, and clothes, but I think you can do better."

Emma's mouth was open in shock, but she didn't get a chance to speak. "I'll pay for it all," he continued. "But you need a whole new look, preferably one that includes clothes that *fit*. I will still be bringing people home with me from time to time, and I expect them to see in you a woman worth marrying, so—"

"What's that supposed to mean? 'A woman worth marrying.'"

"It means that right now you look like a single mother saving her pennies. I want a woman who *looks* like she's caught me." Emma folded her arms and looked away, annoyance and embarrassment clearly showing on her face and in her posture. "I expect you to cooperate and play out your role."

"Fine," Emma said, still hung up on the demands of looking like a *woman worth marrying*. So she wasn't "trendy." Was she really such a hag?

"I will give you a personal allowance of seven hundred dollars a month. That's for school, clothes, hair, makeup, and all that girly stuff."

Seven hundred dollars a month! She quickly forgot the rude comment he had made just moments earlier.

"On top of that," Andrew continued, "you'll have a budget of one thousand dollars a month for food, household items, and any other expenses necessary for this house, not to include the basic bills and utilities—my accountant takes care of those. I expect things to be very good here, no cutting on extras. So long as I'm happy with the way things are, you can keep whatever is left over of the thousand at the end of each month. But if it seems like you're scrimping in order to pad your pocketbook, I'll take it away and do it myself."

"Okay, anything else?" Emma said after digesting that latest bit of info.

"I still expect you to care for the house as you have been. I expect you to play the part of a happy wife when company comes. I don't think separate rooms will be too obvious—it's actually becoming quite popular for couples to not share a room, but you need to help me keep up the pretense with other people."

Separate rooms for married people? That sounded so bizarre, but he *was* from California. And it worked in her favor. "I can do that."

"I'm not going to explain the real situation to anyone. It will be much easier to just play the roles, introduce the marital problems at the appropriate time, and then get it over with."

Emma paused uncertainly. She could see his point and didn't want to be seen as a gold digger, so she finally nodded. "Fair enough. And how is the divorce going to work?"

"As soon as I get the payoff, I'll cut you a check, and we'll file papers."

It was impossible not to reflect on the mangled mess of a divorce she had just lived through. Did she really want to be divorced twice by the age of twenty-two? She didn't answer the question. She was impulsive by nature, and she couldn't think of a better option. She stuck out her hand. "I'll do it."

Andrew smiled widely and gave her hand a firm shake. "Good. I'll get my attorney to start on the papers. Oh, and one more thing. Stop smoking."

Emma didn't like that he even knew she smoked and opened her mouth to convince him that she didn't. He didn't give her the chance. "I'm not stupid, and you can't hide it from me well enough. It's a gross habit."

Emma took a deep breath and finally nodded.

"Deal?" he said, sticking out his hand again.

She regarded it for a moment and then let her eyes scan the study over his shoulder. She was going to live here! A slow smile spread across her face as she took his hand and gave it a good firm shake. "Deal."

CHAPTER 9

"How's my baby sister?" Tally asked as he shrugged off his coat. It was Sunday night, and Tally had brought his family to Chris's house for dinner.

"Fine, thanks," Emma said as she took their coats and glanced quickly at Tally's cane, frowning slightly. Nearly five years ago, Tally had been involved in an accident that had severely damaged his knee. Almost two years ago, he'd had surgery when he blew it out again. But he hadn't healed well for various reasons, and Emma felt sorry for his discomfort—although she knew no one would talk about it tonight. Tally's wife, Janet, greeted her, and Emma smiled and said hello before putting their coats in the closet.

Emma had met Janet for the first time over the Christmas holiday following Janet's marriage to Tally. It had been a very long three days. Janet had been rude and distracted, and everyone had been glad when they left—Emma had thought she was a total . . . well, not a very nice woman. Shortly following that meeting, the family had learned that Janet was struggling with an addiction to painkillers and other prescription medications. Emma hadn't followed the story too closely because she was barely pregnant with Cate and sick as a dog. She hadn't seen Janet again until moving to Utah, and the changes amazed her. Two years after their first meeting, Janet seemed to be a totally different person. But she was still drop-dead gorgeous, and Emma couldn't help but wonder how her brother had landed such a babe.

Emma planned to fill them in on the upcoming change in her life once dinner was over. Her stomach was in knots. All through the meal Emma thought she was going to explode, and she kept picturing their responses to her news. In her fantasies, their reactions ranged from giddy joy to shotguns and handcuffs. She had no idea how they would accept this, but she felt the shotgun scenario was more likely.

When dinner was finished, the men did the dishes while the women got the kids ready for bed. Between the four of them, they had five kids under the age of five and getting them all into pajamas was a circus event. Once that feat was accomplished, the kids were sent downstairs—except for the babies of course—and Tally and Chris entered the living room.

Emma's whole body started to tingle. She cleared her throat and got right to the point, sure that if she dragged it out she would throw up. Her brothers had been such a great support to her since the divorce, and she hated knowing that she was about to disappoint them both. But the truth was that she was more than just their little sister; she was Emma, and she had a life to live.

"I need to tell you guys something," she said, interrupting a conversation about basketball. They must have sensed the seriousness in her voice because they didn't even try to put her off.

All four of them looked at her with polite curiosity, and her heart sank to her toes. She couldn't meet their eyes, so she looked at the brown carpet at her feet, wishing Cate would run upstairs and interrupt.

"Sounds serious," Tally said with a laugh.

Emma smiled and continued to look at the floor. "It is

serious." She paused for just a moment and then mumbled, "I'm getting married."

A team of raging elephants bursting through the wall wouldn't have been a bigger surprise, and they were all frozen as they digested the information. Emma cleared her throat again and told them simply that she was getting married, to Andrew—in a few weeks. She had considered telling them about the trust and the details of the marriage but just didn't know how. Somehow letting them freak out about her marrying someone she barely knew made more sense than telling them the whole truth. When she finished, they still remained silent, staring at her as if she'd grown two heads.

It was Chris who spoke first. "Are you insane?"

Tally was quick to add his own two cents. "You hardly know this guy, and you're going to move in with him? This is the craziest thing I've ever heard."

Chris was shaking his head. He stood and started pacing. "Emma, think about what you're saying. It's crazy, it's dumb, and it's wrong."

"I know that's how it sounds, but . . ."

"But nothing," Tally interrupted. "You just got out of one bad marriage, and you want to jump into another one? I can't believe you're even considering this. It's nuts."

Emma took a deep breath as tears pricked her eyes. She hadn't planned to get emotional, but she hated the reaction of her two big brothers. Lacey and Janet had yet to say a word, which didn't help a bit. "I realize it sounds that way to you guys," she said.

Tally shook his head, and Chris snorted.

"But I'm sinking here." They became quiet, and she looked at them, hoping to show them how sincere she was. "It's taking all I have to keep my head on straight these days. I work my butt off so that I can come home exhausted and try to be two parents to my daughter. I'm barely able to pay my bills, haven't even started paying off my legal fees, and what do I have to look forward to? I want to go to school, but how can I? I want to be with my little girl, but I can't. And now there's this guy who's giving me the opportunity to have all of that. I can go to school, develop a career plan, and spend more time with Cate. I'll get a nice home to live in and enough money to catch up on my debts. Does it really not make sense to you that I might want to do this? Is it really that crazy? Or is it the only option that *isn't* crazy?"

"Do you love this guy?" Janet asked when Emma had finished. It was the first time she'd spoken, and Emma ached for her—for someone—to side with her just a little bit.

"A little," she said. It wasn't a total lie. She loved most of God's children. "But I find a lot to respect and admire." That much was completely true.

"Does he know you don't love him?" Janet continued.

"Yes."

"And he's okay with that?"

Emma let out a breath. This wasn't working. "We both have our reasons for this. I can't explain all of it—but you'll have to trust me on this."

Chris snorted. "Trust you? You're signing up to be some guy's mistress, Emma—why would you—"

"No, I'm not," she shouted. She took a breath, and after calming herself she explained all the details of the arrangement—the things she'd left out.

Those raging elephants would have been nice right about now. No one spoke. In fact, no one looked at her.

Finally Janet cleared her throat. "I guess it might be just what you need."

"Janet," Tally said, looking at his wife in shock.

Oh, thank you, Janet! Emma thought to herself.

Janet put a hand on Tally's arm and turned to look at Emma. "It's quite an opportunity."

"I know," Emma said softly, relieved beyond words to have even the slightest hint of support. "It has the potential to solve a lot of my problems."

"Or create more of them," Tally added.

The room went quiet, and Emma just sat there. They were all so different from her. They didn't understand what it was like. She looked up when no one spoke, and then she stood. Both brothers stared her down. Janet had a softer expression, but her concern was obvious. Lacey looked uncomfortable. At least they weren't yelling at her anymore.

"I'm sorry if you don't agree with my decision," she said simply. "But I'm doing this, with or without your blessing. I've already notified my landlord, and I'll write Mom and Dad about it—though I prefer to keep the details to myself. They don't need to worry about this." She stood and went to the doorway that separated the living room from the kitchen. She paused and, staring at the floor, spoke one last time. "I love you guys, and I hate disappointing you, but two years ago I married the man I loved, and I'm left with a daughter and not much else. Now I have the chance to marry a man I don't love and come out on top. It makes sense to me." She went down-stairs, picked up Cate, wrapped her in a blanket, and slipped out the back door.

It was a lonely walk—all three houses—and she questioned her decision for the millionth time. Was marrying Andrew worth it, if it alienated her from her family? She shook her head. She'd always felt like she was on the outside anyway. She was the only one who had gotten a divorce, and she hadn't been active in the Church. This was just one more thing to add to the list.

An hour later as she was rocking a sleepy Catherine while still contemplating the evening, there was a knock at the door. She lay Catherine in her crib and went to open the door, steeling herself for the possibility of her brothers standing there with a burlap sack, intent to save her from herself. Taking a deep breath, she opened the door. Her eyes widened. "Janet?"

Janet smiled. "Can I come in?"

Emma nodded as she looked past her to see if Tally was with her. "It's just me," Janet replied. Emma smiled and moved to let her in. When the door closed, they stood there for a few moments. "I took Tally home and came back," Janet explained. "I want to know what I can do to help."

"Help?" Emma repeated.

"Your brothers love you, Emma," she said. "But what you're doing isn't their first choice for your future. You can't blame them for feeling protective."

"It's my life, and I'm not a little girl anymore."

"But you'll always be their little sister."

Emma nodded. She knew that—boy, did she know it. She looked up at her sister-in-law again. "Are you here to try and talk me out of it? Because if you are, you're wasting your time."

Janet shook her head. "I told you—I'm here to help, any way I can."

Emma was silent. She narrowed her eyes suspiciously. "Really?"

Janet smiled. "Did I ever tell you about my second marriage?"

"I thought Tally was your second marriage?"

"Third."

"Really?"

It was almost one in the morning when Janet finally left. Emma shut the door behind her with a smile. She'd hardly known Janet a few hours ago, and now she felt like they'd known each other forever. They had decided to start packing the apartment while they talked, and Emma learned more about Janet than she had ever guessed. She'd known that Janet had battled a prescription drug addiction and that Tally had almost called it quits. But she'd never heard about how she and Tally met, fell in love, and got married, nor how devastating the first six months of their marriage had been. Her respect for Tally grew by the minute. When she left, Janet had promised to take Emma shopping, convince Chris to fix Emma's hair, and try to soften Tally a little more. She'd also challenged Emma to pray.

"Not because of me," Janet had said. "And not for Tally or

Chris but for yourself. You'll be amazed at the difference in your life if you let the Lord know you care what He thinks."

The advice to pray continued to haunt Emma throughout the night and all the next day. She'd tried to recapture the gospel principles she'd been raised with, but it hadn't been easy, and she didn't really trust the Spirit yet. She'd been going to church on Sundays when she didn't work and had attempted to read her scriptures. She also hadn't had a smoke since accepting Andrew's offer. After getting home from work the next night, she felt like maybe she *was* ready to pray about this.

Once Catherine fell asleep for the night, Emma put her carefully in her crib. Pulling a blanket up to her young daughter's chin, Emma imagined where she would be two years from now. Without Andrew's offer, it wasn't hard to imagine being exactly where she was right now. Yet, by accepting Andrew's offer, she could be established in a better job and have a home of her own.

Leaving Cate to her slumber, Emma went to her own room and knelt next to the bed. It had been a long time since she'd said a real prayer. She wondered if she remembered how. She took a breath and just started to talk. She couldn't bring herself to ask whether it was the right thing to do—she felt pretty sure she knew the answer to that. But she would like His help, although she wondered if that was possible. There was no lightening bolt, no silence to her doubts, but she felt better for having gotten on her knees. Feeling better about this was more than she'd expected, and it was enough.

CHAPTER 10

On Monday, Emma used her lunch break to check her e-mail. She was planning to write to her mom about her upcoming marriage but was distracted by an e-mail from Jake. For a moment, she considered just deleting it but reminded herself of the mess she'd already made by ignoring his attempts to contact her. After taking a breath, she opened the message.

> *Emma,*
>
> *It's taken me a while to work up the nerve to talk to you, and I finally just settled on this. I'm sorry things turned out so badly, especially in front of Cate. I know things haven't been easy for you, and I shouldn't have taken her without your knowing about it. I wish you'd just answered my calls. Anyway, I'm sorry—for everything.*
>
> *I just reached my ninth month of sobriety, and I've come to realize that it wouldn't have worked for us even if the drinking hadn't become such an issue. But I wish it hadn't ended like it did. I'm also missing Cate a lot. I wish I hadn't allowed you to move, and yet I'm glad you get the chance to start over. I really want Cate to know who I am, Emma, and I want her to know Suzanne. We*

had some pictures taken before we went to dinner, and I'd like to send one of the three of us that you could put in her room. She's growing up so fast, and I don't want her to forget me.

Things were never good between us, Emma. We weren't a good match, and you know it. But can we at least try and get along for Cate's sake? I hope we can; I really do.

Jake

She read it three times. The first time she was angry. The second time she was annoyed, and by the end of the third time she was just sad. She didn't know how to respond, so she didn't. Instead she wrote her mom about her marriage and spent the rest of her day going over Jake's request. He wanted her to display a picture of him and Suzanne? As if they were Catherine's family? The idea made her choke. But then Chris's words came back to her: *"If you rob her of that, it will haunt both of you."*

By the next day, she was ready to respond. It took her a ridiculous amount of time to pen the one-line e-mail, but it was a start, and it was all she felt capable of doing anyway.

Jake,

I understand and I'll do my best.

Emma

After her shift, she checked her e-mail again and found his response.

Emma,

Thanks

Jake

She wondered if it took him as long to come up with a response as it had taken her.

CHAPTER 11

By Thursday things were becoming much more real.
Emma would fly to L.A. on Friday to sign the contracts,
and the next weekend Andrew was coming to Salt Lake. They
would go to the courthouse and get married—just like that.
Her mother hadn't taken the news well and tried to talk her
out of it with numerous e-mails. Lucky for Emma, full-time
missionaries had rules about calling home too often. Then
Camilla, her only sister, found out and took her usual know-it-
all stance trying to convince Emma how ridiculous the whole
thing was. Emma couldn't imagine how either of them would
have reacted if they knew the full spectrum of what she was
doing. She was glad that Chris and Tally had agreed not to
tell them. Finally, Janet stepped in and smoothed things over.
Emma received a short "I don't understand why you're doing
this, but I love you" e-mail from her mom, and Camilla just
stopped calling—which was fine by Emma. She wondered
what Janet had said to them but wasn't sure she really wanted
to know.

A horn honked outside her basement apartment, and
Emma turned to smile at the babysitter. "I'll probably only be

a few hours." Mickey picked Cate up and put her on her hip. Mickey was fifteen and had four little brothers and sisters. Lacey said she was wonderful.

"We'll be fine," Mickey assured her.

"Okay," Emma said, kissing Catherine on the forehead and heading for the door. "I'll see you later." She ran up the steps and waved at Janet, who waved back from inside a brand-new minivan. "This is nice," Emma said as she climbed into the passenger seat.

"I can't believe I'm driving a minivan," Janet said with a shake of her head as she pulled out into the street.

"Are you sure he's going to be nice?" Emma asked a few minutes later after they picked up Lacey and headed for Chris's salon. "I haven't talked to him since Sunday."

"He's under strict orders to be very nice," Lacey said. "He'll be good."

When they arrived, Chris greeted Emma as if she were any other client. She was just glad to be on speaking terms and that her sisters-in-law were there to protect her. Chris spent an inordinate amount of time clipping and snipping before announcing he was finished. Emma's light brown hair had always had a slight wave. She'd worn it long, with no bangs, since junior high. Now it brushed her shoulder. Chris had given it some choppy little layers, but it was still long enough to be pulled up if she wanted. Then he showed her how to blow-dry it properly, as well as several different styles she could do.

"Chris, I don't even own a hair dryer," she confided when he got frustrated with her protests of it being too much work. Chris stared at her in the mirror and shook his head. "I *have* neglected you, haven't I?"

Next he put blond highlights throughout her hair that lightened the color just enough to make it look naturally gorgeous. Emma was amazed that this was the same unruly mane of hair she'd had all her life. After loading her up with a hundred dollars worth of hair care products, Chris made her promise she would do her hair every day and get a trim every six weeks. She promised and was then whisked away to get her nails done.

After the hair and nails, the next thing she did was get fitted for contact lenses. She placed an order and took some samples home. She'd had contacts before, but they were expensive back then and so she had given them up and settled for her glasses. It hadn't bothered her, but now, with all the other changes, she noticed how much not having the bulky frames really opened up her face and showed off her eyes.

Janet then took Emma and Lacey to Dillard's in Ogden, where she worked part time and got a twenty-five percent discount.

Emma wasn't much of a shopper and didn't give a lot of thought to what she wore. After ten minutes, Lacey and Janet took over and started tossing things in dressing rooms. When all was said and done, Emma had a whole new wardrobe and again was amazed that clothes could make her look so good.

"Why don't you try on a couple of swimsuits?" Lacey said while thumbing through a rack.

"No thanks. I hate swimsuits."

"Oh, come on. You've got that pool and hot tub. Do you really plan not to use them?"

Emma thought about it. "I have a swimsuit from high school that's just fine. No sense spending more money on a new one. I look twelve years old in swimsuits."

"Well, you're not twelve anymore, Emma. Try them on. Oh, and put that red one on first. It's got a Wonder Bra in it."

"A what?" Emma asked.

Lacey and Janet looked at one another. Janet shook her head. "Where have you been, Emma?"

When Emma emerged shyly from the dressing room a few minutes later, Janet smiled broadly. "Not many women can thank childbirth for their figure, but for you I think it was a very good thing. You're buying that one."

Emma looked at herself in the mirror and was rather surprised herself. She had hips! And a chest to go with them—

well, sort of. Of course she had noticed that her clothes fit differently after having Catherine, and she did go up a bra size. But she hadn't noticed how . . . well, grown-up she looked. *The things you learn when you take the time to look in the mirror; who'd have guessed?*

It was almost ten o'clock when Janet dropped her off, helped her haul in her purchases, and offered to take the sitter home. Mickey just stared. "You look so good," she breathed, her tone thick with admiration. Emma thanked her and once Mickey was gone went to stare at herself in the mirror. She turned slowly, doing a careful appraisal, and then just stared some more. She was reminded of the Hollywood cliché when the dowdy woman takes off her glasses, takes her hair out of a bun, and is an instant beauty. Weird—that it was exactly what she'd done.

The next day she got a call from Jake—it was delicious. He'd informed her of his upcoming marriage by sending a wedding invitation to her house. She'd reciprocated by asking her attorney to call and tell him about her marriage. Jake asked all kinds of questions about Andrew: Was Emma sure Catherine would be safe? Did Emma plan to leave the two of them alone together? Emma was quite impressed that she endured his questions for so long. When he accused her of getting married out of spite, however, she lost it, and they had a minute or two of name-calling and accusations until she finally hung up. It put her in a very black mood for the rest of the day, but she kept reminding herself that she was starting a new life, and she didn't need to let him control her emotions anymore.

The next morning she felt even more triumphant when she realized that she and Jake would get married within a week of one another. She went shopping again after work to celebrate the realization. It was twisted, but she found a great deal of satisfaction knowing she'd caused him a little angst during his last-minute wedding preparations.

Friday morning she caught a plane and met Andrew at the L.A. airport. He didn't even recognize her until she stopped directly in front of him and smiled broadly.

"Emma?" he asked with his eyebrows raised. "Is it really you?"

She was getting tired of that response. "Was I really such a dog before?"

"Oh, no, I didn't mean . . . you just . . . you look great." He broke into an innocent grin, and she rolled her eyes.

"Thank you," she said pointedly and then started walking, hoping he wouldn't keep making a big deal of it. He caught up with her after a few steps and dropped the subject, although she caught him casting repeated glances in her direction. She liked the power and couldn't help but wonder how Jake would react to see her like this. But she immediately stomped thoughts of Jake from her head. Jake was in her past. This was the here and now, and she was a new person. It was a new day, and she had a whole new future ahead of her. Still, she could imagine his expression if he could see her now—and it made her smile.

Andrew had a cab waiting that took them to the attorney's office. Once there, they read through the contracts, she asked a few questions, then they all signed the forms. Copies were made, thank-you's exchanged, and she was back on a plane by one o'clock. She picked up Catherine from the new day care and drove home. The apartment was full of boxes which would soon be stored in Andrew's garage. Most of the furniture was going to D.I. *One week and counting*, she thought as she put Catherine down and headed to the kitchen to make dinner. *I must be out of my mind.*

CHAPTER 12

*I*t snowed all night, so Saturday greeted Emma with a thick blanket of snow. She wondered if snow on your wedding day was considered bad luck or good luck. Then she wondered why it mattered either way. It wasn't a marriage—it was a merger. That was all. She and Catherine spent several minutes playing in the snow before she took Catherine to day care. Part of her wanted to bring Catherine with her, but she decided against it. Besides, today would be Catherine's last time at day care until Emma started school in January. Yesterday had been Emma's official last day with her nose to the grindstone—at least for a while. She'd miss some of her coworkers and many of the patients she'd come to love, but she wouldn't miss getting up at five thirty every morning and smelling like diapers every afternoon. Starting tomorrow she was a stay-at-home mom. She couldn't wait. She already felt like she'd missed so much with Cate, and she looked forward to making up for that. Today she was taking a load of their belongings to the house where she was to meet Andrew before they went to the courthouse.

Driving in snow was a whole new experience for Emma

because she'd spent every winter of her life in climates with no snow. She drove slow and careful, relieved that the roads had been plowed. It wasn't as bad as she had thought it would be. Letting herself in the front door, she called out for him. "Andrew?"

"Emma," he called from upstairs. "You're right on time. I thought we—" He reached the bottom step and froze.

Emma just smiled. Janet had insisted she dress up, so she'd worn a white linen dress with buff-colored leather boots hidden by the hem. Janet called it casual sophistication. Emma called it nice looking and comfortable but agreed it looked good; she'd always looked good in white.

"It's going to take me a while to get used to you this way," he said.

"What way? Pretty?" she teased, daring him with her eyes to agree.

"Dolled up," he clarified. He finished his assessment and then looked at her deeply. "I know I said it before, but you look wonderful, Emma." She smiled and looked away, but he touched her face and turned it toward him. "Thank you for doing this for me."

Emma swallowed, uncomfortable with his intensity as warmth trickled down her spine. "No problem—it will be fun."

Andrew smiled brightly. "Good." He then turned and headed for the kitchen "I'm just going to grab a Pop-Tart and then we can unload your stuff."

"A Pop-Tart?" Emma said in disgust. "If you'll unload the car yourself, I'll fix something worth eating." He looked at her for a moment and finally nodded. When he was gone, she went to work whipping up a Spanish omelet, toast, and orange juice.

Andrew emptied the car much faster than she had filled it and finished in time to eat a hot breakfast. Once that was done, they climbed into his Jeep Cherokee and headed for the licensing department of the city offices. Within an hour, they were standing in front of a judge who was reading off the marriage vows from a little card. Emma couldn't help feeling guilty as she promised to love and honor her husband; but when the judge read "'til death do you part," she could say "I do" with an almost clear conscience. The first time she'd married, she'd believed it would last forever. She'd been naive and excited back then. This time she knew it was for the term of their agreement. She was anxious but still excited. For just an instant, she wondered if she'd ever marry again. She'd be a twice-divorced single mother by the age of twenty-two. She pushed the thought away. *What a thing to think about during your wedding ceremony!* she thought.

Before they knew it, they were pronounced husband and wife. They turned to face one another and, with the judge looking on, shared their first kiss, sealing their agreement. Emma felt just a tremor when their lips touched, but she chalked it up to nervousness, not chemistry. Then they smiled at one another and left the courtroom.

"So now what?" Emma asked when they got on the road again.

"I decided to spring this on the office. I called this morning and told them I was getting married and wouldn't be in for the week. They took it rather well, I think." Emma laughed lightly. He smiled as he continued. "But I plan to hit the slopes as much as possible and catch up on some paperwork until I go back on Sunday. What about you?"

Strangely, she felt a little disappointed that he was just leaving her, but this was the agreement. "I think I'll get settled, put away our stuff, and then get Cate from day care."

"I'll drop you off at the house then. Will you be doing dinner tonight?"

"Yes, and what would you like for your wedding dinner, Mr. Davidson?"

Andrew laughed. "Mrs. Davidson is a much better culinary expert than I. I'm sure she'll plan just the right thing."

She laughed and looked out the window while

imagining the reactions of the rest of her family and friends
when they found out what she'd done. She wished she could be
like Andrew and pretend it was a real marriage to the people
close to her, but she could never pull it off—no matter how
much she wanted to. *Oh, well,* she thought. She wasn't doing
this for anyone but herself . . . and Catherine . . . and Andrew
too, she supposed.

"Is Emma your full name?" Andrew asked, interrupting
her thoughts. She turned away from the window and looked
at him. The marriage certificate was on the dashboard—she
could see him reading it in brief glances as he drove. "It isn't
short for Emmiline or Emily?"

"No," she answered with a little shake of her head. "Just
Emma."

"I don't think I've ever known a 'just Emma.' Is it a family
name?"

"Not really. Emma was the name of Joseph Smith's wife,
Emma Smith. My parents named me after her."

"Joseph Smith?" he replied blankly. "He's the guy that
brought all his wives to Utah, right?"

Emma paused for a few seconds as she tried to come up
with the best answer. "That was Brigham Young." She wasn't
used to talking much about the Church, especially to someone
that didn't know the basics. And she'd always been suspicious
about the polygamy stuff, so she didn't want to talk about that.
"Joseph Smith was the man who restored my church," she said
slowly, uncomfortable with this topic, especially since she was
on such shaky ground with her testimony anyway. She had to
think way back to her Primary lessons to come up with the
basics. "He was a prophet," she added, almost as if it wasn't an
important detail.

Andrew nodded as he tried to conceal his speculative look.
She hoped he would change the subject. She wasn't any good at
this. "Don't you mean he's the man that *started* your church?"

Emma tried to swallow her discomfort. *Here we go,* she
thought to herself. "My church is based on the gospel that

Christ taught when He was alive, but after He was crucified it broke apart and eventually disappeared. Joseph Smith brought it back."

"And how did he do that?" Andrew asked in a polite, yet suspicious tone. She had no doubt he regarded this whole explanation with as much credibility as alien abductions and reincarnation.

"Well," she said slowly, "Jesus Christ and God visited him and . . . gave it to him."

"Gave it to him?"

"Surely you know all this stuff already, Andrew," Emma said, hoping he didn't detect the slight whine in her voice. "You've spent an awful lot of time in Utah."

"I've heard bits and pieces but never heard the whole thing—I'd like to hear it from you. You were saying that God gave him the church? That doesn't make sense."

Emma let out a breath and continued. "Well, they told him where to find the gold plates that had all the things from the church that Christ had established when He was alive. The gold plates eventually became the Book of Mormon and then . . ." She searched her memory for the rest of it, just wanting to get it over with. "And then some other . . . angels gave him the priesthood and other . . . rules and things so he could start Christ's church again."

Andrew was quiet, and she looked at her hands in her lap. She wanted him to feel positively about the Church, but it just sounded wacky when she tried to explain it.

"And you believe all that?" he finally asked.

It took her several seconds to answer, but she was able to meet his eye when she did. "Yeah," she said simply, glad for the warmth in her chest that testified that she wasn't too far gone to feel the Spirit. "I know it sounds crazy, and I don't live it the way most Mormons do, but I do believe it—I can't seem *not* to."

Andrew nodded. "Okay then," he said, "but if angels start visiting you and stuff, tell them to hold off until I'm out of town."

Emma laughed politely, although she didn't really find the statement funny. "You don't need to worry about angels visiting me. I'm not a stalwart member of the Church."

Andrew shrugged. He didn't care, and she knew it. They turned the corner and pulled into the driveway. The garage door opened and they pulled in. Once the Jeep was stopped, he turned to her and smiled. "Your palace awaits you," he said.

"And the ski lifts await you," she said as she opened her door. He didn't get out right away, causing her to stop and turn toward him once she was out of the Jeep.

"Are we out of our minds?" he asked, showing the first trace of doubt she'd seen so far.

"Probably," she said with a shrug. "But people get married for all the wrong reasons all the time. I'm living proof of that. I don't think we're any crazier than they are."

"I'll remember that," he said, shaking out of his serious mood and opening his own door. He headed toward his bedroom, where all his ski gear was kept in the closet. As he bounded up the stairs, he called back, "I'll be home around seven."

"I'll have dinner waiting."

CHAPTER 13

$\mathcal{T}$he first week went much more smoothly than either of them had expected. Andrew did his thing, and Emma did hers. When he was home, Andrew kept to himself, often in his study, on the phone, or in front of the computer.

Emma had quickly deemed the sitting room off the kitchen as hers. Cate's toys were set up there, and it was the only TV the two of them watched. It kept them out of Andrew's hair and gave everyone some privacy.

After the first couple of days, Catherine started following Andrew around when he was home. Emma apologized and attempted to keep her daughter out of the way, but he seemed to like the innocent admiration. She'd wondered how Andrew would react to having a toddler around and was relieved that he seemed fine with it. She reminded Andrew that all he needed was to say the word, and she would keep Cate out of his way. But he didn't say the word. On Wednesday he brought a little parka back from the ski resort, and the next day he stopped and bought her a toy car. Both were big hits, and he seemed to find a great deal of satisfaction in her babbling excitement over the gifts. Emma warned him not to spoil her. He smiled in a way that said he'd do whatever he wanted.

Jake did mail the picture of himself, Suzanne, and Catherine. It stung to look at it, but Emma couldn't seem to pull her eyes away. She realized that they were getting married on Saturday, and although she tried to tell herself she didn't care, it was impossible to ignore such strong emotions. With the picture was a video that Jake had made. Emma put them both on the top shelf of the closet. She decided to make a cheese soufflé for dinner to keep her mind occupied with something other than thoughts about Jake's upcoming wedding.

On Sunday, Emma went to her new ward and introduced herself as Sister Emma Davidson. A few people came up to meet her, and she found herself feeling quite comfortable there. To her relief, she realized that her life wasn't written all over her face. She was simply another young mother with a husband who wasn't interested in the Church. She didn't smell like cigarettes, no one knew a thing about her, and she felt more positive about the gospel than she had in years. Catherine was even better behaved, which made the church experience a whole new thing for her.

The Relief Society lesson was on attending the temple, so she took it with a grain of salt. The temple was a great goal for most people, but she wasn't anywhere near that point in her spiritual progression—she'd just stopped smoking two weeks ago, for heaven's sake. She was impressed enough with herself for going to church on her own, and knew she had a lot of little things to get used to before she would be ready for the greater understanding and accountability of the temple. Catherine wasn't quite old enough to go to nursery, but the nursery leaders made an exception since there weren't many kids that age. Cate went without throwing a fit—things were looking up.

When Emma got home from church, Andrew's bags were sitting by the door. She kicked off her heels and tried to ignore the disappointment she felt at his leaving. *I'm just used to having him around*, she told herself. But when he said good-bye and shut the door behind him, she felt like a little warmth had left the big house. For dinner she made spinach lasagna and garlic bread sticks. There were enough leftovers to feed her and Cate for a week, but they enjoyed every bite. For the first time since Jake had left, she felt like she belonged somewhere. It was a priceless feeling, and in her heart she thanked Andrew for giving her the opportunity.

Thanksgiving was the next Thursday, and Andrew called to tell her he was flying in Wednesday night but not to make any special holiday arrangements since he planned to ski all day. So Emma went to Chris and Lacey's as she'd already planned. As a group, they all steered clear of the subject of her marriage other than the basic questions of "How are things going?" and "Are you doing okay?" She liked to think that they were even warming to her decision, but she couldn't be sure and tried to convince herself it didn't matter.

Instead, she focused on the medical transcription course she'd be starting in January. She'd already paid the down payment of five hundred dollars and would pay three hundred dollars a month until it was paid off. The classes were Monday through Thursday from nine to one and would last nine months. After that she could get a job doing transcription from home and make pretty good money.

Everything was going great.

Andrew came home every weekend after that, but he was usually skiing or sleeping, so she saw very little of him besides the dinners they shared. It was more like a sibling relationship than a marriage.

The weekend before Christmas, Andrew called to say he was bringing people home with him. It was the first time he hadn't come back alone. "We'll be skiing most of the weekend, but you and I will have to put on the married couple act."

"All right," Emma said obediently, not looking forward to this new facet of "married life" but steeling herself for what she'd always known would come.

"And can you do a dinner for us Saturday?" he asked. "I mean, you'll need to eat with us and everything."

"Okay," Emma said, a bit irritated at his continual reminders that she was not to act like the housekeeper. "I get it. We're married, I'm the blushing bride, and you're the giddy groom; dinner will be fine."

But it was harder than she thought. Luckily Andrew was pretty good at remembering what they should be doing. When he and his guests arrived Friday night, he came right up to Emma and kissed her full on the mouth, giving her a look that said he expected her to play this out. She smiled and gave him a little hug before graciously welcoming his guests to their home. The guy who'd liked her soup the night she'd made dinner last month came this time, and his surprise at her new appearance was obvious. Andrew said his name was Mark. The other three guests were all men too.

The men went out for drinks after dinner, and Emma made sure to be in her room by the time they returned. When they came in, she could hear their loud voices and stumbling steps as they made their way to their rooms. The guests were sleeping downstairs, so when someone thumped into the wall behind her head, she could only assume it was Andrew. She waited several seconds for him to get up and then let out a breath and grabbed her robe. Andrew had already warned her not to make a big deal about the drinking, but it irritated her anyway. He was leaning against the wall in the hallway when she opened her door, but he started to slide almost immediately. She hurried to his side and kept him upright.

"Nice," she muttered as he put one arm across her shoulders. She helped him walk to his bed. Within a few feet of the bed, he fell forward. Emma dodged just in time and avoided being taken down with him. She tried to get him all the way on the bed but finally gave up. "This is not in my job description," she muttered. He was already snoring.

Emma lay awake for at least an hour and thought of all the

things she wanted to say to him. This was too much like her marriage to Jake. She felt like she ought to say something, just to be sure Andrew knew how she felt.

When Andrew came downstairs the next morning, he said good morning and asked if they had any Tylenol. Apparently he had a headache. *Imagine that*, Emma thought. She bit her tongue again and handed him a bottle of Advil. In the light of day, all the things she wanted to say sounded stupid and immature. She decided to keep them to herself. The men were all going skiing again, and she was glad for that. She appreciated being alone.

"Do you still make dinner, Emma?" Mark asked as the men were leaving and Andrew informed them of the schedule.

"Of course. I love to cook." He nodded, but she wondered at his wondering. Andrew ran back in after they had loaded up the car to grab his coat.

"Mark keeps giving me these odd looks," she said as she leaned against the front doorway watching him shrug into his coat. "It makes me uncomfortable."

"Oh, don't worry about that." He paused and then looked at her with feigned concern. "Oh, no," he breathed, his eyes wide. "I hope he doesn't think you only married me for my money!"

"Very funny," Emma said with a dry laugh as she pushed him onto the porch. "You're making a lot more money off of this than I am." Then, purely for Mark's benefit, she pulled Andrew into a kiss on the front porch.

When she finally pulled back, Andrew smiled. "See, now is that so bad?" She merely smiled, turned, and went back inside, trying to ignore the little tremble in her belly.

She and Cate took a walk through the neighborhood, and then Cate went down for a nap around one o'clock. Emma spent a couple of hours in the pool—it was heaven.

When the others returned a few hours later, Emma had whipped up another wonderful meal, which they all sat down to eat. After dinner the men decided to watch a basketball game. Emma was quick to make her excuses.

"I've got to get Cate to bed and then get some presents wrapped," she said, hoisting the wiggling Cate out of her high chair.

"All right," Andrew said with a smile as the men stood and headed for the big-screen TV downstairs.

"We'll be sure not to keep him too long," Mark said with another of his slightly suspicious grins.

Emma just smiled. *Keep him as long as you like*, she thought.

CHAPTER 14

*D*errick and Steve, the other two guests, decided to turn in around ten, leaving Mark and Andrew alone in front of the TV. They were each working on their own six-pack; Andrew was winning.

"So why don't you explain this to me," Mark finally said during a commercial.

"Explain what? Basketball?"

Mark shook his head. "The housekeeper-turned-wife thing."

Andrew didn't risk any eye contact as he considered his response. Mark was his best friend, but Andrew wasn't ready to give it up too easily. "Is it that hard to believe I found the woman to change my life?"

"Yes," Mark said bluntly. "You've made no apologies about being a confirmed bachelor, and then one day you're suddenly married—to your housekeeper."

Andrew cleared his throat and began tapping his fingers on his knee, wishing he hadn't finished off so many beers. He was having a hard time coming up with explanations with the Michelob fog filling his brain.

Mark continued. "You've been married a month, and yet you invite the guys to spend the weekend with you and your wife? She goes to bed at nine, and you stay up until midnight?" Andrew was still refusing to look at him. "Have you forgotten that I have known you for years, Andrew? I've watched your relationships. I know you. What's going on?"

Andrew was silent for nearly a minute but finally realized he had no choice. With a soft groan, he turned to his friend. Mark smiled expectantly and indicated for Andrew to go ahead.

When Andrew finished explaining, Mark just blinked. "You're kidding me." Andrew gave him an impatient look. "Okay, so you're not kidding. I just can't believe that you would be in a sexless marriage."

Andrew sighed heavily. "Is that the only thing that stands out to you in all this?"

"You have to admit—it's weird. I can't believe you didn't tell me about this sooner. I could have given you the names of a dozen women who would have done this *and*—"

"Yeah?" he interrupted, raising his eyebrows and leaning forward to push the point home. "And then what happens? She falls in love, maybe. Then when the year is up, I have a whole new situation to deal with. I'm not a marrying man, Mark. You know that. I don't need or want the complication. Emma's still hung up on her ex-husband anyway. It's a business arrangement and then we go our separate ways. That's what I want and that's what I got. However, I have a reputation to protect, so we've been keeping the arrangement to ourselves."

Mark leaned forward and rested his elbows on his knees. "But don't you . . . I mean now and then just—"

"Emma's great, and yes, she's attractive, but she isn't that kind of girl. It's not that big a deal to me and definitely not a big deal to her."

"Now that's a good point," Mark said thoughtfully, leaning back in his chair. "She doesn't seem interested in you one bit."

"Oh, thanks," Andrew said with sarcasm as he turned the sound back up. "Just don't tell anyone, okay. We've got to keep it a secret."

Mark snorted and smirked but didn't say another word. Sometimes having a best friend was highly overrated.

CHAPTER 15

ndrew came to Utah the day before Christmas Eve, alone and determined to spend the holiday on the slopes.

"They're open on Christmas?" Emma asked as she cleared the dinner dishes while he entertained Catherine by hanging a spoon on his nose. She giggled and clapped, making both the adults smile at her enthusiasm.

Being an only child and removed from his extended family, Andrew hadn't grown up with children around. He had dated a woman once who had two sons, but the relationship hadn't lasted long because they were absolute monsters, and he couldn't stand the screaming—hers or theirs. It was surprising to Andrew how much he liked having Catherine around—but he did. It was fun to have the automatic adoration she dished out so freely.

"Yep."

"No offense, but don't you even care that it's Christmas?"

"Sure I care," Andrew said with feigned offense as he finally gave the spoon to Catherine, who was begging for it. He followed Emma into the kitchen with a stack of dirty dishes. "I love to see all the pretty lights, and mistletoe isn't a bad deal either . . . except this year of course."

Emma shook her head. "I meant that you don't even care that it's a holiday, a chance to celebrate and think of Christ's birth."

"Oh brother, here comes the religion," Andrew mumbled as he put his dishes in the sink.

"That's what Christmas is—the day the Christian world celebrates the birth of our Savior. I'm just surprised you don't care."

"I give generous bonuses to my employees, I donate turkeys to the YWCA, and I can sing the chorus of 'Here comes Santa Claus' without notes. It isn't like I go around telling kids there's no such thing as Santa. Besides, you and I are very different. You've got family and a kid to celebrate it with. I've been on my own for Christmas most of my life. My mom usually worked for the holiday pay, and we didn't have much to celebrate with—when I got older we went skiing together for Christmas.

"Besides, all Christmas really is for the unreligious like myself is kids getting toys they don't need, adults getting junk they'll never use, and everyone pretending to like each other. We went to my grandfather's little dinner now and then when my mom was alive—I much preferred it when we skied."

Emma shook her head. "Your vision of family is cracked."

Andrew opened his mouth in feigned shock and put a hand to his chest. Emma laughed and continued putting dishes in the dishwasher while he made another trip to the table. She was glad for the brief recess. Andrew returned just moments later with Catherine, who quickly wiggled out of his arms and ran for her toys on the other side of the counter.

"Most people look forward to spending time with family for the holidays," Emma said, not letting the conversation drop.

Andrew raised one eyebrow and gave her a disbelieving look. "I highly doubt that."

"Well, I love spending Christmas day with my family. I've gone back home every year except this one, since my parents are in Canada. But Catherine and I are going to get together with my brothers and their families. It's going to be great." She had the dishwasher filled and started wiping down the sink and countertops while Andrew watched her. "But I'll be sure to pick up some Pop-Tarts and a can of soup when I go shopping in the morning so you can enjoy it *your* way."

Andrew made a face, and she laughed and went back to her cleaning.

They'd been married over a month, but it wasn't very often that Andrew really looked at his wife. She was dressed in velvety lounge pants and a white T-shirt. He was reminded how different she was from the women he dated and wondered if in other circumstances he'd have ever asked her out. She noticed him watching her and cocked her head to the side, resting her slender hips against the countertop. He looked her in the eyes—those green eyes that danced when she teased him and froze when she was angry. He looked away and opened the fridge to distract himself. Immediately he spotted a bottle of beer and grabbed it. Even though she'd never said anything about his drinking, he knew she hated it and had little doubt that the conversation would end quickly now that he had a brew in his hand.

It worked. Her eyes narrowed, and she went around the counter to play with Cate. Andrew watched as she sat on the floor in the living room. He could only see the back of her head from his position in the kitchen, but he continued to watch her anyway. She pulled a box of blocks over and started stacking them up for Catherine to push over. He wondered if she knew he was still in the room. She didn't seem to, so he stayed.

Watching Emma and her child this last month had been a new experience for him—one he found rather fascinating. There was such tenderness when Emma dealt with Catherine, and although she lost her cool now and then, he never doubted that she loved her daughter very much. Suddenly he recalled a photograph he hadn't looked at in years. The photo was of his mother and himself. It was his first day of kindergarten, and they were in front of their apartment. Andrew was standing and his mother was kneeling at his side, smiling broadly at the camera with an arm around his shoulders and the other holding his book bag. She was only twenty-five years old then, and his father had been dead for almost two years. She looked so vibrant, so alive and proud.

When his mother had cleared out her home in preparation to move in with him during her chemotherapy, she had come across the picture and given it to him in a silver frame. But as she slipped away, he had found it harder and harder to look at, and he didn't know where it had ended up. He'd like to find it now that the pain of his mother's death wasn't so raw. Maybe he'd bring it back here. For some reason, he wanted Emma to see it.

Emma laughed as Catherine toppled another tower. Emma was only twenty-one, a young single mother trying to care for her daughter—her circumstances quite similar to his own mother's. He didn't know much about Catherine's father, only that the divorce wasn't Emma's idea. She never talked about it.

Did my mom love me like that? he wondered nostalgically. It was impossible to think she hadn't—she must have. She had made the same sacrifices Emma was making. She had certainly felt the same anxiety over caring for him by herself. To see Emma made it so real, so penetrating, and for the first time in his life he felt the tiniest glimmer of wanting to be a part of that kind of love again. His mother had sacrificed everything, yet all her life she told him he was the best thing that had ever happened to her. He had no doubt Emma felt the same way about Catherine, and it was a rather amazing thought.

Those thoughts were oddly tempting, yet he quickly shook them off. That life wasn't for him. He was married to his career. His projects were his babies, and he was realistic enough to see that nothing would change that, not in the long run anyway. For him, falling in love was optional in a relationship, and having a child required more than admiration and respect. Children required stability, commitment, and he wasn't made for that type of thing—at least not yet. Maybe some day he'd be ready, but he wasn't even thirty—he had years of freedom to enjoy and plenty of time to choose the right woman. As he made these justifications, however, he felt strangely irritated that he didn't have those abilities now, that the most important things in his life were things, not people. He could see just a glimpse of a whole new existence—but his current existence was fine, he quickly reminded himself. His needs were met, and he was content.

Again he looked at Emma. She was lying on her back now, watching cartoons with Catherine, who had apparently tired of the destructive game. Her hair was splayed out across the carpet, and she was either ignoring him or really thought he had left. Deciding he didn't want her to see him watching, he left the kitchen for his own TV. Emma's laughter rang out behind him, and he quickened his pace through the dining room and down the stairs to his entertainment room before his thoughts started running away from him again.

CHAPTER 16

*A*ndrew spent Christmas Eve on the slopes just as he had planned; Emma spent it in the kitchen just as she had planned. Although the mountains had plenty of snow, the Salt Lake Valley hadn't had a good snowfall in a couple of weeks, and the old snow was gray and patchy. Emma had hoped to have a white Christmas for her first one in Utah and had all but given up on it when she noticed the first few flakes. She opened the drapes throughout the house so that she could watch it fall and smiled to herself. It would be a white Christmas after all.

Catherine slept while Emma baked, and she wondered if life had ever been this good. Out of habit, she wanted to think it had been better when she was married to Jake, but in all honesty she couldn't say it, even if just to herself. She had thought that being married to Jake would make everything wonderful, that the imperfections of life wouldn't matter once she was Jake's wife. But it hadn't been that way at all. From the start, they'd both had a lot of growing up to do, and the more they grew up the more they grew apart. For the first time since the divorce, she admitted that she had hung onto the marriage for all the wrong reasons. She hated to fail at anything, and she hated being wrong—that's exactly what had happened, and it had hurt her pride and made her question everything about herself.

But she was doing better now. She felt good about what she was doing with her life. She loved the house and loved being home with Catherine. In a few weeks, she would start school and finally be working toward her future. Even though Andrew provided for her, she felt as if she was in charge of her own life. She wasn't dependent on Andrew for her self-worth.

When Catherine woke up from her nap, Emma took the picture Jake had sent out of the closet and put it on the dresser. Catherine noticed it right away and pointed at Jake saying, "Da-da." Emma almost froze, surprised that Catherine still remembered. But then she forced herself to relax and face this. Jake was her daddy. Emma had chosen him once; she'd loved him enough to have this child. Didn't she owe it to both of them to do better? She pulled Catherine on her lap and pointed at Jake's new wife.

"That's Suzanne," she said.

Cate slapped the face in the photo, and Emma chuckled, although she knew that Cate didn't mean it that way. "San?" Catherine asked.

"Yes, that's Suzanne,"

"San," Cate said proudly. She took the photo and grinned at it—that's when Emma finally realized she *had* to do better. There were really no other excuses. It wasn't worth it to keep being petty.

She retrieved the video that had come with the picture. "Do you want to see a daddy movie?"

Catherine scampered off the bed chanting, "Dada—dada— dada."

Emma put the video on when they got to the sitting room but left Cate to view it alone. She might be doing better, but she wasn't ready for this yet.

While Catherine watched the video, Emma wrote Jake an

e-mail, thanking him for the picture and video and the Christmas gifts he'd also sent. She'd told him how excited Catherine had been. He must have been online because she got his reply almost instantly.

> *Emma,*
>
> *Thank you—I can't tell you how much I appreciate it. I hope all is well. Give Cate a hug for me. I hope she likes her gifts.*
>
> *Jake*

It felt good to do something unselfish, and Emma was proud of her personal development. Maybe one day she'd even watch the video—well, maybe not anytime soon.

CHAPTER 17

Emma seemed surprised when Andrew walked in the door at four on Christmas Eve. "Merry Christmas," he called cheerily when he entered. Emma was fiddling with the Christmas tree she had put up in the front room a few days before and gave him a surprised look as he placed three packages under it. *When was the last time I had a Christmas tree?* he wondered. *Did I ever have a Christmas tree in my own home?*

"Well, hello," Emma said as she moved more decorations. "Here I thought you were Scrooge, and you turn out to be Santa."

Andrew smiled. "Just needed a little Christmas spirit."

"I'm guessing the snow ruined your skiing."

"Well, that too," he said as he dropped onto the couch. He watched her for a few moments before determining he hadn't a clue what she was doing. "Why are you messing up the tree?"

"Cate is having a hey day throwing these ornaments against the wall. She's shattered four already. I'm moving the decorations up so she can't reach them."

Oh, Andrew thought. He decided not to tell her how stupid the tree looked now.

She was dressed in a red sweat suit, and her hair was done in two pigtails. On most adult women he knew, it would have looked silly, like she was trying to relive her youth, but on Emma it seemed to fit. Red-painted toenails peeked out from beneath the hem of her pants, and he couldn't help but reflect on how different she looked than when he'd first met her. He seemed to reflect on that a lot lately. Too much, in fact.

"You look awfully festive today," he finally said. She turned to look at him and rolled her eyes before going back to the tree. That bugged him—he wanted her to take his comment seriously.

"You don't believe me?"

"I'm in sweats, Andrew, and I know a suck up when I hear one. What are you about to tell me—that five people are coming over for dinner tonight, and I'd better get busy?"

"No," Andrew said with a chuckle. "I just think you look cute—cozy. And I've noticed that you've become very comfortable in this house. It's come alive having you here."

She peeked at him for only a moment, and he noticed her cheeks were pink. It encouraged him. "No one's coming over. I'm thrilled to have you all to myself."

She risked a glance in his direction again and he winked, causing her to blush again. "I better go finish dinner," she said.

Andrew appreciated that she didn't flirt with him, but at the same time he loved getting off topic with Emma. She was a puzzle for him. Emma was smart but not educated; sweet but not a pushover. It didn't bother her to be the typical cooking, cleaning, child-rearing woman so many of her gender fought not to be. And the blushing—it had been years since he'd been with a woman who blushed over anything. The tenderness surprised him. It was refreshing—and far too distracting. He was annoyed with how often his thoughts had turned to Emma. He decided to take a shower and then get some work done in order to get his mind back where it belonged.

CHAPTER 18

*A*ndrew," Emma said in a loud whisper. The voice came from the doorway. "Andrew."

He groaned and rolled over, opening one eye to see Emma standing in the doorway, with one hand still on the knob. "I wondered if you wanted to open presents with us?"

"Hmm?" he mumbled, pulling a pillow over his face and groaning.

Emma spoke louder. "Presents—it's Christmas—we're opening ours. Do you want to come?"

Andrew rolled onto his back and immediately wished he hadn't moved so fast—his head was killing him. "Uh, yeah," he finally mumbled. "I'll be down in a minute."

"Okay, we're just having some cereal first."

Cereal. The thought made his stomach turn. After dinner the night before, he had escaped to the basement with a couple of bottles of *Lindemans* wine, his Christmas present to himself. There had been a tension at the table that made him uncomfortable, and he had determined not to dwell on it or try to figure out why it was there. He had intended to drink a bottle and save a bottle, but judging by the freight train in his head, he suspected he'd drunk them both.

Coffee, I need coffee. He sat up ever so slowly, wincing as he did so. With his legs dangling over the side of the bed, he waited nearly a full minute and then stood. His stomach lurched, and he sat again, fell to his side, and clutched his nauseated belly. It took nearly five minutes before he made it into the bathroom and into a freezing cold shower. When he stepped out, he felt a little better but was still in desperate need of coffee.

If Emma noticed his cautious step as he passed her on his way to the kitchen, she didn't comment. Right away he remembered that Emma didn't brew his coffee, and he went carefully through the routine of preparing the machine. As it brewed, he folded his arms on the counter and dropped his head on them. At the moment, he couldn't think of one good reason why he should ever drink again in his life.

"You okay?" Emma asked loudly from behind him. He clenched his teeth and cringed, wishing he had the guts to tell her to talk quietly. He feared he would get a lecture if he did—not that he didn't need one. But he wasn't in the mood.

"I'm just ... just fine," he said as he lifted his head and checked his coffee.

"We're ready when you are," Emma said, and then as if sensing his need to be alone for a moment, she left the room.

His coffee finished brewing, and he drank it as quickly as he could stand to, burning his tongue in the process. There was some Advil in the cupboard, which he swallowed with the help of another cup of coffee, and only then did he feel capable of leaving the kitchen.

"She couldn't wait any longer," Emma said when he arrived in the living room. Catherine was pushing buttons on a little machine that made animal sounds, which in turn caused her to giggle and laugh before pushing another one. "I think I could take everything else back, and she wouldn't notice," Emma added as Catherine pushed the cow button and mooing filled the room. Andrew was about to agree and suggest they all go back to bed when Emma pushed a package at him. "This is from Cate."

Andrew smiled his thanks, feeling somehow guilty that she was spending money on a gift for him when there was nothing he needed or wanted. Obligingly he tore open the wrapping to find a box that contained an inflatable pool raft that looked like an arm chair. He smiled at Catherine, who wasn't paying any attention to either of them as she tried to stick a bow on her tummy. "That was very thoughtful of her."

"We tried and tried to think of some junk you'd never use, and this happened to be our first choice," Emma said with a flippant grin.

"I guess I deserved that one," he said, and she just smiled as she fished out another gift for Catherine. This one was a toy that, when pushed across the floor, made the most obnoxious popping noise. Andrew closed his eyes and prayed she would stop before his head exploded. Thankfully Emma distracted her with another gift. It was a baby doll in a stroller, and it made no noise at all; it was easily Andrew's favorite.

"Open one of yours, Emma," Andrew said after she handed him another package. *When did we decide to exchange gifts? What if I hadn't stopped yesterday and bought those? I'd have been a real loser then!* Andrew thought.

Emma opened a box containing a black leather coat. She put it on over her pajamas, and it fit perfectly. "Andrew, you shouldn't have done this. It's way too expensive."

Andrew glowed, temporarily forgetting about his physical condition. "No biggie. Open the other one."

"Two?" Emma said with almost a scowl.

Andrew waved her on, and she found the other professionally wrapped package with her name on it. Hesitantly, she opened the package, and her eyes went wide as she turned the box. "A KitchenAid?"

"With all the attachments," Andrew added, wondering what all the attachments were since it had been the sales associate's great idea. Emma ripped it open and pulled out all the plastic-wrapped pieces.

"Holy cow," she said with a wide grin. Then she looked up at Andrew with an almost pained expression. "Andrew, you shouldn't have spent this much money on me."

"Who else am I going to spend it on? Besides, that mixer thing was for my benefit. The sales lady said you'd go crazy with it."

Emma smiled again, "She's right. I can save so much time with this. Thank you."

"No problem," Andrew said lightly, finding himself strangely embarrassed by the praise.

"No, really, Andrew, thank you. This was all very sweet of you."

Andrew nodded nervously and held up his own package to distract her; it was cologne. He tried to pronounce the name: Xyrius.

"The X makes a Z sound. Zeerus," Emma helped. "I noticed you only have cologne on when you come in from L.A. I thought I'd get you your own bottle to keep here."

She noticed the way I smell? "Thanks. I keep meaning to get some."

"If you don't like it you can take it back and get what you want."

Andrew sprayed some on the sleeve of his robe and smelled it. "No, this is great."

"Take it back if you don't like it."

"I said I like it."

"It won't hurt my feelings."

"Okay, but it's great."

"Really, Andrew, fragrance is a very specific—"

"Emma," he broke in. "I like it—thank you."

Emma smiled and quickly handed Catherine her last gift, from Andrew. While she tore at the paper, Andrew smelled his sleeve again and wondered if Jake had worn this fragrance. The idea made him feel strangely jealous even though he tried to talk himself out of it. Cate finally pulled the box apart to reveal a red sweater with a short kilt-type skirt to go with it. Also included was a bow for her hair, tights that had little ruffled lace on the bum, and black patent leather shoes. Emma ooed and awed, and Catherine made Andrew put the shoes on over her footed pajamas. Her role as Santa over, Emma plopped down on the couch next to him, causing Andrew to be adequately reminded of his hangover.

"Thanks, Andrew. Those gifts were wonderful and very thoughtful."

"You can thank well-trained sales associates for the thoughtful part."

"You're the one who went looking, and I appreciate it." She put a hand on Andrew's knee, and he looked at it in surprise. "Well, I better get cooking. I've still got rolls to mix and a pie to bake." She patted his knee and stood, picked up her new mixer, and went into the kitchen. He looked at his knee again and then rubbed it as if he could erase the tingle she had left there. *Now why did she have to go and do a thing like that?*

Andrew tried to play with Catherine, but her new toys were killing him, and he finally had to excuse himself and take another shower. The water this time around was hot and relaxing, so he put his head back and just soaked up the warmth, glad that his nausea had passed enough that he no longer felt on the verge of throwing up.

He was drinking too much again; it was time to admit it. Not that he was a recovering alcoholic or anything, but he didn't exactly have a clean record behind him, and he could see that he was giving in again.

It was during college that he had started drinking regularly. Everyone drank, and it was a stress relief, a way to unwind. But it resulted in a DUI his sophomore year, and he sobered up quickly when his scholarship was put on probationary status. For the next few years, he only drank occasionally, but after graduation he found himself in a relationship with Lora, a woman who *was* an alcoholic, and he started a big downward spiral. For nearly a year, they got drunk every night they were together. The mornings were horrible. There wasn't coffee strong enough to revive him nor pills capable of allowing him to function. He was just starting his company then, and his schedule was flexible, so he started planning around his nights with Lora. She wasn't the best influence, but she was fun. Unfortunately the buzz of it all didn't last long. Getting drunk quickly turned into passing out, which led to blackouts. When Andrew realized he was losing hours from his memory, he began to get nervous. And he got another DUI.

When Lora began introducing cocaine into her routine, he tried to pull away. Parties were a backbone of their relationship though, and he was beginning to think he was in love. It wasn't easy to find the motivation to change. He attempted to talk to Lora; he tried to make changes in their routines so they weren't at the bars and clubs all the time, but it didn't work as well as he'd hoped. When she slept with a dealer because Andrew wouldn't give her money, they both hit rock bottom. To know her addiction was that strong stung him like nothing he had ever experienced. He broke away from her and cleaned himself up, trying hard to put Lora and his feelings for her far behind him.

Andrew stepped out of the shower and wrapped himself in a large, terry cloth robe. He needed to be more careful. He needed to stick to his limits again and stop medicating himself, before it got out of control. Having made this new resolution, he felt much better about the whole thing and decided to take a little nap. What else did he have to do?

It was nearly four in the afternoon when he woke up from his seven-hour nap. He felt much better and realized Emma must be worried about him. Remaining cautious, he went downstairs, and only when he saw the note on the table did he realize she wasn't home. *Of course, she had the Christmas thing to go to.* The house was uncomfortably quiet without them.

The note said she wasn't sure what time she would be home but that his soup was on the stove. He looked around and noticed she had cleaned up the living room before she left. Catherine's toys were no longer there—in fact the only gifts still visible were his. He walked over to the chair where his new cologne had been left and sprayed it on himself again. He imagined her at the counter of the department store, buying a gift for him, and it made him smile—even though he wondered again if Jake smelled like Xyrius too. He picked up his gifts and took them upstairs as he brushed off his sudden feelings of loneliness. He was always alone in L.A. There was never anyone but himself in the apartment there. Then he remembered certain perks to being alone that he hadn't enjoyed for a long time. Without a moment's hesitation, he dropped his robe in the middle of the hallway floor and continued into his room where he put away the cologne and pulled the inflatable chair thing out of the box.

On his way to the swimming pool, he blew up the chair. He'd enjoy his time alone. He'd bask in his freedom. He'd spend the afternoon lounging naked in his own pool. This was going to be a very merry Christmas!

CHAPTER 19

$\mathcal{E}$mma hadn't seen Tally since Thanksgiving, and although he didn't agree with her decision, he was being tolerant. Janet, however, made her support just as clear as was Tally's tolerance. Emma soaked up the encouragement and ignored Tally's silent disapproval. No one came out and said she was making a mistake. For that she was grateful.

Around three o'clock, their parents called. She talked to her dad for a few moments and ignored the concern in his voice as she told him how well things were going. Before handing the phone over to her mother, he told her he loved her, and she got a little lump in her throat. She wished they were here. Christmas just wasn't the same without them.

After the phone call, they exchanged family gifts. Chris gave Emma the game *Stratego*. "Oh, I love this game," she exclaimed when she opened it. "Remember when we were growing up? We would play it for hours."

"How could we forget?" Chris replied. "You're one of the worst winners I have ever known."

Emma laughed brightly. "Who wants to play?"

She beat Tally and gloated merrily. But then Chris beat

her, leading her to seriously doubt that she was the worst winner in this family when he hoorayed and danced around with his tongue stuck out. Catherine found her during that last game and put her head on her mother's lap. It had been a long day, and she hadn't taken a nap.

"I think it's time for us to bug out," Emma said, smoothing down Catherine's hair that had fallen out of her ponytail during her playtime with cousins. "What can I do to help clean up before I leave?"

They shooed away her offers, so after fixing a plate of leftovers and loading their gifts, she left.

"There you are."

The sound of Emma's voice as the door opened startled Andrew and lucky, for both of them, reminded him that he had nothing on. In a flash, he rolled off the chair and plunged into the water. *Did she notice? Did she guess?* A moment later, he broke the surface of the water and pulled his floating chair to his chest to obscure her view.

"Sorry if I startled you," Emma said as she eyed him strangely. She had Catherine on her hip, and the baby immediately started straining toward the water. Emma had always been nervous about the pool and hadn't let Catherine venture in very often. That made it all the more tempting. "Are you all right?"

Apparently it seemed odd to her that he would plunge into the water for no apparent reason. *If only she knew!*

"Uh, yeah. Just fine," he sputtered, giving her a nervous smile. "You're home early."

"Cate was tired, but then she took a nap in the car," Emma said as she slipped off her shoes. She sat on the bench, one arm holding Catherine firmly against her chest despite the toddler's protests. She also removed Catherine's pants and began rolling up her own.

Oh, please, don't tell me she's staying, he pleaded silently. Sure enough, she came to the side of the pool, made sure it wasn't wet, and sat on the edge so she could dangle her feet in the water. "The pool's warm," she commented. She lifted Catherine down so that her legs went into the water. Cate giggled and kicked, splashing water all over her mother.

"Did you have a good time?" Andrew asked while trying to figure out a solution to this problem.

Emma smiled. "I had a great time."

Andrew was relieved when Emma stood as if to leave. "Do you mind if we get our suits and join you?"

Andrew raised his eyebrows as he thought about how to answer that question. In his grand display of freedom, he hadn't bothered to bring any clothing down with him. Not even a towel. His mind worked quickly, figuring out a solution, and he smiled. "Sure."

"I'll be back in just a minute then," she said as she left the room.

Andrew waited until he heard her footsteps disappear up the basement stairs before diving for the side of the pool and climbing out—with one eye on the door in case she came back. He left the pool room and carefully made his way up the stairs, dripping with every step. *No problem,* he thought, just as he got to the base of the stairs leading to the upper floor. He was on the second stair when the door to Emma's room opened. He flew back down and hid behind the sofa, listening as she babbled to Catherine about how fun swimming would be. He heard the door to Catherine's room shut a few seconds later. *Now or never,* he decided. He sprinted up the stairs and into his room, shutting the door behind him. *I made it,* he thought with relief as his heart pounded in his chest. He quickly found his swimsuit and hurried back downstairs before Emma could get suspicious.

Emma and Cate joined him a few minutes later. Emma was holding Catherine on one hip and blowing up a bright orange float as she entered the pool room. She took a minute to put

Catherine in a life jacket and then placed her in the flotation device. Catherine wiggled and fussed, but Emma didn't seem to notice.

"She won't even feel the water with those things," Andrew pointed out.

"Better safe than sorry," she said as she lowered Cate into the water. She jumped in right after her. Catherine kicked and splashed while Emma went completely under. There was something incredibly attractive in the way she emerged, water dripping from her eyelashes as she pushed her hair back with her hands. Andrew didn't like that he was noticing, and yet he couldn't seem to look away.

"What?" she asked as he continued to stare. She grabbed Cate's flotation device and started pushing her around the water.

"Uh, nothing," he said quickly as he pulled his eyes away. "I'm going to do some laps."

They stayed in the pool for nearly an hour. He got over his tongue-tied appreciation of her in a bathing suit enough to hold a decent conversation, and she told him about the afternoon while they both took turns entertaining Cate. He finally convinced Emma to take all the gear off, and they threw her back and forth, much to Catherine's delight.

Emma looked up at the clock and moved for the ladder. "I hate to be a party pooper, but I need to get Cate something to eat, and then she really should go to bed. She's had a big day."

"Will you come back when she's in bed?"

"Aren't you about waterlogged? You were already here when we came down."

Andrew just shrugged, realizing that he was being too forward, and began stroking his arms backwards as if it had just been a casual question on his part. "I love the water—what can I say?"

"It'll be a while until I get her down—but I'll come see if you're still here. Too bad the Jacuzzi's broken." She smiled. "Then I'd definitely come back."

Andrew was grateful she'd changed the subject a little. "When are they coming to fix it?"

"First of the year," she said with a shake of her head. "I swear the only thing they did was drain the stupid thing. It's been two weeks already. You'd think they could have gotten the part and fixed it by now."

"Yeah, well, money doesn't solve all of life's problems," he said.

"But it helps with most of them." She put Catherine on the edge of the pool and climbed out after her, much to Catherine's displeasure. "I'll see ya later," she said as they left the room.

"Yeah, see ya," he said. He hated how disappointed he was that she'd left. In fact he was starting to worry himself. He needed to get back to California—all this time with Emma wasn't such a good thing.

CHAPTER 20

*E*mma fixed Catherine some leftover yams from the family lunch, but the toddler was upset about being ripped away from the pool, so she threw them on the floor and banged on the tray of her high chair.

"Catherine," Emma said with exasperation, "just eat something. It's been a long day." She didn't say that she was also a little ticked off at not being in the pool anymore, but she knew it was Catherine's fault, not her own. She finally resorted to cereal, which Catherine ate between pouty glares, and then whisked her off to bed. For the first time in a long time, Catherine put up a fight, and by the time Emma finally got her situated, she was glad to pull the door shut. Staying home had been great, but she didn't know what she'd do if she never got a break.

When she returned to the kitchen, Andrew was pilfering leftovers. He had wrapped a towel around his waist and looked up with a grin. "You don't mind, do you?"

"Just save me some trifle," she said.

"Some what?"

"That cake-whipping cream-fruity-layer-stuff."

"Oh, I hadn't seen that," he said, finding the bowl of dessert. He smiled mischievously at her, and she scowled. "I'll save you a little," he said.

"You'll save me a lot or you don't get any at all."

He rolled his eyes. "Fine," he said with dramatic flair. She shook her head and retuned to rinsing dishes while he ate. As she began running out of things to do in the kitchen, and he helped himself to ham, she had an idea.

"Do you want to play *Stratego?*" she asked.

"What's that?"

Emma brightened considerably. "It's a game. I got it for Christmas. It's fun."

"Sure, I'm a quick study," he hurried to interject before she got too cocky.

Emma cast him a sidelong look. "We'll see."

They set it up in the living room, and she explained how it worked. The first two games she won easily, the third he gave her a scare, and then on the fourth he beat her soundly. Emma was shocked. "I've played this game all my life."

"I told you I was a quick learner," Andrew said with inflated arrogance as he set up his players again.

Emma narrowed her eyes a little. "I say we change things this time."

Andrew lifted an eyebrow. "How so?"

"For every man of yours I kill, you have to answer a question."

"What for?" Andrew asked in response to the playfulness in her voice.

"There are a few things about Andrew Davidson I'd like to know—and I always play better when there's a prize to be won," she said with a grin.

With a crisp nod, he answered, "It's a deal, so long as it goes both ways."

Emma nodded and shrugged—what did she have to hide? Emma killed one of his captains first and smiled broadly. "Okay, tell me the name of your best friend growing up."

"Brandon Faraday," Andrew answered quickly while studying the board. "He lived across the street from our apartment complex. He moved when I was ten though, and I haven't seen him since."

"Where did he move to?"

He looked up and narrowed his eyes. "You'll have to kill another soldier for that information, missy."

The game continued. She killed two more of his men, found out where Brandon Faraday had moved to, and asked her next question. "Where did you attend college?"

"University of Southern California," he answered comfortably before they continued. Emma's army was the next to suffer casualties, and she smiled, expecting the same type of bland question that she had been throwing his way.

"Why did you get a divorce?"

Emma blinked, and her stomach burned slightly as the smile faded fast. She had become good at ignoring that part of her life lately. She had stopped missing Jake and obsessing about his new life, and she preferred to keep it that way. Andrew definitely noticed her hesitation, but he didn't back down, so she straightened and tried to act like an adult. *Who's idea was this anyway? Oh yeah, it was mine.*

"He met someone else," she said simply.

Andrew was silent for a moment. "I'm sorry. How long were you married? You were awfully young."

"Just under three years, and yes we were young," she answered. "We struggled almost from the start."

"Why?"

Emma was silent for a moment, until finally deciding that Andrew of all people wasn't going to judge her. "I was pregnant when we got married, and—"

Andrew raised his eyebrows. "I thought Mormons didn't do that sort of thing."

"We're taught not to, and now I know why. I mean, we were planning to get married eventually, but . . . Jake wasn't a member of my church, which is a big deal for Mormons, and well ... I got pregnant, so we decided to get married right away and deal with explaining to our folks when I was further along. We married just a week after graduating from high school. Then I got really sick and miscarried a few weeks later." She glanced at him briefly, realizing he probably didn't want all the details, but he looked interested, not embarrassed. "All of a sudden, the reason we got married was gone. So we made a new plan. Jake started school, I went to work, and we decided to wait to have children. Our parents never knew, and we pretended it had never happened. But we weren't ready to be married, and we fought a lot. I got pregnant twice more that first year and miscarried both times."

"I thought you said you'd decided to not have kids for a while?" Andrew interrupted.

"We did," Emma said with a dry chuckle. "I get pregnant like that." She snapped her fingers. "We were young, and I was horrible at taking birth control pills consistently. And then when I get sick it's just too much for my body to handle. That's why I miscarry." She shook her head and looked back at the game board. "I don't know why I'm telling you all this."

"But you had Catherine?" Andrew asked, ignoring her attempt to end the conversation.

"It was just lucky, or unlucky depending who you ask, and it put more pressure on Jake than he could handle. He wasn't prepared to handle me when I was that sick."

"*He* couldn't handle *your* morning sickness?" Andrew asked.

"For normal women, morning sickness is irritating. But what happens to me is not normal. It got better around the sixth month, but I'd still throw up once or twice a day. Before then I threw up constantly. I was hospitalized a dozen times and ended up on a feeding tube for a while. I was only four pounds heavier when Catherine was born than I was before I got pregnant, and she weighed six pounds."

"So will you have more kids?" Andrew asked. "Later, I mean."

"Probably not," she said. "I would love to have more. But I don't think I could go through that again. It's due to a sheer miracle that Cate was born healthy and normal. It took almost three months after she was born for me to regain enough strength to go back to work, and I lost my husband in the process. I don't think I'm up to paying that price again. If I ever find Mr. Wonderful, I'd consider adoption. I'd really like to have more kids." She looked up at him again and smiled widely, signaling the conversation was over. "But I don't have to worry about that for awhile, do I? Anyway, now you know more about me than you ever wanted to. Is it my turn to go?"

Andrew nodded but looked at her a little too long, making her wonder if her hair looked okay. She killed another soldier and got the next question. She followed his lead and went for the throat.

"Since you now have my life history, it's your turn. Have you ever been in love with anyone?"

It was his turn to be reticent, but he had started it so she didn't feel bad. "I'm not sure."

"What do you mean?"

"You'll have to wait until the next causality," Andrew answered with a grin.

"I gave you a lot of freebies."

Andrew shrugged. "You didn't have to."

She scowled at him playfully as she watched him move his piece into one of her bombs. She made an explosion noise, gave him his piece, and smiled. "What do you mean you're not sure?"

Andrew looked down at the game board. "It seems to me that if you're ever really in love with someone, you would never lose that—that it would never go away. There have been a couple times that I wondered, but then things went bad, and now I'm not sure. How about you? Have you ever been in love?"

Emma paused. "Of course I have. Remember, I've been married before."

"We're married and not in love. You said yourself you got married because you got pregnant."

"That's totally different. I loved Jake very much." When she finished, realizing she had given him a free answer, she made her next move. The game was silent for a few minutes until one of Emma's men got whacked.

"Are you still in love with him?"

"I don't know," Emma said simply and indicated for Andrew to move.

"I don't accept the answer. Try again."

Emma gave him an irritated look. "I really don't know. Most of the time I'm convinced I hate him, but then sometimes when I'm alone or frustrated with Cate, I think, wouldn't it be nice if he were here, if that comfort of having someone to share all this with was still a reality for me? Or sometimes I catch myself thinking about the happy times—our wedding day or the trip we took to Disney World—and I miss him terribly. But I've come to think that true love comes after years together, after sacrifice and mutual growth. When Jake and I got married, I thought he was my soul mate, the one person in the world created just for me. I thought love was some magical thing that had happened between us because it was our destiny." She paused and shook her head. "But I don't think that's what love really is. I think two people grow into it, not fall into it, and Jake and I never grew into it. We rushed things, didn't lay the right foundation, and expected things to be easy. They just aren't—and because we expected it to be, we didn't work very hard at making it work between us. Then he found a way out, and here we are."

They both paused, and her cheeks colored when she realized the lecture she'd just spewed forth. She smiled apologetically, and Andrew made his next move. With his current luck, he walked into her marshal and lost his man.

"Tell me about your mom," she said quickly.

"You already know about my mom," Andrew said as he shifted uncomfortably.

"I know she didn't marry well, filed for divorce, and took good care of you. I know she died a couple of years ago. There's got to be more than that."

"She was a remarkable woman," Andrew said. "She gave up everything to take care of me. She taught me to be independent and resourceful. She was always supportive of my decisions but not afraid to tell me when I screwed up. We were very close."

"It must have been awful when she died," Emma said.

"The actual moment wasn't that bad," Andrew said quietly. "It was watching her go for those last six months that was awful." Emma didn't move. She was watching him intently and asked him to tell her about it. Strangely, he did so. "When she got sick, she was living with a man she'd been with for almost a decade. They used to travel a lot—they loved sailing and were always together, although he didn't want to get married. He was great when she was first diagnosed with breast cancer. They stopped traveling so much, settled down, and concentrated on getting her better. But the sicker she got, the more removed he became. One day he came to me and said he was moving across the country, and Mom wasn't going with him. I was furious with him for abandoning her, and she was devastated. That's when she first started giving up on her recovery. Her heart just wasn't in it anymore. She moved in with me, and eventually I had to hire private nurses to stay with her when I was working. But she kept getting worse. She did two different rounds of chemotherapy, her hair fell out, she lost both breasts and a substantial amount of muscle and lymph system. She was so embarrassed by the way she looked. She wouldn't let me see her without her wig until the very end when she was on so much morphine she couldn't care."

He paused for a moment and kept his eyes on the game board. Emma stared at him, almost startled to find this kind of depth in him. "I remember leaving for work one morning and looking at her while she slept. She couldn't have weighed more than eighty pounds. Her nightgown was flat on her chest, and

her head was covered with soft, patchy fuzz. She had tubes
in her arms. I couldn't believe she was the woman who had
cared for me all my life, the woman who had taught me to ski,
and who sent me postcards from all over the world. And then
her face contorted with pain, and she whimpered softly, as she
often did, and I was finally able to let go of the fear of losing
her. I wanted her to die, to leave the pain behind. When I came
home, she was in a coma. Three days later she died."

"Were you with her?" Emma asked as she wiped a tear
from her cheek. She'd been watching his eyes as he talked, and
felt like she'd just seen more than most people who knew him
had ever looked for.

"I was. The nurse called me at the office. Mom's breathing was uneven and her pulse was dropping. I made the thirty
minute drive in just under twenty. An hour later, she passed
away, peacefully."

"Did you cry?" It was hard to imagine Andrew in that
situation, but the tenderness in his voice and the pain in his
eyes convinced her of the depth of his feelings, and she wanted
to give him a hug—to offer comfort in some way. But she
didn't. She couldn't, and she doubted that he wanted her to.
She thought for a moment about her belief of life after death
and tried to imagine what it would be like to lose someone you
loved and not know what happened next.

"Not then," Andrew said with a small smile. "On that day
I had watched her sleep, though, I had bawled like a baby.
Never even made it to work. I found the closest bar and got
trashed."

Emma's sympathy all but disappeared, and she was glad
she hadn't hugged him, as the fire rose in her chest. "Doesn't
that bother you?"

"Didn't bother me a bit," Andrew said, suddenly the tough
bad boy.

"Your mother is dying, and you get drunk?" Emma
summed up in disgust.

"Alcohol is a good way to calm anxiety."

"No it isn't—it's a way to hide," Emma said bluntly. "It's a depressant. It slows the ability to think and feel. It doesn't solve anything—it just pushes it away."

"It relaxes *me*," Andrew said with a touch of defensiveness.

Emma snorted. "Then you wake up sick and miserable so that you have to recharge yourself with coffee in order to function. So the next time you don't want to face your feelings you drink again, pass out, wake up sick, load up on coffee. It's a continuous cycle, and the problems never get solved. In the meantime, you make a fool of yourself and kill off brain cells. What a great way to relax."

"You just don't understand," Andrew said.

"No, *you* don't understand because you are the drinker. The drinker never understands. It's the people cleaning up after you and putting up with the distance who figure it out. You think everything is okay because you didn't have to work out your problems. I mean, isn't your dad a pretty strong example of this? Didn't he throw everything away for the high?"

Andrew watched her as though he was figuring out a puzzle. "I'm not Jake, Emma," he said with more compassion than she'd expected. "And I'm not my father. I don't make it anyone's problem. Don't guilt-trip me for Jake's weakness."

Emma contemplated further battle but finally nodded in surrender. "Sorry," she said, although her ardor hadn't completely disappeared. She was quiet for nearly a minute and then she spoke again. "Jake started drinking heavily when I was pregnant with Catherine. The sicker I got, the more he drank. After she was born, he started going to AA. That's where he met his new wife. But it isn't good for you."

They were both silent, wondering where all this had suddenly come from. "Sorry," Emma said penitently once more. "I guess the game wasn't such a good idea."

Andrew shook his head, but he stood up and then reached a hand toward her. She regarded it for a moment before looking into his face and taking his hand, allowing him to pull her up. "We learned a lot about each other," Andrew said as she came quietly to her feet. "That was the point, right?"

Emma blinked, and they stared at one another for a few moments. Just then Catherine started to cry, and Andrew let go of her hand. "I'd better get to bed," he said.

"Yeah, me too," Emma replied. He turned to leave, and she went to her daughter, the connection broken.

Emma patted Catherine's back for a few minutes until she fell back to sleep. When Catherine's even breathing replaced her wiggles, Emma went downstairs to clean up the game. She was preparing herself a piece of pie in the kitchen when Andrew entered. He went to the fridge, although he couldn't seem to help eyeing her plate of leftovers.

Emma watched him and smiled as she ate her pie, her hips against the counter. Finally he gave in and asked if he could have some. She laughed and helped make him a plate. Rather than go into the dining room, he leaned against the counter too, and they ate their Christmas leftovers in silence. She finished her pie and served herself some trifle.

"How do you stay so thin when you eat like a pig?" Andrew asked.

"Good genes, I guess," she said. She finished her food and rinsed her dish before putting it in the dishwasher.

"Emma," Andrew asked just as she put her hand on the door. She turned and looked at him expectantly. "Does Jake wear Xyrius?"

She made no expression at all but cocked her head to the side. "Jake was allergic to cologne," she said simply. She looked away and left the room but not before seeing the smile on his face.

CHAPTER 21

$\mathcal{A}$ ndrew spent the next four days on the slopes. Emma spent them using her KitchenAid to make breads, cakes, cookies, and anything else that required mixing of any kind. She also did some deep cleaning. She would start school the day after New Year's, and she wanted to accomplish as much as possible around the house before then. Andrew headed back to L.A. a few days before New Year's and said he wouldn't be back the next weekend. He had a big project that needed his full attention.

A week later, Emma accepted a calling in the ward as a Cub Scout leader. Why she would be called into Scouting when she had a young daughter was beyond her, but she accepted and agreed to attend a training meeting the following Thursday.

That evening she also received a call from a Brother Epperson who claimed he was her home teacher. He wanted to set up a time he could come visit on a night when Andrew was home.

"Andrew works in L.A.," she explained. "He's only home on the weekends."

"That's fine with me," Brother Epperson said quickly.

"Will he be home this weekend?"

Andrew hadn't called yet to confirm, but she doubted he would skip two weekends in a row, especially with all the snow the city had received in his absence. She also didn't want to look like an idiot who didn't know her husband's schedule. She could always cancel if Andrew didn't come.

"Andrew will be home Friday night, but he won't want to visit. He's not interested in the Church. But you can—"

Brother Epperson interrupted. "All the more reason for us to meet him. We'll be there around seven."

She hung up with a snort. *This ought to be fun*, she thought to herself. From just one phone conversation, she was sure that Brother Epperson embodied all she didn't like about members of the Church—but hopefully she would be proven wrong.

The next day she started school. It was great, although she had homework every day that week. She was excited about what she was learning. It was nice to be getting on with her life. Whereas before, thoughts of Jake had been such a part of her everyday life, now she found herself getting better and better at not thinking of him at all. Now and then she would remember the anger and hurt, but it was nothing like it had been, not nearly so overwhelming—she was grateful for that.

Thursday evening she attended her Cub Scout training, learned some weird little applause things they did, and came home feeling overwhelmed. What could she possibly know about little boys? Luckily there was another leader, Gloria, who had been doing it for a while, and although Emma had only met her briefly, she seemed nice. Holding a calling was a new thing for Emma. She'd never been this active in her adult life. When she said her prayers that night—a habit she was still working on—she prayed for the motivation to keep it up. Church activity didn't come easy for her, but she wanted very much to change that about herself. She really wanted her future to be better than her past, and she believed the Church was her best way to make that goal a reality.

CHAPTER 22

*A*ndrew came through the door a little after six on Friday night. She met him with a smile and took his bag. "You're not a bell boy, Emma," he said somewhat gruffly. He'd had a horrible day at the office and hadn't worked out the tension yet. What he really wanted was some alone time. For the first time since this marriage began, he wished she wasn't there.

"I'm heading upstairs anyway," she said with a little irritation.

Andrew grabbed the small suitcase out of her hand. "Well, don't."

"Fine!" she said and turned back to the kitchen with the familiar glint in her eye that showed she was ready for battle. "Dinner's on the stove."

Andrew sighed. Just what he needed—a fight with Emma. He took his bag up to his room before going into the dining room where his dinner sat waiting. She had fixed chicken enchiladas, Spanish rice, and corn bread. He sat at the table for a few minutes but found it lonely and depressing enough that he decided he ought to explain. It would be a long weekend if he and Emma were fighting. As he pushed the chair away from the table, he reminded himself that this kind of thing was exactly what he'd been hoping to avoid by marrying for convenience. So much for his bright ideas.

Emma was in the kitchen sitting room on the couch with her feet tucked underneath herself, holding a glass of ice water and watching TV with Cate. He sat on the opposite end of the couch, but she didn't look up.

"I'm sorry, Emma," Andrew mumbled before taking a bite of his dinner. She didn't say anything. Andrew let out a breath. She wasn't going to make this easy. "I had a really lousy day." She ignored him and took a sip of her drink. "I'll let you take up my bags next time."

She gave him a withering look. "Ha, ha," she said dryly before turning her attention back to the screen.

Andrew continued to eat his dinner, wondering if he should just go back to the table. He reluctantly admitted to himself that he would rather be with her and Catherine than be alone, even if she wasn't speaking to him.

Catherine wasn't being nearly as stubborn as her mother. She climbed up next to him and grabbed a handful of corn bread. He flinched, not used to children grabbing his food, but he noticed that Emma flinched too, and that sent his thoughts in a new direction. "That's good, huh, Cate?" Andrew cooed, glancing briefly at Emma who was totally absorbed in a Colgate commercial. "Your mama's a good cook."

Catherine smiled a corn bread crumbly smile and pointed at her mother while attempting to say "Mommy" as more crumbs fell from her mouth. "But she's also very stuck up, Cate," he said with another quick glance.

Emma's jaw tightened, but she didn't give in. He cut Catherine a bite of his enchilada and blew on it before giving it to her, ignoring his disgust at sharing his food with a slobbering child. "Your mommy's so stuck up she isn't protecting you from my germs." Catherine smiled, loving all this attention, and a bit of tortilla fell out of her mouth. "She's *so* stuck up she isn't throwing a fit about all the food you're getting on the couch. She's *so* stuck up she—"

"Andrew."

He smiled victoriously. He had gotten her. He looked up just as the water and ice from her glass hit him in the face. In the moment of shock that followed, he couldn't breathe. When he caught his breath, he looked down at the dinner now swimming on his plate and then looked up—but Emma was gone. Catherine had gotten a good dose of water too and started crying. He vacillated for a moment before finally picking her up and taking off after Emma. He ran through the kitchen, still absorbing what she'd done, and pushed the door open to the dining room only to get another cup of water in his face.

This time he took it all. Catherine was unscathed and just blinked at him, forgetting her earlier discomfort as water dripped off his nose. With Catherine in his arms, he ran to the stairs Emma had just disappeared down. By the time they got downstairs, Emma was nowhere to be seen, and everything was silent.

"Where'd she go, Catie-did?" he asked.

"I-ne-no," she said. Andrew couldn't help but chuckle. He'd never understood her toddler talk before. But he didn't have time to dwell on it. He was on the prowl. Rather than looking wildly, he took a breath and decided not to react blindly. He'd think it through. Going into any of the bedrooms would leave her cornered, and a quick glance assured him she wasn't in the family room. Those options dismissed, the pool room was the only possibility left. Of course! It was the door closest to the stairs, and if he had automatically started searching bedrooms she could have just run back upstairs. He punched in the code on the number pad above the door, and when he heard the click of the magnetic lock, he pulled it open.

Emma squealed from her spot only a few feet away, and she ran to the opposite side of the pool. He didn't chase her. There was no need. The sliding glass doors that opened to the back yard were locked up, and she wouldn't be able to get them unlocked before he got to her. That meant that there was only one way out of the room, and he was standing in front of it. She looked at him with part playfulness and part fear, and he liked it.

"Ma-ma!" Catherine said triumphantly. Andrew smiled again and looked around. The mini life vest was on the bench, and he took a moment to strap her into it—just to be safe. He put her down but almost as quickly picked her up again, scanning the room to see if there was anywhere he could contain her. He spotted the Jacuzzi and smiled to himself. The repair people still hadn't fixed it, and it was empty—making a perfect playpen. Watching Emma closely, he walked over and put Catherine into the empty hot tub. She was thrilled.

"Do you want to explain yourself?" he asked as he pulled his wet shirt off his chest, the fabric making a slight sucking noise in the process. He liked how Emma closed her eyes for a moment, as if berating herself for starting this whole thing. "I assume you have a really good reason?"

"Uh, not really," Emma said in a high-pitched, nervous voice as she folded her arms and shifted her weight from one foot to the other. She was wearing jeans and a sweatshirt with the sleeves pushed up to her elbows. Her hair was pulled up in a twisty kind of thing. She looked young and . . . cute was the word that fit her best. He forced himself not to dwell on it. He had a score to settle. Andrew started walking along the edge of the pool, and in response she walked away from him, looking hopefully toward the door.

"Okay," Andrew said slowly, stopping his pursuit and turning in the opposite direction, which caused her to do the same. "So then you must have a really *bad* reason—let's hear it."

"You were being a jerk."

"And you were being a—"

"I was reacting to your mood," she cut in as they continued their semicircles around the pool. He never let her close enough to the door to get her hopes up.

"And I was reacting to *your* mood."

"And I reacted to your reaction."

"By throwing water at me?"

"I couldn't think of anything else," Emma said nervously.

"I suppose I should be grateful that you didn't have a blow torch in your hand."

"I'm sorry—it was a bad idea."

"You're sorry," Andrew repeated thoughtfully. "I have spent three months putting together a project that fell apart this week. I've worked eighteen-hour days trying to salvage it, and today I finally accepted that it's gone. I lost over a hundred thousand dollars, making this the worst single day of my career. I come home to this, and you're sorry?"

Emma paused, not liking the serious tone of Andrew's voice. "I really am sorry."

Andrew gave her a sarcastic nod. "So what should your punishment be?"

"I said I was sorry," Emma reminded him, wondering why she *had* thrown that cup of water at him anyway.

"Yes, you did say you were sorry, didn't you," Andrew said as he rubbed his chin thoughtfully. "But that still isn't restitution."

"I'll make you another plate of dinner."

"Not good enough," Andrew said, shaking his head.

"I'll whip up some of that chocolate mousse pie."

Andrew looked up to the ceiling, deep in thought, and then sat down on the bench that ran the length of the wall on his side of the pool. He began removing his shoes. Emma watched him with growing dread and glanced again at the door. She still wouldn't make it there without being caught, and she had no doubt that he was going to throw her in the pool. She felt bad that Catherine had gotten caught in the crossfire. She looked over at her, but Catherine was having a great time walking on the seats in the empty Jacuzzi. Emma realized she should have run when Andrew still had Catherine in his arms, but she hadn't. If she ran now, he would still have to get up and then grab her. If she waited, he would be ready for her. It wasn't rocket science.

She bolted, barely glimpsing Andrew struggle to his feet as she flew toward the door. It was right there—she was going to make it. She reached out for the doorknob and was just feeling victorious when an arm caught her around the waist, and they both toppled to the tile floor. Still, she wasn't giving up. She fought and flailed as if it were lava, not water, he was intending for her. But he was stronger than she was—a lot stronger. It took him less than a minute to lift her up, with her back pressed against his chest and arms. He pushed her toward the edge of the pool as the wetness from his shirt began seeping through the back of her sweatshirt. *This was a very bad idea!*

"Andrew!" she begged, wishing she could fully hide the laughter in her voice. *This isn't funny,* she told herself. "Please don't."

"Don't what?" Andrew said just behind her ear, giving her chills and making her realize just how close they were. "Don't get *you* wet?"

"I'm sorry," Emma said and then shrieked slightly as they got to the edge of the pool. "I promise I'll never do it again, I'm—"

"You're right, you won't," Andrew said with a light laugh as he pushed her further over the edge. She was pulling back as hard as she could but was going over anyway.

"What about Cate?" she said with mock fear for her daughter's safety. Just then Catherine giggled. Perfect timing. They both knew she was safe. "Come on, Andrew," she tried one last time. She was now bent over at the waist, staring into the water. At any moment he would simply let her go and her own weight would pull her in . . . unless . . .

With one quick movement, she put one foot behind his ankle and plunged forward. She heard a grunt of shock and felt his hands release in an attempt to save himself.

The water was like a vacuum, and her clothes weighed her down, but she swam for the shallow end of the pool with all her strength, which once again was no match for Andrew's.

She hadn't made it ten feet before she felt his hand grab her ankle. There was just enough time to get a lungful of air before being pulled under.

Andrew pulled her toward him, moving his hands up the sides of her body as if climbing a ladder. Once she was completely underneath him, he moved forward, letting her surface for air before pulling her under again. This time however, after being sure she was dunked, he grabbed her around the waist and swam toward the shallow end. When they surfaced, he had his arms wrapped tightly around her, pinning her arms to her sides and her entire body against him. They both gasped for air, and then she started squirming.

"I went to college on a swimming scholarship," he finally said when he had caught enough breath to speak.

"What a shock," she said sarcastically, still not showing the humility she was sure he was looking for. "Are you going to let me go now?"

Andrew squinted up at her. "Uh . . . no."

Emma laughed and tried to squirm again, but he simply pulled her more tightly against him. She realized just how close to one another they were—again. Both their smiles faltered. She stared into his face and saw something in his eyes that she'd never been close enough to see before. It was like a void—no, a hunger—and she wasn't sure she wanted to know what it was he wanted that badly. She forced a smile and tried to ignore the buzz she felt being wrapped in his arms. "So we're just going to stand here all night?" she asked after a moment.

He seemed unsure of how to proceed, and she felt his grip relax. She wondered if he was letting her go. "I might let you go for a price," he finally said.

She didn't have to ask what he wanted, and without questioning whether she was right or wrong, she dipped her head and kissed him quickly on the mouth. He shook his head.

"Not good enough."

Without further invitation, he moved one hand to the back

of her neck and pulled her face gently to meet his own. From the first touch of their lips, they both knew this was different than the crowd-pleasing kisses they had shared, and for a moment Emma felt pure fear that this was not a good thing. But that feeling only lasted a moment. Then the fear was drowned in the sweetness of it all. Andrew released his encompassing grip, and when his hands came up to cradle her face, she may as well have melted in his arms. She put her dripping arms around his neck, and as the kiss deepened, wrapped her legs around his waist to keep her balance. His hands left her face and wrapped around her back, pulling her even closer as the water rippled with their movements. All thought that this was wrong, all realization that this was not the right thing for them to be doing, had fully left her mind. How could it be bad when it felt this good? For the briefest of moments, she imagined a life as a true wife to Andrew. It caused the tremble in her stomach to nearly throb, and she intensified the kiss herself, unconscious until now of how badly she wanted more of this.

The doorbell ruined everything. *Dang*! Catherine yelled out, "Doe," just in case they didn't hear it.

They didn't break apart instantly. Rather it was a slow release of feelings and sensations as they realized that the moment had been just that—a moment. Andrew's eyes were dark, and he looked somewhat surprised. But whether the surprise stemmed from his actions or hers, she didn't know. When the doorbell rang again, reality descended completely. "The home teachers," she said softly as Andrew relaxed his grip and let her drift away from him.

"The what?" he asked in confusion.

"Men from my church," she said and began swimming toward the ladder, completely unsure of how to act around him now that this had happened. Her heart was still thumping, and she couldn't help reliving the moments spent in his arms.

"Oh, this will be wonderful," she added to herself as she looked at her drenched and dripping clothes. She quickly retrieved Catherine from the Jacuzzi. Catherine threw a fit over being taken out and held by her wet mother, but Emma didn't have time to pacify the baby. She held Cate on one hip and hurried for the front door.

"Don't drip on the carpet," Andrew called as the door to the pool room swung slowly shut. She snorted and shook her head.

The two men gaped when she opened the door a few seconds later. She tried to smile sincerely, but between the moment they had destroyed, the comprehension of what had just happened, and the freezing air gushing into the room, she feared it didn't seem very sincere. Catherine started to wail and tried to push away.

"I'm sorry. I . . . uh . . . we just fell in the pool," she tried to explain as she ushered them in. "I'll be down in just a minute."

She peeled off the wet layers of clothing and put dry ones on. It took only a minute to wipe her face off on the towel and pull her hair up into another ponytail. Catherine was all wet now too, so she quickly changed her into her pajamas. When she came out of Catherine's room, Andrew was waiting for her.

"What are they doing here?" he whispered with annoyance, making Emma wonder if the feelings from the pool escapade were completely her own. Water ran down his face, and his clothes were stuck to his skin. She forced herself not to look at the way they clung to his well-formed chest. His face was hard, and she worried that he already regretted what had happened. She wished they could discuss it, but that wasn't about to happen right now.

"Our church designates people to watch over one another. They're supposed to visit once a month," she whispered back, looking toward the stairs but not wanting to make him mad by running off.

"Couldn't they have come when I was out of town?"

"For propriety they're not supposed to come unless you're here," she said as she shivered in the hallway. "I should have told you sooner. I'm sorry."

"Another apology," he said with a groan before closing his eyes briefly. He turned to his room, and Emma hurried back down the stairs.

The home teachers didn't look any happier than they had in the beginning, and she wondered if she should reschedule. If she hadn't bothered to answer the door, she could still be downstairs in the pool with Andrew—the thought made her cheeks flush pink as she sat on the couch across from the two men.

"Is Brother Davidson going to join us?" the older man said, although *older* was a bit far fetched. He didn't look any older than Andrew.

"I'm not sure," Emma said with a smile. "He isn't a member."

"Home teachers are placed in stewardship over families, Sister Davidson—part member or not."

His preachy tone put her instantly on guard, but then he smiled, and she decided to ignore it. "I don't think he's interested in joining us."

"Have you made the invitation?" he asked, giving her a patronizing look that again raised her ire.

She forced a smile and sat up a little straighter. "He knows you're here. If he comes down, he comes down—if he doesn't, he doesn't."

Brother Epperson looked annoyed by her answer, and she impulsively looked to the other man for some help but quickly concluded he couldn't be more than eighteen. Brother Epperson then immediately opened an *Ensign* magazine and began reading word-for-word the First Presidency's message. It was four pages long. Emma tried to pay attention, but her thoughts were far away. Every minute or so, she had to force herself to focus on the lesson she was being taught. Brother Epperson droned on for what felt like hours. It had been years since she'd had a home teaching visit, but she didn't think it was supposed to be like this.

To Emma's surprise, Andrew, dry and dressed, entered the living room and sat next to her on the sofa in time for the last few paragraphs, at which time Brother Epperson sat a little taller and made frequent eye contact with Andrew as he read. Emma was acutely aware of Andrew's proximity and found it even more difficult to pay attention.

When he had finished, Brother Epperson looked directly at Andrew. The article was about having a testimony centered on Christ. "Do you believe in God, Brother Davidson?"

"Brother Epperson," Emma interrupted, "I told you Andrew isn't really interested in the Church right now. He—"

Brother Epperson turned to look at her. He looked truly angry as he spoke. "You are the example here and know that we owe God everything, including our obedience to the simple commandment of baptism—"

Emma couldn't believe this was happening and stood quickly, cutting off Brother Epperson. "Well, it was nice meeting the two of you," she said loudly.

That shut the man up but only for a moment. "It is my stewardship to be sure you are being spiritually fed. I don't think you—"

"I will ask you to leave," Andrew said with forced calmness. "Now."

Brother Epperson finally stood. His companion followed, looking pale and ready to collapse. Brother Epperson turned and walked out, stomping on the welcome mat as Emma closed the door behind them.

"What was that?" Andrew said, casting fiery eyes at Emma.

Having his anger directed at her was surprising. "I have no idea."

Andrew's eyes narrowed, and his nostrils flared just a little bit. "You set this up?"

Emma's eyes widened. "No, of course I didn't."

"You asked these men to come and preach to me."

Emma shook her head, wondering how exactly to get out of this. "No . . . not at all. Everyone gets home teachers.

They're supposed to—"

"And is that why you kissed me? Your way of drawing me in?"

"What?" Emma countered angrily. "I told them they could come over, but I didn't expect to be accosted anymore than you did! And the kiss was your idea. I was just—"

"What? *Playing along?*"

They both went silent, and Emma wondered again what exactly had happened in the pool. What were her motives? What were his? Why *had* she given in?

"I'm going back to L.A.," Andrew said suddenly and then disappeared up the stairs, leaving Emma confused. He returned with his bag a few minutes later and slammed the door on his way out.

Emma pulled the door open almost as soon as it had shut and hurried after him, ignoring the stinging pain of the frozen cement on her bare feet and the way the frigid air clung to her wet hair. She called out, but he wouldn't stop. Finally she caught up with him and grabbed his arm.

"What is your problem?" she demanded. "I don't know what that guy was doing. He's some kind of wack job—I've never met anyone like that in my church before. I'm so sorry, and if you want me to be, then I'll be sorry about the kiss too, but I am not trying to manipulate or convert you, Andrew. I never have."

Andrew just stared at her with no expression at all. "Don't play games with me, Emma. I told you that a long time ago, before any of this happened. I want the whole picture all the time. I don't want to guess at your motives or wonder what's going on in my home. Do you understand that?"

"Yes, but this wasn't my fault," Emma whispered, resisting the urge to cry.

"And that kiss was just stupid," Andrew said bitterly. "I never want *any* of what happened tonight to happen again—do you hear me?"

Emma swallowed the lump in her throat. She'd never seen

Andrew angry, and she hated the way it reminded her of Jake when he got mad. "Okay. None of it will happen again."

"Good," Andrew said with a nod as he threw his bag in the car. "I'll see you next weekend."

Emma didn't say anything as Andrew got in the car and pulled out of the driveway. *What just happened?* she asked herself as the tears fell from her eyes and the burning in her feet finally reached her brain.

CHAPTER 23

*A*ndrew whipped around the turns and then slammed on his brakes when he came to the first red light. He struck the steering wheel with his fist and cursed Emma in his mind. But he knew his mood wasn't entirely her fault. If anything, she had provided him a temporary break. If only she hadn't brought those preachers over to make a horrible day worse than ever.

There was no doubt in his mind that she had choreographed the whole situation, but it was possible that it turned out to be more than she bargained for. Her irritation had seemed sincere—but she was the one who invited them over without his knowledge, and even she admitted they were supposed to teach. *What a mess,* he thought as he slammed on his brakes for another stop. He had thought coming to Salt Lake today would clear his head, but now he was more confused than ever. Not only was he worried about his business, but now Emma was making his life even more complicated.

Why did I kiss her? Stress relief maybe, or simple entertainment. He worried that it was more than that, but he was still too angry to think about it. He should never have had those drinks on the plane; alcohol heightened whatever he was feeling, and he'd been in a very bad mood all day.

Then he had an idea. If he got completely plastered, his mood would no longer be a problem.

With that thought, he got into the right-turn lane and headed into downtown Salt Lake instead of getting on the freeway for the airport. He slowed down at the first bar he came to, pulled into the parking lot, and turned off the car. People said that drinking never helped the situation. Emma said it was simply running away. But what did they know? They just weren't as good at it as he was.

Emma put Catherine to bed and then went through the house and straightened up as she tried to review the evening. Maybe she was all wrong about Andrew. Maybe he wasn't a nice, kind-hearted guy. Maybe he was simply a spoiled, arrogant man. From their first meeting, he had been condescending and snobby. There were episodes when they had gotten along really well, and most of the time she felt quite comfortable with him. But now those occasions seemed like a sham, little speed bumps that delayed her final judgment.

He had asked for that kiss, deepened it, held her, and sent her swooning. Then he had said it was stupid as if it meant nothing. In her experience, no kiss like that could mean nothing. But she wasn't Andrew Davidson, and she certainly hadn't had the kind of experiences he had. She had slept with one man in her life, and he had been her husband, eventually. Andrew was a modern man who saw sex as a natural part of the dating process; so she realized it was quite possible that to him a kiss like that *would* mean nothing. The thought made her feel sick inside, and she fought back tears.

That jerk of a home teacher had been the icing on the cake. Her insides burned as she reviewed Brother Epperson's behavior. She had known zealots before but hadn't ever been confronted like that. How could a man like that believe the same things she did? If only she had warned Andrew that they were coming. It still would have ended badly, but at least he wouldn't have been able to accuse her of playing games.

She justified and rationalized until almost midnight before finally getting ready for bed. *I really screwed up this time. I should be used to it by now. What a mess!*

She looked at her scriptures but found she was too upset to find the right spirit. *I'll read tomorrow*, she told herself and then she got into bed, ignoring her prayers as well.

The clock said 2:46 A.M. when she was awakened by pounding at the door. If she had allowed herself enough time to wake up, she would have been frightened, but the fog of sleep allowed her to hurry to the door before thinking the situation all the way through. Andrew tumbled into her when she opened the door, nearly causing her to fall over. It took only a moment to realize he was incredibly drunk.

"He owes me twelve bucks in cab fare," said a voice from the driveway. She looked past Andrew to see the cab driver. Still trying to figure out exactly what was happening, she stumbled with Andrew to the couch and emptied his pockets. She found a fifty in his wallet, handed it to the cabbie who had come to stand in the doorway, and told him to keep the change.

"Thanks, lady," he said in a much nicer tone than he had used previously. "He's supposed to pick up his car at *The Dead Goat* tomorrow."

Emma forced a smile. "Thank you." He nodded, and she shut the door.

Turning, she looked at Andrew pathetically sprawled out on the couch. *How disgusting.* It took several attempts to get him into a standing position and then nearly five minutes to lead him up the stairs. He was only semiconscious, and when they finally reached the bed, he fell toward it, pinning her beneath him.

Just what I need, she thought as she tried to get free. His warm mouth on her neck made her shiver, however, and she froze for a moment as the feelings from earlier that night descended upon her.

"Emma," he breathed. She swallowed as his hand came up to her face in the darkness. His hands were clumsy as he tried to caress her face. She looked away but didn't pull away like she knew she should.

"Andrew," she said in a slightly squeaky voice as sensations she'd all but forgotten seemed to overtake her, "you're drunk."

He ignored her and kissed her neck again, washing her body with heat. *The kiss was stupid*, she chanted in her mind. But she wasn't fighting him, and his hands were beginning to roam. By the time his mouth met hers, she had almost dwindled into submission, but the strong smell of alcohol brought her back to her senses in a hurry. She pushed him away and tried to get up, disgusted with him for being drunk and with herself for being so lonely as to entertain the thoughts she was entertaining. Was she truly that desperate to feel wanted? The answer frightened her.

"Emma, please," he moaned as she pulled herself away from him. He didn't try to stop her. "Please stay."

"You're drunk," Emma repeated and shut the door behind her just as he screamed her name. The frustration in his voice frightened her, and she wondered if she was really safe with him. He didn't say anything more, and after a few minutes she opened the door just enough to see that he was asleep.

Tears came unbidden to her eyes, and she put a hand to her face, overcome with confusion. *What is happening?* She stood in the hallway staring at him and wondering why she was feeling so helpless.

Then a thought struck her. She thought back to just after Jake had left and how empty she felt without him—how badly she longed for him. She had been forced to realize the feelings were entirely hers, that he didn't want her. That one-sided love, that singular need, felt something like this. She thought back to that kiss in the pool, the fulfillment she felt being in

Andrew's arms, and she found a rather frightening similarity. There were more reasons not to admit this than she could count. It was completely wrong and unintentional. But in the dark hallway, by herself, she admitted that the time she had spent with Andrew had done something to her she hadn't expected.

Sleep was hard to come by once she got around to returning to her room, until the wayward thought that she could possibly be developing these types of feelings for Andrew all but disappeared. *It's late. I'm confused and lonely. That's all.*

The next morning Andrew didn't wake up until almost noon, and when he finally stumbled out of his room, he said he had a splitting headache.

"What a coincidence," Emma said blandly as she finished cutting up Catherine's hot dog for lunch. "So do I."

Andrew sat at the counter heavily and put his hands over his face. Then, as if just realizing that he was not in California, he lifted his head and looked at her. "Did I drive back here?"

"In your condition? Hardly," she grunted in disgust. "The bar was kind enough to call you a cab. The Cherokee is waiting for you to pick it up."

Andrew groaned and dropped his head onto his folded arms. "I need coffee," he mumbled.

"I don't do coffee," Emma said as she plopped a spoonful of applesauce onto Catherine's plate.

Andrew was quiet for a few minutes, making Emma wonder if he had fallen asleep. Finally he lifted his face but wouldn't look at her. "Did I embarrass myself horribly?"

"If 'horribly' translates into being unable to stand on your own and barely conscious as I helped you stumble to your room, then, yes, you horribly embarrassed *both* of us."

Andrew groaned. "I'm sorry, Emma," he said quietly.

Not half as sorry as I am, Emma thought to herself. Aloud she tried to change the subject. "As soon as you're ready, I'll drive you downtown. You do remember what bar it was, don't you?"

Andrew didn't bother answering, and soon he went up to his room, without coffee. Within an hour he returned, showered and shaved but not looking too much better. Emma loaded Catherine up, and they drove her car to the bar's empty parking lot in silence. Once she pulled up behind his Jeep, they sat there for a moment. Andrew seemed to be trying to decide whether or not to speak, but she beat him to it.

"Go back to California, Andrew. Next week we'll both pretend none of this happened, and everything will be fine."

"I am sorry, Emma."

"Well, then we've both made our apologies," she said without looking at him. "I'll see you next week."

Andrew nodded and got out of the car. She watched him climb into the driver's seat and pull away, not wanting him to see the tears in her eyes. She tried to come up with all the things she hated about Andrew, but it didn't help. It was impossible for her to deny how much she admired him, how impressed she was by all he'd done with his life. He was a good man, a kind man. Until this weekend, he had always treated her with respect. But he was also a selfish, materialistic drunk—nothing like the kind of man she needed in her life. By the time she got home, her eyes were dry, and she had convinced herself that she wished the weekend hadn't happened at all.

CHAPTER 24

March

"Emma," Andrew called as he entered the house.

"Yes," she said as she came around the corner of the dining room.

"Some of the guys came. I forgot to call."

Emma nodded. "No problem. I'll just whip up a few more servings." She could hear the myriad male voices and retreated to the kitchen. It was now March and not the first time Andrew had popped in with extra guests. After that first weekend of the New Year, and *The Dead Goat* incident, as she thought of it, he hadn't come alone. She figured it was just as well. What had once been a comfortable and easy relationship had turned awkward. As long as he was surrounded by his friends, they didn't have to bother one another much.

They never discussed what had happened that night, but she noticed he didn't drink as often or as much. She'd forbidden herself to think of the kiss, how badly it had hurt to have him leave angry that night, or how much she'd wanted to stay in his room when he returned. Sometimes the memory would sneak into her thoughts, but she pushed it away as soon as she realized it was there.

The Sunday following the home teacher problem, Emma had attended church and been asked to meet with the bishop. Apparently Brother Epperson had informed him that the situation at her home was not good, and the bishop wanted to know what was wrong. She had been instantly offended and told him of Brother Epperson's badgering. The bishop said that the man was new in the ward and did have a tendency to get a little theatrical. He apologized profusely and said he would assign another companionship. "Don't bother assigning anyone else. Andrew won't allow it now."

She came home feeling empty. The next week she hadn't bothered to go to church, and in the weeks that followed she found more and more excuses not to attend. The Relief Society presidency came by to see her, and the entire bishopric even came by one night. But that only seemed to make her feel that she was a project; she didn't want that. The one week she finally went, due to Chris's encouragement, she had the good fortune of running into Brother Epperson in the hall where he introduced her to his "eternal companion" and "children of the covenant." *What is it with this guy?* But it was the last straw. She felt she'd given her best. Sometime in the future she'd go back, when she was in another ward, but it wasn't worth her energy anymore.

Her calling as a den mother fizzled out too. Gloria, the other den leader, was nice, but Emma made herself unavailable and stopped answering Gloria's phone calls. Gloria was then called as Emma's visiting teacher, but when she stopped by, Emma kept the visits short and on the doorstep. She liked Gloria but not the reasons for her interest, and therefore blew her off as often as possible. When Emma dared look at herself, she knew she was not in a good spiritual situation, but she assured herself it was only temporary. And she couldn't deny that she was more comfortable right where she was. Church was unsettling. She hadn't had a positive experience in quite some time, and it seemed ridiculous to force it. The teachings were sound, and she was grateful to have the knowledge she had, but she just didn't fit in with the society of Saints. She never had, and she was beginning to believe that she never would. Surely God could see that. *Wasn't it Nephi that said God wouldn't ask us to do more than we are capable of?* Activity in this church right now was an incapability for her. Everything seemed to be steering her toward that realization.

The guests Andrew brought home with him were always the same, though in different groups, and she'd gotten to know them well enough. Occasionally one of the guys would bring a girlfriend, and Emma was careful to have family obligations that kept her time at the house limited during those weekends. The men didn't seem to notice the distance between Andrew and his wife, but the women paid much more attention.

Mark had come this weekend, as well as Derek and a man named Gordon. She had become pretty comfortable with all of them but was still relieved when Catherine did her the favor tonight of being a royal pain during dinner, allowing Emma to escape into the kitchen for the rest of the evening. Most mothers wouldn't appreciate an attitude like Catherine's, but Emma found it worked to her advantage more often than not. Cate went to sleep shortly thereafter, and Emma started on the dishes. When Mark entered the kitchen, she threw him a washrag and instructed him to wipe down the countertops. He came nearly every weekend and had made a habit of helping out after dinner. At first it was odd, but with Andrew's withdrawal, she found she enjoyed the companionship. Mark was friendly and easy to talk with and listen to.

"So anything interesting happen this week, Emma?"

Emma smiled and continued putting dishes in the dishwasher. "Aced a test and got my roots done. You?"

Mark shook his head. "Just another work week with nothing more to sustain me than looking forward to another good meal."

"Oh, listen to you," Emma laughed as she rolled her eyes.

"Your flattery might just make an impression, if I didn't know you eat at five star restaurants every night."

"And that is exactly why you should take my compliments very seriously. I *do* eat at the best restaurants, and believe me, they are highly overrated when compared to the culinary excellence I experience here."

Emma shook her head and laughed again.

"What's so funny?"

She looked up to see Andrew standing in the doorway, and she smiled at him, not perceiving the displeased look on his face. "Mark was talking fancy."

"I was telling her that her food is better than any place in L.A., and she doesn't believe me," Mark said with a little wink in her direction. She shook her head again and pushed a lock of hair back behind her ear.

Andrew watched for another moment, but no one spoke, and tension seeped into the room as the seconds ticked by. "I can finish up, Mark."

They both looked up at him. Andrew looked directly at Mark and raised his eyebrows which apparently was all the explanation Mark needed. Once he left, Andrew began scrubbing at the stove.

"I'd be careful around him if I were you," Andrew said after a minute.

Emma creased her brow and stopped working on the dishes. "Careful around Mark?"

"He knows."

"Knows what?"

"That we aren't for real," Andrew said, turning to face her. "He figured it out months ago."

"Thanks for telling me," she said with annoyance. "I thought you were keeping it quiet."

"He's my best friend, and he figured it out. I didn't find it necessary to tell you before now."

"And what does *now* have to do with it?" Emma said with growing irritation. All her frustration with his coolness wanted a release, and she was tired of suppressing it—especially when he tried to act like her father.

"Now he seems to be developing a bit of a crush on you."

Emma blinked. "Because he helps me with the dishes?"

Andrew didn't answer for several seconds. "Just watch out, okay?"

Emma turned her back to him and began scrubbing a pan. "Oh, I'll be sure to watch out for nice men who offer to help me with my chores. Mighty dangerous. Thanks for the warning, boss."

Andrew remained quiet for several seconds. "You're the one that made the no-sex stipulation, Emma. I'm just—"

Emma spun around as the fragile rein she held on her emotions broke completely. All the "making nice" with one another had worn her down, and she hated having him talk to her as if she was the pupil and he was the teacher. The suggestion that she would have some kind of relationship with Mark was way over the top. "You think I'm going to sleep with him?" she said indignantly.

"Things happen, and you don't know the kind of guy Mark is."

"You mean the kind of guy *you* are?" she spat back. "The kind of guy that balks at having to take a year off of having sex! Let me set the record straight—I'm not the kind of girl that thinks sex is a sport, Andrew. I'm not the kind of girl that even thinks about having a relationship with your best friend. Don't transfer your sexual frustrations to me—okay?"

Andrew clenched his jaw and threw the washrag on the counter. "I don't know why I even bother talking to you. You can't help but start an argument."

"You're the one that came in to warn me about Mark's *passionate* intentions. I'd better be careful or he might serenade me with the blender or tantalize me with a pastry brush—please."

"Oh, forget it," Andrew said in defeat, and he left the room.

Emma threw her scrubber in the sink and took a deep breath. This was getting ridiculous. She went to bed long before Andrew did. Sometime during the night, a movement by the bed awoke her, and she rolled onto her back with a groan before bolting upright. Who was in her room and why?

"I'm sorry, Emma," Andrew said quietly.

"Wh-what?" she asked, only half awake but glad to know it was Andrew standing over her bed.

"I'm sorry about the whole Mark thing. I was out of line," he explained.

Emma blinked her eyes a few times. Without her contacts or glasses, she could barely make out his form in the dark. "That's okay."

"But I want to clear something up," he continued.

"Okay," Emma said in confusion.

"I'm not a playboy."

He spoke quietly, and since she had no idea how to respond, she didn't respond at all. "My mom taught me better than that." He paused. "I just wanted you to know that."

Emma felt a little confused yet strangely relieved. "I'm sorry I freaked out," she finally said after arguing with herself. She preferred the "he's wrong, she's right" ending, but it didn't fit. She'd overreacted too. He didn't respond to her apology, and she settled back into bed. "Good night," she said when he stopped in the doorway and looked back at her.

"Good night," Andrew repeated. He shut the door quietly behind him, and Emma had a hard time getting back to sleep.

CHAPTER 25

*E*mma was up long before Andrew and his guests and had breakfast ready when they wandered in one by one. Andrew was the last one to sit at the table, but they all lingered over their coffee as they discussed the snow from the day before and made plans for the day. Emma listened to their conversations while she fed Catherine.

Out of the blue, Gordon asked, "So how is it you're married to Andrew, yet you don't ski?"

Every eye, including hers, turned to Andrew, and she felt just a little satisfaction at the slight flush in his cheeks. She said nothing, just waited for him to answer that one. Andrew didn't skip a beat. "I'm teaching her next weekend," he said in a completely believable voice as if it had been planned since the day they said "I do." "I've just been waiting for the season to wind down so there wouldn't be so many people."

Mark rolled his eyes and took a bite of his bacon.

Emma just smiled and gave her husband a sparring look, wondering just how serious he was about this, or if he would back out when his friends left. Still, it did sound fun. "I'll get a sitter."

"Good," Andrew said before turning his attention back to his coffee as if nothing out of the ordinary had happened.

Later, she asked if he meant it, and he said he did. She decided not to argue.

Andrew came back the following Thursday night, with Mark in tow. The next morning Emma dropped Catherine off at Lacey's where she was going to spend the night. Then she headed up Parley's Canyon to meet the two men at the ski resort in Park City. They had taken Andrew's car up earlier. Andrew had decided to spend two days teaching her, instead of the original one they had planned, and had booked some rooms. He was afraid that one day wouldn't be enough, and he didn't want her coming up with excuses to skip out on the second day. She was excited about the new experience but apprehensive at the same time. The only reason Andrew was doing this was to impress his friends, and that made her want to resist. But she had agreed to the weekend and planned to follow through.

Since Mark was well aware of the marital situation, it made no sense to keep up the farce, so Andrew booked them each their own room. And due to the hotel being nearly full, they ended up scattered throughout the building. Emma decided that having space to herself for an entire night made it worth all the coordinating she had done. It had been a long time since she'd had a break, and she looked forward to a long evening in front of the fireplace, watching the snow fall and reading a book. The only drawback was that before that could happen, she was supposed to learn to ski.

As soon as she checked in and met up with Andrew and Mark, they escorted her to the ski shop where she was fully outfitted in ski gear. She refused to let Andrew buy her anything. "Rental only," she said. She wasn't going to be guilt-tripped into making this a habit just because he'd sunk five hundred dollars into ski gear for her. Once she was ready, they hit the slopes. By noon Emma was wondering what anyone saw in this stupid sport. She was freezing, her legs were like jelly, and she was wondering how long before she gave into her urge and slapped Andrew silly.

"Can't we get something to eat?" Emma whined after he demonstrated once again how to get up without taking off the skis.

"As soon as you can go ten feet without falling, then we will," Andrew said in frustration.

Emma let out a breath and lifted her ski goggles. "Get me an instructor, Andrew. Another hour of this and I'll be requesting a divorce."

Andrew smiled with patronizing understanding, showing that he wanted out of the instruction as badly as she wanted him out of it. She watched him ski smoothly down the hill, returning a few minutes later with a woman named Tonya. They were introduced, and then Emma was given permission to eat lunch before they got started. *Finally!* Emma thought as she tried to unclip her boots from the skis but ended up in the snow—again. Andrew helped her and then carried her skis to the lodge where they had a lunch of chili and corn bread. About halfway through, she looked up to see him watching her.

"What?" she asked self-consciously.

"Nothing," he said with a shake of his head before looking back into his bowl. When she looked up at him again, he was watching her again.

"What?"

"You're very pretty," he said.

She felt herself blush. "If you think I'm going to give you my corn bread in exchange for sweet talk, you're wasting your breath."

Andrew chuckled and went back to his meal. When she caught him looking at her again, she put her spoon down and leaned forward. "Take a picture—it lasts longer."

Andrew smiled. "I'd love to."

Emma shook her head in disgust, but her stomach fluttered at his not-so-mild flirtation. She wondered why he was being so brazen all of a sudden. "I wanted you to know"—he paused, waiting until she looked up at him—"how much I appreciate all you've done."

She looked away, embarrassed by the praise and wondering where the compliments were coming from—she wasn't used to this kind of attention from Andrew and wasn't sure how to respond. Andrew continued. "You've taken great care of the house, of me and my friends. That means a lot to me. I haven't been very good at thanking you, and as I watched you today I realized just how much you've done for me. You're even trying to learn to ski, and . . . so . . . thanks."

She smiled shyly and stirred her chili, not meeting his eyes but feeling them on her. "It's been fun."

"I'm glad you think so. After everything that happened after New Year's, I was worried I'd ruined everything. I appreciate your forgiveness."

Forgiveness? She'd never thought of it that way before but supposed it fit. "I appreciate that you've cut back on the drinking when you're here."

Andrew shrugged. "Limits are good," he said simply. They both fell silent, as if trying to find a way to continue. After a few moments, his eyes met hers. "I'm glad you're here with me today, Emma. I'm glad we get a chance to spend some time together."

A little shiver went down her spine, and she smiled a little too easily. "I'm glad I'm here too."

Andrew smiled back and time seemed to stop for a few moments.

"Hey guys, whatcha eatin'?"

They both looked up at Mark. Emma wondered if Andrew was relieved to have been interrupted. She wasn't. She was glad to get the events of January out in the open, glad he was repentant and that they could both put that night behind them. Mark went to order some lunch after giving Andrew a hard time about leaving him on the slopes by himself. As he walked away, Andrew smiled at her again—that somewhat sideways grin of his that accented the slight dimple in his chin. "He's got great timing, doesn't he?"

Emma could only smile. He'd read her mind.

CHAPTER 26

The afternoon was better than the morning had been. Tonya was a far better teacher than Andrew, and within an hour Emma was beginning to feel like a prodigy. She could actually do the bunny hill without landing on her backside! After almost three hours of instruction, Emma begged off. She was exhausted. Tonya agreed to meet her in the morning, and Emma waited at the bottom of Andrew's favorite run to tell him she was finished. Mark got there first, however.

"I'm going to take a shower and go down to that Olympic-sized Jacuzzi I heard about. With any luck, I'll be feeling my legs again before the night is over. Will you let Andrew know where I went?"

Mark smiled. "I'll let him know," he said.

She thanked him and trudged toward the hill.

Andrew thought he saw Emma and Mark talking at the bottom of his run, but he couldn't be sure. He headed in that direction however and pulled up beside Mark as the other man was unclipping his boots a minute later. When Mark looked up to see Andrew, he looked almost angry, as if Andrew had interrupted something.

Andrew lifted his goggles off of his face and looked around for a moment. "Was that Emma? I thought I saw her from up the slope?" he said, still breathless from the run.

"She went in," Mark almost mumbled. Andrew looked at him for a moment, and Mark looked away but not before Andrew could read his guilty expression.

"And so you thought you'd get a little time alone with my wife, huh?"

"I'm beat," Mark retorted.

"Well, so am I," Andrew said emphatically as he bent over and unclipped his boots. "And I'm still married to her, Mark."

"Really?" Mark countered sarcastically.

They stared one another down until Andrew stomped ahead of his friend.

Within twenty minutes, they were both in the Jacuzzi, but Emma hadn't arrived. They waited in silence, and when she walked in, they smiled at her in unison.

"The slopes just aren't the same without you," Mark said with a wink that made Andrew's jaw clench. *How unfair!* Mark could get away with that kind of comment, but Andrew couldn't.

Emma just smiled and sat on the stairs, an adequate distance from both of them. Mark was the first to move closer. "So what do you think so far?" he asked as he slid onto the lowest stair just a few feet from her. Emma smiled and then told him all about the day, laughing at herself and making sarcastic comments about Andrew's teaching abilities, which he didn't appreciate. Andrew attempted to get in on the conversation, but each time he tried, Mark seemed to overthrow him with some witty comment that would make Emma laugh. Andrew was boiling after half an hour and finally said he was going to the outdoor pool, located on the other side of the glass wall. Mark and Emma watched him leave.

* ✳ *

Is he okay?" Emma asked once Andrew was gone.

Mark shrugged and slid next to Emma. "Ah, he's fine. I think you in a swimsuit is difficult for him to take."

Emma colored darkly and sank lower in the hot tub. "He seems upset about something," she said in an attempt to discover the truth. Surely it wasn't her in a swimsuit. Maybe he was mad that she hadn't let him finish teaching her. She *had* made some possibly rude comments when explaining it to Mark. Maybe he didn't realize that she was kidding. Then she thought back to the comments Andrew had made about Mark having a crush on her, and she replayed the banter they'd been exchanging. It wasn't hard for her to see it from Andrew's point of view, and yet she wondered if that could really be the cause of his mood. The mere thought that he might be jealous made her toes tingle.

"Nah, he just thinks I'm making a go for you. It's driving him crazy."

Emma looked at him. He had echoed her own thoughts. Suddenly she found herself uncomfortable with Mark and worried that she'd led him on somehow. "I think I'd better go make sure he's okay," she said after a few seconds.

Andrew brightened when Emma came to see him in the pool. As they shared a look, Emma was reminded of their last pool encounter. *It was nothing*, Emma repeated to herself. She dove in, slicked her hair from her face, and swam over to him. They started talking—had a very nice conversation in fact— until she suggested they return to the Jacuzzi. She explained she was cold, but Andrew seemed suspicious, and she hoped he didn't wonder if she just wanted to get back to Mark.

Back in the Jacuzzi, things got tense, due at least in part to the glares both men were shooting at one another, and after only another ten minutes they all decided to get ready for dinner.

Emma was trying to decipher the men's moods as she got ready, wondering if she had done anything she shouldn't have. She dressed in black, straight-leg slacks and a black sweater that hugged her figure. Her hair hung loose around her shoulders, and she took extra care with her makeup. How often did she get the chance to dress up? After a final inspection, she smiled to herself and left the room, wondering if Andrew would approve of how she looked tonight.

He opened the door to his room just seconds after she knocked. All he had on was a pair of nicely fitted jeans that allowed half an inch of the waistband of his boxer shorts to show. Emma tried to look away, but when she finally met his eyes, she could tell he was well aware of her taking notice and seemed to enjoy it. She found that irritating but was still highly disconcerted by being so close to his half-nakedness and having no one else around.

He invited her in, and she entered with a little hesitation. *It's just Andrew,* she reminded herself. Still it felt odd being in his bedroom—intimate somehow.

"You look wonderful," Andrew said with an appraising look that brought the color to her face. He looked too long and too slowly for her not to be embarrassed, and when his eyes met hers, she felt transfixed. There was a glimmer there—a look of anticipation and appreciation that was quite stunning. It left her speechless. He seemed to like it.

A few minutes later, Mark arrived and gave Emma nearly the same compliments Andrew had, although he didn't look at her quite the same way—thank goodness. She pushed aside her ponderings as they headed for the restaurant.

Emma had the grilled salmon and spinach salad. It was divine, and she decided to see about finding a really good recipe she could replicate at home. Andrew and Mark sat on either side of her, and the meal was wonderful until the men finished their fourth glasses of wine. Emma had ignored the drinking, but both men were loosening up. She couldn't help but feel uncomfortable. Mark scooted closer to her and brazenly ran his fingers up her arm, resting his hand on her shoulder. She stiffened at his touch and wondered what to do. All three of them went silent for a moment or two.

"Get your hands off of her," Andrew said the next instant. The conversation had been light and fun until now, but it turned almost ominous with his words.

"You don't own her," Mark said glibly.

"Sure I do."

"Oh, for heaven's sake," Emma chimed in. "Let's not go there." She wriggled out from under Mark's hand and tried to get back to the story Andrew had been telling about a recent meeting he'd had with a finance company. "Uh, so then what happened?" she asked. It didn't work. The men continued to glare at one another.

"You know, Cate did the cutest thing the other day. I was washing dishes and—" Mark put his arm across her shoulder, cutting her off.

"Move it," Andrew hissed.

"No," Mark spat back.

Suddenly Andrew slammed his glass onto the table, making Emma jump. "I'm tired of you making passes at my wife," he yelled, causing several heads to turn in their direction.

"Andrew," Emma whispered, humiliated by his words. "What are you—"

"Like you haven't noticed," Andrew spat back. He moved closer to her, wedging her between the two of them. "I've had all I can take."

Several tables were watching them now, and Emma had had enough. In one quick movement, she slid under the table and stood up on the other side. The two men seemed to have a hard time keeping up with her. "I'm going to bed," she said with a fake smile. "Thanks for dinner."

"I'll walk you up," Mark said.

"No thanks," Emma replied, putting her hand up in a stopping motion she hoped would help make her point. "I'll go up alone." With that she spun around and hurried away. As embarrassed as she was, however, she liked that Andrew felt protective of her. In fact, she liked it a lot. She hoped they would resolve their issues though and wished she hadn't ignored the continual flow of wine. Still, she couldn't help but smile to herself. She'd been wondering about Andrew's feelings toward her, if there were any. Somehow she felt she had part of the answer. His jealousy and anger at Mark's advances seemed to be a sign that she wasn't the only one getting emotionally involved in this relationship. But was that a good thing? She couldn't decide.

CHAPTER 27

The bartender refused to sell Andrew another drink, and Andrew cursed at him. That little incident got him a one-way ticket out of the bar. The nice blonde who had been sitting next to him most of the evening helped him out, since Mark had left right after Emma had—right before Andrew had traded his booth for a bar stool. The blonde had kept him company after that. She even talked the bartender into giving him another drink, or two, maybe three—he couldn't remember just how many. When he started to nod off, the blonde asked him what room she should take him too. He gave her Emma's room number.

The voices woke Emma, and although she couldn't hear what they were saying through the heavy wooden door, they weren't going away. *It's probably some dumb kids playing hotel hallway games*, she thought as she got up, went to the door, and pulled it open in order to tell them off.

"Andrew!" Emma said with surprise, causing both him and the blonde who was holding him up to look at her with varying degrees of shock. Andrew smiled a drunken grin, and the blonde quickly tried to put some distance between herself and Emma's husband.

"I was just helping him upstairs. He had a little too much to drink," she explained slowly as if making up the excuse as she went. She had illegal limits of cleavage showing, and Emma wondered why she'd bothered to wear a shirt at all.

"Yeah, sure you were," Emma said darkly. She stepped out and took over as Andrew's crutch. Emma moved him inside and looked over her shoulder for only a moment. "Better hurry back to the bar and try again, honey," Emma said. The blonde scowled but turned toward the elevators.

The door shut behind them and cut off all light. Andrew had one arm draped over her shoulders, and she helped him to the bed. She turned to look at him and shook her head in disgust. She'd thought these episodes were a thing of the past.

"You've got five minutes here while your girlfriend catches the elevator, and then we're going to your room." She leaned toward the bed and let him fall. Once free of him, she went into the bathroom and tried to repair her hair—not that anyone cared at this hour. When she'd come back from dinner, she'd changed into her flannel pajama bottoms and a T-shirt and then decided to lie down, just for a few minutes. A glance at her clock told her the few minutes had turned into almost five hours. *Perfect*, she decided in a positive attempt to ignore the situation. After putting her drunk husband to bed, she'd make some hot chocolate and try to retrieve the evening she'd nearly lost. Hard as it was, she swallowed the anger she felt at Andrew in his drunken state, telling herself it wasn't any of her business.

"She's no-ot my girlfriend," Andrew mumbled from the bedroom almost a full minute after she'd stopped talking. "She was jus heping me."

"Yeah, she was about to be a *big* help," Emma said with irritation, wishing she just didn't care. Oh, she hated it when he drank! If that girl had taken him to his own room, who knows what would have happened? The thought both saddened and disgusted her. *That kiss was nothing*, rang in her ears, *nothing at all*. "Why are you at my room anyway?" she asked bitterly as she sat on the edge of the tub and pulled on her shoes. "Yours is at the other end of the hall."

"She said what room did I want to go to, I say six-seven-one."

Emma poked her head out of the bathroom. Did that mean what she thought it meant? But seeing him sprawled on the bed cut short her pondering. *I hate it when he's drunk*, she repeated silently.

She pulled her hair up in a ponytail before helping him to his feet once more. "Okay, playboy, it's time to go to bed."

"Mmm," Andrew said contentedly as he tried to nuzzle her neck. *Boy, does he get frolicky when he's wasted*, she thought.

It was a long walk down the hall, but they finally reached his room. She found the key in his back pocket after nearly a minute of searching that he seemed to enjoy too much. After going inside and turning on the bathroom light, so as not to hurt his eyes with the intensity of the room lighting, she helped him to the bed. He just slumped there, and she was about to leave when she realized he would be awfully uncomfortable in his shoes. She hesitated as a little voice told her to leave. She couldn't understand why it mattered since he was unconscious, so she ignored the warning and headed for the bed. He seemed to be asleep, and she looked at his face for a long time. His expression was calm, peaceful, and the hair hanging in his eyes intensified his already attractive features. Her mouth went a little dry as she looked him over from head to toe. He really was a good-looking man. Memories of their kiss, of the intense chemistry it had created, came to mind, and she found herself wishing things hadn't turned so ugly between them. She thought of the conversation they'd had at lunch and sighed. His apology had been powerful.

Slowly she began removing his shoes and socks. As she took off the last one, she ran her hand briefly up his calf under his pants for no particular reason. Then she then looked up at his face again. *Wow, but he's a handsome man*, she thought, and her heart thudded a little bit. He looked so vulnerable, so innocent.

She couldn't help but think of the kiss, the way it had felt to be in his arms, and the momentary fantasy she'd had about being his wife—in every way. The memory sent a little tingle down her spine, and she smiled to herself. It was just a fantasy. She moved to lie alongside him on the bed, propping herself up on an elbow. Hesitantly at first, then with more intent, she ran her finger along his chin, slightly scruffy with a day's growth of beard. Her heart was beating faster. She knew she should leave, but something was driving this sensual behavior, and she couldn't seem to stop herself. His eyes didn't open at her touch, so she got a little more daring. She touched his hair softly and then ran her fingers through it. It was so soft, and she liked the rumpled look she had just given it. She moved a little closer and could smell the Xyrius cologne she had bought him for Christmas. He was wearing a sweater with a couple buttons at the top and the slightest hint of chest hair showing. She was playing with fire. She knew she was, but she slowly undid the buttons anyway and then put her hand on his chest.

Emma could feel his heartbeat beneath his warm skin, and the little fire in her own belly seemed to grow stronger. *He really shouldn't sleep in such a heavy sweater*, she told herself, and so she carefully wiggled him out of it. He remained unmoving and unconscious. When she looked down at his half-naked body, she told herself more strongly than ever that she needed to leave—*now*. She put her entire palm on his chest, feeling the rhythm of his heartbeat again. It was a relaxing rhythm. She lay down beside him again and closed her eyes, propping her head up with her elbow as she concentrated on the beat of his heart in the silent room. Feeling close to him without him even knowing it gave her a bit of a rush.

Thud-ump, thud-ump, thud-ump.

Had she not been so lost in her relaxation, she would have

noticed that he had opened his eyes and was watching her. She didn't even notice the slight increase of his heartbeat. In fact until he touched her, she didn't notice anything. But when his hand covered hers on his chest, her eyes flew open. They stared at each other in the semidarkness as he turned on his side to face her, still holding her hand against him. His face was so close she could smell the fruity alcohol on his breath. She swallowed as his hand moved up her arm to her shoulders and attempted to pull her closer to him. His eyes were glazed, the alcohol smell growing stronger as his face moved closer to her own.

She was finally ready to leave. *He's drunk*, she told herself. *It's like that time when the cabbie brought him home. He doesn't know what he's doing.* She pulled away.

"Emma," he whispered quietly, "please don't go." He sounded convincingly sober. His words washed over her, and she stared at him for a few moments.

Emma swallowed again and closed her eyes briefly in an attempt to gather strength. In the next moment, Andrew's lips were on her neck, causing her to inhale sharply. His mouth moved to her ear, and she tried a verbal protest this time. "You're drunk, Andrew. You don't know what you're doing."

"I know exactly what I'm doing, Emma," he said as he somewhat clumsily pulled the elastic from her ponytail and then put both hands in her hair as it fell around her shoulders. "Stay," he whispered. Then he captured her mouth with his own, stifling the next protest forming there.

"I—I can't," she said against his lips. Her willpower was fading fast.

"You can," he reassured, kissing her neck again as he rubbed her back and pulled her closer. "We're married."

He has a point, she thought, and then just as quickly she pulled back. "This isn't what we agreed to," she replied, pulling out of his grip and sitting up on the edge of the bed with her back to him as she tried to control her breathing. Andrew scooted toward her and ran his hand under her shirt and up her back, giving her chills.

"We made the rules, Emma. We can break them," he said, raising himself to kiss her neck again. Her eyes fluttered closed. His lips were at her ear. "Please stay. Why won't you let me love you?"

Love me? she repeated in her mind. *Did he mean . . . ?*

"Emma," he whispered deliciously, the sound of her name on his lips destroying any desire she had to be anywhere but right here. The feelings she'd been trying to ignore were alive and well, and in that she wasn't alone. *This will change everything*, she thought to herself. *Nothing will be the same after this.* She couldn't imagine anything better than that.

When Emma awoke the next morning, she just lay there staring at the ceiling, unsure if she dared turn her head to the side. Would he be there, confirming that this was real? Or would she realize this had simply been a very realistic dream? He moved, and his arm brushed her naked shoulder, sending a shower of impulses to all the nerves in her body. It was real! She had spent the night with Andrew! Her mind was a jumble of thoughts and feelings, but instead of trying to sort them out she simply closed her eyes and remembered. She bit her lip slightly as she relived the tenderness of his touch, the heat of his skin, and the sweetness of hearing her name on his lips over and over again.

Her eyes opened again, and she turned to look at him. He was asleep, blissfully asleep, and she smiled as she whispered what she had said out loud to him the night before, "I think I'm falling in love with you, Andrew Davidson." He didn't seem even close to wakefulness.

How will he respond when he wakes up? she wondered. In her mind, she reviewed all the movies she had seen, all the "morning afters," and wondered how she should act. As the minutes ticked by, her nervousness grew. How long was he going to sleep? Her watch told her it was nearly 9 A.M. She was supposed to meet Tonya on the slopes at 10. She wondered if they would even ski today—the wicked little angel on her shoulder suggested that she and Andrew should just stay in his room.

I'll take a shower, she decided after a few more moments of increasing nervousness. The skiing had left a sore and aching impression on her, and the hot water on her body felt marvelous. She wished she had time to hit the jacuzzi. It would be nice to relax. Maybe later. Maybe Andrew would come. She wondered what kind of changes this meant for them. Another smile played across her lips as she tipped her head back and let the water wash over her face. What did the future hold now? She wished Andrew were awake so that some of her questions could be answered.

CHAPTER 28

*T*he sound was at first unfamiliar, like a rushing wind or the continual rubbing of a plastic bag, but soon he determined it was some source of water. *The sink? No. Too much spray. The shower, that's what it was. Someone was taking a shower.* He shot up in bed, reviewing where he was. He was at the ski resort, in his own private room, and someone was taking a shower!

"I went to the bar with Mark," he muttered as he tried to remember the events from the night before, trying to figure out what had happened, who was in the shower. His memory was foggy and unreliable but started coming back to him slowly. "I got drunk and . . . the blonde." He groaned before closing his eyes as his whole body tensed. He remembered her helping him out of the bar, and then he remembered nothing. Wildly he looked around the room for evidence of the thoughts forming in his mind. His clothing lay scattered on the floor, and he remembered having his shoes removed, the relief of the cool air on his feet, and the feel of a hand moving up his leg.

Moments came rushing back in a blurred kind of recollection, more like a series of small bursts of consciousness, and he groaned with dread. He'd brought the blonde to his room with him, and yet in the brief memories it was Emma he'd been with—wistful fantasy of a drunken mind. "I thought it was Emma," he muttered, and then he clenched his eyes shut as his stomach sank to his toes. "What have I done?"

Mark was just putting the finishing touches on his packing, deciding he had no desire to continue this weekend any longer, when the pounding on the door began. "I'm coming," he called as he quickly zipped up the suitcase. The pounding continued. *Boy, housekeeping is getting ornery these days.* As soon as he opened the door, Andrew rushed past him, wearing only jeans. His hair was a mess. Was he here to apologize about his comments in the restaurant?

"I'm in trouble," Andrew said quickly before he laid out all the details.

"You are such a putz, Andrew," Mark said when Andrew finished telling him the story. Mark was sitting on the bed while Andrew paced around the room.

"I can't believe this. I just can't believe it," Andrew moaned, finally collapsing into a chair and covering his face with his hands. "If Emma finds out . . ." He looked up at his friend with desperation. "What if she comes to my room when she gets up? What if she calls?" His frantic eyes widened. "What if that girl answers?"

Mark said nothing.

Andrew just stared at him. Finally he begged, "Mark, you've got to help me."

"Me?" Mark said with a snort. "Me, the guy you humiliated in the restaurant? The guy you think is after your wife?"

"I'm sorry, man. You know how I get when I'm drinking. Please, Mark, go explain everything." He stood and started fumbling in his pockets, finally pulling out his wallet. "Offer her whatever she wants—I don't even know her name. I thought . . ." He stopped and shook his head. "I barely remember what happened. Just tell her to leave right now."

"I'm tired of cleaning up your messes, Andrew. Do it yourself."

Andrew looked at him with tortured eyes. "Please, Mark?" he said softly, in a tone of such regret that Mark couldn't help but feel compassionate. "If I see her again, I think I'll die. And Emma will be devastated if she sees us together."

Mark finally stood. "Fine, but I'm doing it for Emma, not you."

CHAPTER 29

*E*mma spent as much time as she could in the bathroom. With every moment, her anxiety was increasing. She got dressed and used Andrew's brush and the built-in blow-dryer to do her hair—all the time hoping he would knock and let her know he was awake and ready to confront this. Her stomach was in knots. The more she thought about it, the more nervous she became and the more convinced she was that she shouldn't have stayed last night. Sure he had been tender and passionate, but how was she to know he wasn't this way with every woman he had ever been with? The thought made her sick.

After waiting as long as she could, she decided to just face it head on. She opened the door, planning to wake him if he was still asleep, but he wasn't in the bed. She looked around the room, but he wasn't there. She went to the door, her stomach sinking even further as the panic began to rise. Why had he left?

Well, I'm not going to stay here and wait for him, she decided, moving quickly toward the door. She needed some time to figure out what to do. She was nearly at the door when she heard the card key slide in and out of the lock. She stepped back and took a deep breath. The moment of truth had arrived.

"Emma?" Mark said as he opened the door, startled.

"Mark?" she replied with just as much surprise. She looked at him wide-eyed. They both just stared at each other for a moment and then looked away. Her cheeks burned, but she couldn't think of anything to say.

"Uh . . . what are you doing here?" he asked finally, a look of confusion on his face.

"I . . . uh . . . this is embarrassing," she muttered as she kicked at the carpet.

Mark's brow furrowed, and she closed her eyes and shook her head in resignation. It was more than obvious—she might as well take responsibility. She looked up and forced a smile. "Things can change pretty fast, can't they?"

Mark continued to stare at her for a few moments. "You . . . stayed here last night?"

Emma wished she could melt into the floor—this wasn't quite the way she had pictured things. "Andrew had too much to drink, and this woman brought him to my room, and I brought . . . him . . . back . . . here." Her face was burning. It sounded so idiotic to say out loud. She wished Andrew was here to help her explain. Where was he anyway? Then she remembered that Mark had let himself in. Maybe he knew where Andrew was.

"Have you seen Andrew?" she asked quickly, trying to suppress her embarrassment. "He left while I was in the shower. I *really* need to talk to him."

Mark shook his head and looked at the floor. "Emma," he said in a sigh. Then he said nothing.

"What?" she asked, her nervousness beginning to edge toward full panic. "What is it?"

Mark closed his eyes for a moment and cursed under his breath. "He sent me here to pay off the barfly he thought spent the night with him."

Every muscle in her body froze. She couldn't breath. She couldn't blink. Then she felt as if she was imploding, shrinking within herself like an aluminum can being crushed. "No," she finally whispered, reliving the night in a single moment. She stepped back, hit the bed with her legs, and sat down. Mustering every bit of courage she had left, she looked up at Mark's pained face. "Tell me everything he said. Every word."

A few minutes later, Emma was still sitting on the edge of the rumpled bed staring at the floor. She looked at the wallet Mark was holding in his hand and willed herself not to cry. *Why did he say my name then?* But it really didn't matter. Even if he had *wanted* it to be her, it didn't change the fact that he believed it was someone else.

The moments ticked by as the realization fully sunk in. Finally, sitting up a little straighter, she put out her hand for the wallet. Mark didn't seem to understand.

"Give me that," she said. He did as she asked. She opened it and removed all the bills. Mark creased his brow as she stood and went back into the bathroom. She returned a few seconds later with her shoes.

"Tell him she's gone," Emma said quickly. "Tell him I called while you were talking to her and that . . . uh . . . Cate's sick and I have to go home." She wiped fleetingly at a tear, and her chin trembled as she looked up at Mark, whose eyes were full of sympathy. "Promise me you won't tell him it was me."

"Emma, I don't think—"

"PROMISE ME!" she shouted and then lowered her voice and wiped her face again. "Don't let him think for a *moment* that I am in this marriage for anything other than my ten percent. Surely you can understand this, Mark."

Mark watched her face for a few more moments before stooping to pick up the wallet she had dropped on the bed. "I won't say anything," he agreed quietly. "But for what it's worth, I *do* think he cares for you a great deal."

"To hell with that," Emma said as she turned and looked at the bed one more time before leaving the room.

CHAPTER 30

When Mark returned to his room, Andrew hurried to open the door. "Well, what happened?"

"She took all your money, but she's leaving," Mark said as he tossed the wallet to Andrew. "Emma called your room. Catherine's sick, and she's going home."

Andrew dropped onto the bed with relief. "Oh, thank goodness. I don't know how I'd have faced her. Mark, you have no idea how much I appreciate this."

Mark turned away and walked to his suitcase. "I'm not much in the mood for this anymore. Can you take me to the airport?"

Andrew nodded. "I'm really sorry, Mark. I don't know how it happened."

"You should have never married her in the first place, Andrew," Mark said. He looked at Andrew hard. "You should have seen the look on her face yesterday when you went out to the pool. She couldn't keep her eyes off of you."

"I care about Emma, Mark," Andrew said as he stared at his hands in his lap. "I care for her more than I ever thought I could."

"And yet . . ." Mark let the words hang in the air, unfinished.

Andrew wanted to explain everything, or at least defend himself. But how could he? He had made promises to Emma, and he'd broken them. He knew that his feelings toward her had changed, that he'd been flirting and wondering just how much of a relationship he and Emma could establish. With that in mind, however, how could he try to explain that he really thought it had been Emma he was with last night? The fact was that he'd betrayed her.

Part of him wanted to admit it to her, just so it wouldn't eat him up inside, but his heart screamed against the very idea of watching the censure in her eyes. And then, on top of everything else, he would lose the trust money that started this whole thing. *Damn that money.* If he hadn't been greedy, he'd never have married Emma, never admitted how empty his life was without her. If only he could believe there was some chance for them to try again, the right way. But he knew he had ruined it. He had ruined everything.

Emma went straight home, rather than picking Catherine up right away. She needed some time alone and only stopped to buy a pack of cigarettes which she smoked until she was sick to her stomach. It had been months since she'd lit up, but she didn't care if everyone smelled it on her. She didn't care if she got lung cancer and died tomorrow. She needed some relief—something. After parking the car in the garage, she went inside, hurried to her room, and threw herself on the bed. *I am so stupid,* she berated herself as the tears began to flow freely and her chest began to tighten. *How could I have done this? How could I have stayed with him? And how could I have allowed myself to fall in love with that man, a man so different from what I need?* In a brief moment of self-forgiveness, she reminded herself that he was her legal husband, that it hadn't been some petty act on her part. But then the moment passed. Husband or not, she had no right to do what she had done. In her heart, she knew it was wrong. Perhaps she was in love with him. Perhaps she was willing to make the first step toward a future together, but she'd made that decision alone. He believed he had shared what she saw as special and sacred with a stranger. How many other times had it happened to him that way? How long a list had she just joined?

CHAPTER 31

May

*A*re you sure you're all right?" Lacey asked for at least the third time in the last two hours. They were tying a baby quilt for Camilla, Emma's only sister, who was due with her fourth child next month. Camilla was sick—sicker than she'd been with the others. The Blair family curse, she called it. She and Emma were both very fertile and paid for it dearly, though Camilla's sickness had never been as bad as Emma's pregnancy with Catherine.

Emma forced a smile. "I'm fine, just tired."

Lacey looked at her with concern, but Emma wasn't paying attention. After a few minutes, Lacey tried to start yet another conversation. "I got an e-mail from your mom yesterday. She said she's been trying to contact you."

"I know," Emma said. "I've been meaning to e-mail back. I've been really busy."

"She's not very happy about missing the birth of her new grandkids."

"Grandkids?" Emma asked, almost panicked that Lacey

knew something more than she should.

Lacey looked confused. "Didn't Janet tell you?"

Emma paused. "Janet's pregnant?"

"Can you believe it?" Lacey said with a shake of her head. "Miranda is only nine months old."

Emma looked back at the quilt and felt the numbness descend again—it had become common, and she hardly noticed it anymore. "I guess it was a surprise then."

"Big surprise. She's trying to be a good sport, but I don't think she's too excited about it. I thought she'd told you."

"I've been meaning to return her calls too," she answered slowly.

A long silence ensued until her sister-in-law changed the subject to the only thing Emma was less interested in discussing. "Have you heard anything from Andrew?"

Emma paused as she finished the knot she was tying at the moment and then continued. "Not since that message he left on the machine," she said quietly. It had been just over a month since the ski trip. When Emma had returned home from picking up Catherine that day, there had been a message on the machine from Andrew saying he had to head back to California and wouldn't be around for a while due to business reasons. He hadn't even come home to get the rest of his luggage. Emma had told Lacey about it a couple weeks ago.

"If I didn't know better, I'd say you were missing that husband of yours," Lacey said in a playful voice.

"I miss him terribly," Emma admitted in a faraway voice. She stood. "I need to check on Catherine."

A few minutes later, Emma returned and said she wasn't feeling well, that she needed to get home. Lacey helped her get her things together and load Catherine into the car.

"Are you *sure* you're okay?" Lacey asked one last time.

Emma didn't bother to answer the question directly. "Camilla's almost eight months along now. Is she starting to feel better?"

Lacey shook her head. "With the other pregnancies, she

got some relief around the seventh month, but she's still sick this time. Her doctor told her to gain two pounds by next week or he'll induce her. You know better than I do how she's feeling though," Lacey said with a little laugh. "Wasn't your pregnancy with Catherine just like that?"

Emma swallowed and forced a socially acceptable smile. "Sick from the sixth week on and couldn't gain weight for anything."

"I don't know how you guys survive it," Lacey said compassionately, as Emma let herself into the car. "You're sure—?"

Emma avoided her eyes. "I'm just fine, Lacey. I'll see you for Sunday dinner."

CHAPTER 32

*J*ust as Emma expected, the nausea hit a couple weeks later. With the other pregnancies, it had been the same—fatigue until about six weeks, then the gut-wrenching nausea. She got up on a Tuesday morning and felt light-headed but went to school as usual. When she got there, however, she knew she wouldn't make it through the day. The Rice Krispies she'd managed to eat for breakfast sent her running for the bathroom by nine. She revisited the bathroom twice more with dry heaves before asking her teacher if she could be excused. She spent the remainder of the day on the couch or the bathroom floor at home. Besides her nausea, she was aching for a cigarette. But when she went outside and lit up, the smell made her vomit all over the back porch. She stared at the mess for nearly a minute as tears filled her eyes. Then she threw the remaining cigarettes in the garbage and gave in to the misery of wanting what she couldn't have—the story of her life.

At five she picked up Catherine from day care and spent the rest of the evening on the couch listening to endless Disney videos with her eyes closed. The movement of the cartoons would make her sicker if she watched, so she laid there and wished she'd never met Andrew Davidson.

For the rest of the week, she tried different things in order to make it through the school day. She skipped meals, knowing that whatever she ate would be thrown up later, but it didn't keep her from heaving into the toilet bowl anyway. She tried to eat several small meals, but it only sent her to the bathroom with greater urgency. No matter what she tried, she threw up—whether there was anything in her stomach or not—and it left her lethargic and light-headed.

After determining that there was no solution, she tried to force herself to keep eating, despite the complete absence of appetite. The baby within her needed any nutrition it could get, and that meant she had to eat.

The baby. Andrew's baby. It was unbelievable that this had happened. Her feelings ranged from guilt, to anger, to panic, and finally to just plain disbelief. How could God allow this to happen to her?

But she knew it wasn't His fault. She knew it was hers, and hers alone.

After three more days of the same routine, she requested an early meeting with her instructor. But finding herself too sick to drive, she had to call her on the phone. She explained the situation and how her pregnancy with Catherine had started this same way and never gotten any better. To her relief, the instructor said she could drop out and return later as long as she could pass a skills test at that time and that she reenroll within a year. Emma thanked her and hung up. Then she lay there as Catherine whined to be picked up and wondered what she was going to do. How long could she keep this to herself? There was only one thing she knew for sure—she would keep it a secret as long as she could. Hopefully no one would find out until she knew what she was going to do. Maybe she would be lucky this time. Maybe it was just morning sickness, and it would go away. She could only hope. Until then she would take care of herself as best she could and try to formulate a plan.

Another thought crossed her mind, and she admitted that

despite the heartache, it would probably be best if this pregnancy ended like the others had. She could handle a miscarriage better than she could handle a pregnancy. But it was impossible to hope for something that depraved, especially when she looked into the eyes of her daughter. She put a hand on her belly and said a little prayer that whatever happened she'd be prepared to handle it. She didn't feel she had any claim on heaven's power right now, but she was praying for the baby, the innocent one in all this, and so it seemed okay. That was the best she could do.

By the end of the next week, she was sure she was going to die. She barely had the energy to fix food, much less eat it, and she was losing weight. Lacey or Janet had called nearly every day this week, leaving messages saying they were worried and wondering if Emma was okay. Emma hadn't returned their calls.

The day care she had been using would pick Catherine up at nine and drop her back off at five. It was expensive but necessary. Each morning Emma would drag herself out of bed to get her daughter dressed—she rarely finished the routine without getting sick. After Catherine left, Emma would lie on the floor next to the bathroom, with a pillow and blanket if she had thought ahead, and wait for the day to wind down, throwing up continually. If she was lucky, she would be able to sip on a glass of water throughout the day and get some sleep. If she was really lucky, she would be able to drink some chicken broth or eat some crackers without vomiting. Her hopes that it wouldn't be as bad as her pregnancy with Catherine had been quickly squashed—this time it was much more difficult. With Catherine she could eat a little bit every day if she timed it right and lay perfectly still afterward. This time around Emma considered it miraculous if anything stayed in her stomach. As she lay there, she wondered how she could possibly live through this. Her body was starving itself to death. Her doctor with Catherine had told her that the baby would draw whatever nutrients it could from her, like a parasite. But Emma wondered just how much was left for the baby to draw from.

Around noon, only three weeks after the nausea had started, she pulled herself up at the sink and tried to drink a glass of water. It immediately came back up. An hour later, she tried again and had the same reaction. All day and into the evening after Catherine had come home she tried and tried to keep the water down, but she couldn't. The subsequent retching that accompanied every attempt made her throat burn and her body ache. *I need to see a doctor,* she told herself and determined to find one the next day as she drifted off to sleep on the floor. She lacked the energy to make it to the bedroom for the night. Catherine had already cried herself to sleep on the living room couch.

The next morning she managed to get Catherine off to day care in clothes that didn't quite fit since she hadn't done laundry in weeks and had turned to the ones Cate had grown out of. Then Emma laid down on the floor and reminded herself to call a doctor. It was Friday, and she knew there was no way she could take care of Catherine over the weekend—last weekend had been nearly impossible. She decided she would call Janet or Lacey after she took a nap. Maybe one of them could take Catherine without her telling them everything. Maybe she'd feel good enough to drive when she woke up. She had no energy for anything else right now, and her thoughts were becoming fragmented the more she tried to focus on anything in particular.

CHAPTER 33

*J*anet answered the phone on the third ring. "Hello," she said quickly, shaking the bottle she'd just prepared for Miranda.

"Yes, is Janet Blair there, please?"

"This is she," she said blandly, preparing to hang up if it was a solicitation.

"This is Tiny Tot's Day Care—Emma Davidson put you down as an emergency contact."

Janet stood a little straighter as she handed the bottle to the baby and turned her full attention to the phone call. "Has something happened?"

"Well, we're not sure," the woman said. "We tried to drop Catherine off, but no one answered the door. We've called from a cell phone several times as we've dropped off other kids, but there's been no answer. We're on our way back to the day care now, and we need you to come pick Catherine up."

Janet let out a breath and cast a quick glance around her kitchen. Dinner wasn't ready, the baby was whining, and Josh, her five-year-old son, was fighting with the neighbor kid over what TV show to watch. Tally was in Provo photographing a wedding. "I'm in Willard, so I'll try and call my sister-in-law. One of us will be there as soon as we can. What's the address?"

Lacey didn't answer her home phone or her cell phone, and Chris didn't know where she was and said he couldn't leave work. Janet hung up with an irritated sigh. By the time she got there, Lacey would probably be home, and Lacey was much closer. But then she wondered what was happening. She and Lacey hadn't had any luck getting in touch with Emma since the family dinner three weeks ago, and they finally backed off and decided to give her space. But they both knew something wasn't right.

With traffic it took over an hour to get to the day care, and the workers were not happy. Janet assured them it wouldn't happen again, put Catherine in a seat belt between Miranda and Josh, and headed for Emma's house. When she got there, the house was dark. Leaving the kids in the car, she went to the front door and knocked loudly before ringing the bell. No answer. She knocked again before trying the door-knob. Locked.

Peering in the windows, she couldn't see a thing. She pounded on the front window and called Emma's name. Nothing. A feeling of urgency came over her, and she hurried around the house, trying the windows and doors as she went. When she realized it was shut tight, she went back to the car and got her cell phone out of her purse.

Five minutes passed before the first police officer arrived. She explained what was happening, and he proceeded to pick the lock on the front door. They both entered hesitantly, looking around as if someone might jump out at any minute. The smell of old garbage was thick, and Janet's anxiety over the situation continued to rise.

"Emma?" Janet called from behind the officer. "Emma, are you here?" There was no answer. She entered the living room, still calling Emma's name. On her way to the kitchen, she happened to glance up the stairs. In seconds she was kneeling next to what looked like a pile of blankets. The officer was right behind her.

"This is her?" he asked as Janet shook Emma's shoulder. She looked so thin and pale, and she didn't open her eyes.

Janet continued trying to get a response while the officer began talking into his radio, calling for an ambulance.

CHAPTER 34

Against her fervent hope that she never would, Emma began to wake up. Gradually she began to realize she wasn't at home as the fluids dripping into her body began to repair her faculties. She wanted to curl up and stay in this semiconscious state forever—until she realized that it was dark outside the window and that Catherine was still at day care. Only then did she begin forcing herself into consciousness. When she did come to an understanding of the full reality of what was happening—that the secrets she needed to keep hidden were secrets no longer—she started to cry.

A young intern met Chris, Janet, and Lacey in the hall some time later and updated them on the situation. Janet's children were with Kim, a friend of Janet's in Salt Lake, and Lacey had sent her kids to a neighbor's house. Emma was dehydrated and malnourished, the intern said. They were giving her fluids through the IV, and although she was responding, they wanted her to stay for a few more days so they could push more fluids, run some tests, find some medication to take the edge off the nausea, and make sure the baby was all right. Then she could go home.

They blinked at him. "The baby?" Chris said dumbly.

The intern looked uncomfortable. "Mrs. Davidson is about two months pregnant."

Lacey knocked a few minutes later. Emma just shook her head and looked away as Lacey approached the bed. She was so embarrassed. All this time she'd been assuring her family that marrying Andrew had been a good thing. And now this. How would they ever trust her decisions again?

"It's going to be okay, Emma," Lacey said quietly. Silence filled the room, interrupted only by the hum of the IV and muted voices from the hallway.

"I didn't know how to tell you guys. I didn't know what to say," Emma finally explained.

"I know," Lacey said with tears in her own eyes.

"I don't know what I'm going to do," Emma whispered as her face crumpled, and she turned away again. "Andrew doesn't want it."

Lacey closed her eyes and took what seemed like a deep, cleansing breath. "It's going to be okay," Lacey said again, rubbing Emma's thin arm awkwardly.

Chris stayed in the hall, pacing and boiling inside while Janet talked to Tally on a cell phone. Chris was fuming. He had been right all along. This was too much for Emma to handle. She was too young to know how to deal with a situation like this, with a man like Andrew. Now she was pregnant. By the time Lacey returned, he felt ready to explode. Janet said she would stay for a while. Chris and Lacey had to get home to their children. Once they were in the car, Lacey explained what Emma had told her.

"He doesn't want it!" he shouted. "It's way past that now."

Lacey took a breath. "Emma's prepared to handle this herself."

"That is just ridiculous," Chris ranted. "He's a part of this too. He should be the one visiting her here. He should be the one taking care of her during this pregnancy, not us. This nearly killed her, Lacey! If Catherine hadn't gone to day care, Janet would never have found her in time. Do you realize that? I'm calling him as soon as we get home and telling him to get his sorry butt back here to finish what he started."

"And what good will that do?" Lacey returned. "He doesn't want a family. He isn't going to change his mind just because you tell him to. And we *did* find her, Chris, and she *will* be all right." She paused for a moment. "We need to focus our energy on Emma and the baby. Did you know she had three miscarriages when she was married to Jake? All of them because she was so sick. She could still lose this baby, and if she doesn't, she's got seven months of hell to look forward to." Chris closed his eyes and shook his head. Lacey continued, "Andrew wouldn't be any help if he were here anyway. They had a one-night thing. It isn't like they're in some committed relationship, if—"

"They're married, Lacey, and he slept with her. That's a commitment."

"But look at the logistics, Chris. This is the man who took advantage of her in the first place. Do you really think the fact that she is going to give him a child, one he doesn't want, will change him so much? She knows she made a mistake, and she's prepared to face the consequences. We need to support her in this."

"We supported her already," Chris said with a forced calmness. "She has shown that she can't make good choices. She needs to insist that he be a part of this, and I'm tired of trying to deny how I feel about her decisions."

"Well, big brother, I don't think you have much of a choice. She's accepted his opinion. We don't have to like what's happened, but we do have to love her, more than ever. If we continue to push the issue of Andrew, she's only going to pull further away, and that won't help anyone."

"I can't believe this has happened," Chris finally said after a long pause.

"Neither can she."

CHAPTER 35

Two days later, Janet and Tally picked Emma up from the hospital. They signed the papers, talked to the doctor, and then helped get Emma into the car. Once they were driving, Janet turned around in the front seat. "How are you doing?"

Emma looked out the window. "I'm okay," she said. The hospital had pumped her full of anti-nausea medication before she left, but it would wear off in about an hour. Physically, she felt better, but she knew it wouldn't last, and mentally, she felt numb. Everyone had tried on different occasions to convince her to call Andrew and make him do his part. She lied and told them they had already discussed it, and that he said she could keep the baby if she wanted to, but he didn't want any part of it. They had been horrified, and she looked away to avoid the fire in their eyes. She felt bad for lying to them, but she wasn't willing to tell them the truth. They'd be more horrified by what had really happened. The truth was she had made a dumb mistake, possibly the biggest and dumbest mistake of her life, and now she had to pay for it. And the explanation wasn't completely untrue. Andrew didn't want a family. He'd been very clear about that. And keeping it from him was only temporary. She knew he'd eventually find out. For now it was best kept to herself. She didn't have the energy to deal with him on top of all of this. Her family dropped the subject of Andrew, and for that she was grateful. She could hardly think of him without wanting to cry, and yet she seemed to think of him all the time.

"We fixed up the guest room for you," Janet continued. "It's in the basement, away from everyone, so it will be quiet. Lacey got a hold of a local housekeeping service called *The Broomstix Girls*. They're supposed to excellent, and she's meeting them at the house this afternoon. Is there anything you need her to get while she's there?"

For a moment, Emma didn't answer. She didn't want to stay with Tally, she didn't want someone else cleaning the house, and she didn't want anyone packing her things. But the doctor had insisted she stay with someone for a few days while he evaluated her and learned how effective the medication was going to be. "Catherine and I need clothes and personal stuff," she finally said.

"Maybe you could make a list," Tally added. Emma nodded, still looking out the window and feeling like a twelve-year-old.

Staying at Janet and Tally's didn't end after a few days. By the following Wednesday, she'd lost over five percent of her pre-pregnancy body weight, and the doctor stopped being conservative. The medication she'd brought home didn't seem to be helping, and it was the final symptom they needed to make a diagnosis. The name of her condition was Hyperemesis Gravidarum, meaning basically that she threw up continually—and it could kill her. Her doctor sent her to the hospital to get what he called a TPN line—Total Parenteral Nutrition. The IV was hooked into her arm, and a digital pump fed a feeding solution directly into her bloodstream. It pumped these nutrients all day everyday, and if she was able to move from her bed, the pump went with her. For now it was impossible for her to stay at the house alone, so she would continue staying with Janet and Tally.

They would try other medicines, but the doctor wasn't hopeful. Emma felt like she had the flu, every minute of every day. Smells, bright lights, even sounds increased the nausea. She drifted in and out of sleep all day, interrupted by perpetual vomiting. The TPN would make sure she had enough nutrients to grow her baby and to keep her alive. Also included in the solution was liquid Zofran, the Cadillac of antinausea medications. It definitely made things better. She could eat some things and not throw up. But it didn't make it go away completely.

Janet had taken Emma to the hospital and stayed with her through all the treatments and tests. As soon as they were in the car, Emma cleared her throat. "I'm going to call Jake when we get home."

Janet looked at her in surprise. Emma continued, "I can't take care of Cate, and you guys shouldn't have to." She paused and her chin quivered. Sending her daughter away was heartbreaking. But she couldn't expect Janet and Lacey to do everything. They had already agreed, reluctantly, to oversee managing Andrew's house. They had been disgusted that Andrew would still require her to be the housekeeper but had agreed, so long as they didn't have to talk to him. Emma assured them that he would be in L.A. for the summer and ignored her guilty conscience. She couldn't think of what else to do.

"Between Lacey and I, we can take care of her. You don't have to send her to Jake."

"With Catherine I felt better around the sixth month, so it will only be for the summer. You have enough to do with me there. I think it's best."

Janet was quiet.

"He's her father. If I can't take care of her, he should get the first opportunity to fill in. He's been sending videos of himself every month and e-mailing to see how she's doing. It will be a good thing."

Janet nodded. "If he says no, Lacey and I will be happy to help."

Emma smiled and hoped they got home quickly. She could feel the medication wearing off, and she didn't want to use the ice cream bucket again.

Jake was supportive. He didn't say anything at first, but as she continued to explain, he softened. Of anyone, Jake understood just how hard this was going to be for her, and she figured he was grateful that he didn't have to be the one taking care of her this time. She left out the fact that Andrew wasn't involved, but Jake didn't need to know that. Jake said he would need a week to get things figured out, but he'd be happy to take Cate for the summer—a contingency of his visitation he was actually entitled to but that Emma didn't have to comply with until Catherine turned five. Emma thanked him with her heart in her throat and hung up the phone before the tears came. Part of her had hoped he'd say no so that she could selfishly keep Catherine with her. But she knew this was the best thing for everyone, even Catherine. It felt like a knife in her chest, but sometimes the right thing was harder than the wrong thing.

Ten days later, Saturday, Tally brought Cate into Emma's room to say good-bye. Jake was flying in from Texas. Tally was meeting him at the airport where Jake would gather Catherine and her things before taking another flight back home. Emma managed to sit up so she could hold her baby for the last time. Tally handed Catherine over, and Emma tried to find a position that would work for a few minutes. It was hard for Emma to even hold her daughter these days. She was so weak, and Catherine was always trying to pull on the IV. After only a few seconds, Tally had to take Catherine from her. Emma leaned forward and planted a lingering kiss on Cate's soft hair. "You be a good girl," she whispered in a trembling voice. "And don't forget your mommy loves you."

Catherine put her chubby hand to her own lips, pulled it back and blew. This was her new trick, blowing kisses. Emma did the same and then watched Tally take Catherine away. She squeezed her eyes shut and willed herself not to cry. But soon she was sobbing, which led to vomiting, which left her exhausted and wishing she could be unconscious and wake up six months from now when it was all over. She knew exactly what lay in store for her in the months ahead, and she was frightened. Could she really live through this? Was it possible to survive on vitamin water?

Then she thought of how much she loved her little girl, how grateful she was to have her. And when she finished this, she'd have another child to love. She clung to that thought with all her might. She could do this for her child. For him, or her, she could do anything.

CHAPTER 36

September

*A*ndrew stood as soon as Mr. Austin entered the room. It was September and work was crazy, but he'd put off everything to come here today. They shook hands and sat down. Andrew didn't bother with pleasantries. "What is this?" he asked quickly as he tossed a letter on the table.

"I think it's obvious what it is, Mr. Davidson," Mr. Austin replied. "Your thirtieth birthday is only six months away. This is a statement making you aware of your current status."

"It says that I'm not eligible for the payoff," Andrew pointed out. "Why not? I've fulfilled every detail of the requirements." *Have I ever*, he thought to himself. When he received the letter yesterday, he'd been ready to explode. Rather than discuss it on the phone, he'd caught a plane, spent the night in a hotel, and arrived for an appointment with Mr. Austin first thing in the morning.

"You and your wife are not living together."

Andrew paused. "I own a home in Utah and an apartment in L.A. She lives in Utah, and we're together on the weekends."

"You were together on the weekends during the winter, but you haven't booked a flight to Salt Lake for almost five months. We also looked over your taxes. The Utah house is listed as your second home—the apartment in L.A. is your primary residence."

Andrew paused and tried to keep his temper in check, something he hadn't been very good at lately—just ask his employees. "She prefers to live in Salt Lake. She has family there. I work in L.A., and I've had such a busy summer I haven't made it back."

Mr. Austin removed his glasses and rubbed the bridge of his nose as if he were very tired. "Mr. Davidson," he began, "I realize how frustrating this is to you, and I apologize for that. But the trust is very specific, and you're welcome to read all the provisions and regulations outlined therein. Our law firm is required to substantiate every requirement. In congruence with the trust, we had an investigator verify your situation last month, and this is what he found. You'll find that mandate on page fifty-nine. We have the choice at this point to cancel the payoff if we feel inclined to do so. It takes a lot of paper-work and time to retrieve this amount of money, and because you don't fulfill the requirements, we can stop the process. However, because your failure is a repairable detail, we chose to inform you of your status. We wanted to give you a chance to make the necessary adjustments. You have time to make a more permanent living arrangement, with data we can track, to prove that you and your wife reside together.

"On your thirtieth birthday, the investigator will complete another report, a detailed report designed by Edward David-son eighty-five years ago. It's on page ninety-two. You should have already read it the first time you were here. It specifies that you and your wife reside in the same residence—and not just on weekends. The investigator will then review the infor-mation with me, and then we will send it to an independent law firm. Only after they double check all the information will we sign the report. We don't put our signature on legal documents lightly. If you are not living with your wife, you will not meet the requirements, and you won't get your payoff. It's as simple as that."

Andrew stared at the shiny desk top, trying to keep his annoyance at bay while he thought of the correct response. When he didn't speak, Mr. Austin continued, "If I may say so, you're not the first heir to find himself in a marriage of convenience for the sake of this inheritance."

Andrew's head shot up, but then he wondered why he should be surprised that Mr. Austin had figured it out. He looked back down rather than endure the man's stare.

"That is your choice of course," Mr. Austin said, "and the will couldn't specify you marry for the right reasons, but it demands everything else, and you're simply not meeting those specifications."

Andrew stood quickly and turned to face the windows, clenching his jaw as his annoyance took over. "This is ridiculous," he finally snapped, turning to look at the other man. "How can it possibly be this detailed?"

"Two years, three lawyers, a lot of money, an obsessed old man, and two wayward sons," Mr. Austin said. "Edward Davidson was brilliant. He thought of everything, even in 1918. He had nothing to lose. It's his money. He set it up exactly as he wanted to, which is his right. You either fulfill the requirements or you don't. If you do, you get paid; if you don't, you don't—it's that simple." He stood. "Is there anything else?"

"What am I supposed to do?" Andrew asked heatedly, spreading his hands wide. "Turn my whole life upside down for this?"

"Yes, Mr. Davidson," Mr. Austin returned with the first hint of irritation he'd shown thus far. "It's two and half million dollars. It will take some *sacrifices* on your part." He tossed the folder on the table. "Give the folder to my secretary when you're done."

He left the room, and Andrew turned to look at the folder. He picked it up and threw it against the wall. It fell to the floor, papers bent and splayed in every direction. He cursed Edward Davidson in his mind as he turned to the window again. With everything he'd been through so far, he wasn't sure it was worth two and a half million.

Half an hour later, he returned the rumpled folder to Mr. Austin's secretary and took a cab to the airport. He upgraded to first class and attempted to get comfortable while trying to come up with a plan. The plane took off for L.A. a short time later, and the flight attendant came around to offer him a drink. She reminded him that in first class, alcoholic drinks were free of charge. Then she went on to list all the beverages available. Andrew listened and then said he'd like a ginger ale. He hadn't had a drink since that night in Utah, and yet he doubted there had ever been a time in his life when he needed alcohol more than the last few months. But the price he had paid for that last night in the bar was too high. He wasn't willing to try his luck anymore.

When the plane landed, he picked up his car from short-term parking and headed for the office. The rest of the day was spent trying to concentrate on anything but the trust, but it continued to loom over him like a threatening rain cloud. It was late when he left for his favorite restaurant. They showed him to a table by the windows. The red-headed waitress asked him his opinion of his dinner a while later, and he said it was fine, but he couldn't help thinking that Emma could blow it out of the water.

Emma, he thought to himself, *what are you doing right now?* He imagined her at home, with Catherine, watching videos and building block towers, and he ached to see her again. It amazed him that he could miss her so much. The more he'd tried to talk himself out of it, the more he longed to be with her again.

The meeting with Mr. Austin hadn't helped. To fulfill the trust, he would have to find a way for them to live together full time. He didn't know how he'd missed that information the first time he read through the documents, but apparently he had. The thought of living under the same roof as Emma excited him, but he feared it just as strongly. Surely she would see his betrayal in his eyes. Surely she would know. That's why he'd avoided her for so long. He'd hoped that time would help him justify his transgression, but his guilt was as fresh and strong as it had ever been. The longer he stayed away, the more impressions from that night returned.

And as they did, his guilt ate him up. He had been convinced it was Emma; he could remember calling her name, and yet it hadn't been. It was some tramp he had met in a bar. What kind of man could feel for Emma the way he had finally admitted he did and yet spend the night with someone else? As his guilt increased, so did his fear at seeing her. If he felt like this now, a thousand miles away, how would he feel when he looked her in the eye? He couldn't fathom it, so he made more excuses to stay away.

In the early morning hours, after sleep had proved hard to come by, he made the final decision to go to Salt Lake. At the very least, he needed to discuss the living arrangements with Emma and see if she had any ideas. He'd known all along that facing her was inevitable, and he'd run out of time. In the morning, he'd call and let her know he'd be coming home for the weekend. The knowledge that he'd be seeing her caused a juvenile thrill of anticipation to run down his spine, a tingle he hadn't felt in many years. For just a moment, the fear retreated, his guilt disappeared, and he thought only of how great it would be to see her again.

CHAPTER 37

$\mathcal{J}$anet knocked lightly and entered the room. Emma was lying on her left side as the doctor had prescribed. The physiology of the body offered better blood flow to the baby if she lay on her left side. It took a few seconds for Janet's eyes to adjust to the dim light of the room. Bright lights aggravated Emma's condition. Almost anything did, and so she stayed in her room most of the time with the shades drawn, a fan pointed at her bed, and headphones over her ears. About the only stimulus she could stand was listening to the radio or tapes on her headphones with the volume turned low. It was going on three months now. It was hard to believe it had been that long.

"Emma," she said quietly as she approached the bed. She sat down in the chair beside the bed and placed a hand on Emma's arm. Emma's eyes opened, and she reached a thin hand to her headphones and pulled them to rest on her shoulders.

She smiled. "Hey there."

"Hi, how are you doing?" Janet asked with compassion.

"Pretty good," Emma said. Her eyes appeared huge and her cheeks were sunken. Her emancipated appearance made it hard to believe that she was doing as well as she was. Janet's eyes traveled to Emma's stomach. The slightly protruding mound testified that although Emma appeared to be wasting away, the baby was growing and developing just fine, although Emma wasn't nearly as big and round as Janet was.

"Lacey went by the house, got the mail, and checked the messages. Andrew's coming home for the weekend."

Emma closed her eyes briefly and rolled onto her back, her hand automatically moving to rest on her growing abdomen. She said nothing. Janet waited a few seconds and then continued. "She wrote a note that said you were staying with us."

"Was there anything in the mail?"

"Some insurance statements and a bill for Broomstix. I went ahead and paid it over the phone from your account. The house looked good. Mark also called again. I wrote down the number in case you wanted to call him back this time."

Emma shook her head, as she had every time Janet had told her that Mark had tried to contact her. "Thanks, Janet," Emma began, ignoring the subject of Mark's call completely. "I don't know how I would have survived without you guys." Her chin started to tremble, and she waved a hand through the air. "I can't even say thank you without getting emotional. I'm such a mess."

Janet rubbed her arm. "We're happy to have you here, you know that. I brought you the phone. It's almost six o'clock." She stood and then snapped her fingers. "And Lacey met your visiting teacher, Gloria. She saw the car and came over to introduce herself. Lacey explained a little of the situation, and she gave us her number in case you ever needed her to do anything."

"Does she have the magic bullet to beat this thing?"

Janet shrugged. "Anyway, it might come in handy. I'll hang onto it."

Emma smiled her thanks, the first real smile she'd given since Janet entered. "And here's your cocktail." She placed the cordless phone on the bed next to Emma and put the jug of grape Kool-Aid on the bedside table. The Kool-Aid was the only beverage that Emma didn't throw up, so they kept the house well stocked. Kool-Aid, dry wheat toast, clear chicken broth, and citrus-flavored Jell-O were the main ingredients of Emma's diet. Any fats, spices, or dairy products caused her to throw up, sometimes over and over again for hours on end. The TPN line continued to fill her bloodstream with the vitamins her body needed while she laid still, sleeping eighteen to twenty hours a day.

Janet stood. "I'll come get the phone in a little while. Can I get you anything?"

Emma shook her head and met Janet's eyes. "No," she said softly. "Thank you." Janet turned and left the room.

Emma waited until the door shut before rolling onto her side and taking a long drink of Kool-Aid. It was cold and felt good as it filled her mouth and traveled to her stomach. Within a couple of minutes, she felt revived by the sugars, but she took a Zofran just to make sure she didn't interrupt her weekly call to Catherine by retching into the bucket beside the bed. She waited another five minutes until the clock radio said 6:02 P.M. before she punched in the number.

"Hello," said the female voice on the other end of the line two rings later.

"Hi, Suzanne," Emma said. "It's me. Is Catherine there?"

"Sure, let me get her." At first Emma had called every day, but it seemed like overkill, so they agreed once a week was sufficient. Emma had made her own peace with Jake and his marriage. In fact, most of her anger and bitterness had been replaced by gratitude and relief that they were willing to rearrange their lives to help her. She was in no position to be prideful anymore.

"Mama," said a little angel voice. Emma smiled widely. She'd been so afraid that Catherine would forget her somehow. But Jake and Suzanne had put up pictures of her, just like she'd once put up pictures of them, to ensure the two-year-old would remember who her mother was. Whether or not

Catherine missed her was still up for discussion. Not only did Jake and Suzanne give her plenty of attention, she stayed with Jake's mom while they were at work. Catherine was her only grandchild and got plenty of love.

Emma cleared her throat. "How's my baby girl?" Catherine went on to babble excitedly. Emma picked up the words "doggie," "gwink," and "daddy." Everything else was indecipherable. Then as suddenly as it began, it stopped. Suzanne was on the line within a few moments. "I guess she's done."

"She doesn't give much warning," Emma said. "How are things going?"

"Good. Jake got his promotion last week."

"Oh, that's great. Congratulations." It was weird to think that only a few months ago she had wanted to rip this woman's eyes out.

"But they want us to move to Chicago."

Emma paused. "Wow," she said. "When?"

"Next month. I am wondering how you are feeling, if you are ready for Cate to come home. We've loved having her here. It's been great. But I'll be getting a new job, and we won't have Grandma to babysit."

The relief that overcame Emma was beyond words. Her one fear had been that they would want to keep Catherine forever. "Actually, it sounds perfect. I should be feeling better soon, and Lacey said she's ready to help out anytime."

"Are you sure?"

"It'll be fine. Just tell me when."

When Janet came in, Emma talked to her about Catherine coming home. Janet agreed to call Lacey. Between the two of them, it would work out just fine. "They'll remove the TPN next week, right? When you're twenty-two weeks?"

"Yeah, most women feel better by then. Although with Catherine, it never went totally away."

"He didn't say it would go away, just that you'd feel better— be able to eat more." She didn't add that keeping the TPN line in would increase her risk of infection and her veins collapsing.

It had been twelve weeks already, and it had to come out.

"I'll ask him at tomorrow's appointment. You're sure Catherine won't be too much?"

"Lacey and I will work it out," Janet said. "Don't worry about it."

Emma managed to hold down some toast and Jell-O, but around nine o'clock she was bent over the bucket again. Janet checked on her around ten and helped her back to bed where she prayed for sleep. It wasn't quick in coming. Knowing that Catherine was coming home filled her with more joy than she thought was possible, but that didn't suppress her worries about Andrew's visit. She'd wondered about his silence the last five months but couldn't complain. It had worked to her advantage. Now that fall was coming, he'd be coming back more often, and she knew it was only a matter of time before he found out. Her stomach tightened every time she thought about it, until she had to force herself not to dwell on it any more.

The next day Janet helped her into the waiting room of the doctor's office in Ogden and then left to run some errands. A neighbor was watching Janet's children. Emma was shown to a room and assisted onto the exam table. The lights were dimmed; she put on her headphones. Every week was the same. She waited for the doctor to come in while the nurses took her vital signs, changed the TPN line, and measured her belly.

"Twenty weeks," the nurse said as she removed the measuring tape. "You're measuring within normal limits. The doctor will be in soon."

Emma's head began to spin. "Can you leave me a basin?"

The nurse nodded and retrieved a large emesis basin from a cupboard. Emma began retching immediately and didn't stop until a few minutes after the doctor entered the room. As she lay back down, her face was flushed, and she felt overwhelmed with fatigue.

"Are you okay now?" the doctor asked. He was an OB/GYN that specialized in high-risk pregnancies, and she liked him because he never did anything without her understanding exactly what it was and why it was necessary. She nodded, and he continued, looking at her chart as he spoke. "Everything seems to be going pretty well," he explained. "But it's time we discussed something. Have you considered having your tubes tied? I've mentioned it before, but it's time to make a decision."

"Quite frankly, Dr. Evans, I never plan on having sex again."

Dr. Evans chuckled, but his tone was serious. "I know this is a big decision, and that you're very young, but it's a decision you need to think about."

Emma didn't answer for a few seconds. "I'm only twenty-two years old. I'm not sure I'm ready to make that choice."

Dr. Evans leaned forward and looked at her sternly. "Emma, I'm going to be very frank with you. If you get pregnant again, you would be putting your life, as well as the life of your child, in jeopardy. HG is usually worse with each subsequent pregnancy. You've been lucky so far. You haven't had severe tearing of your stomach lining or esophagus. You haven't had hallucinations, and you were put under my care in time to save your life. But I've had patients who have ruptured their placentas from vomiting. It's not uncommon to get serious infections from the TPN tube—infections that can kill you. There are many women who have had no choice but to terminate their pregnancies five months along in order to save their own lives. You've lived through hell these last few months, and you're not out of the woods yet. Next time . . ." He left the sentence hanging.

She didn't answer him. She was busy wiping the tears from her cheeks. She thought back to the time she'd told Andrew she didn't plan to have any more children. She'd been so confident back then. She wished she felt that confident now. "You don't have to make a decision right now. Just keep it in mind."

Emma promised that she would. Later that night, after the usual evening wave of nausea, she stared at the ceiling and let the tears fall. She'd argued with herself for hours, going back and forth between what she wanted and reality. In the end, she knew she really had little choice. Andrew's child would be her last.

It wasn't until her tears had passed and she was just drifting off to sleep that she noticed the flutter in her belly. Her eyes flew open, and she lay very still, willing a confirmation. Within a few seconds, it came again, and a wide smile spread across her face. Slowly she placed a hand on her stomach and then inhaled sharply as once again she felt the flutter of life within her. Within seconds she was crying again, but not with grief. After a few minutes, the movement stopped. Her baby was at rest again. She closed her eyes and gave a brief prayer of gratitude. She'd been adequately reminded of just how lucky she was.

CHAPTER 38

*A*ndrew came home and entered the house Saturday morning, listening for the sound of voices. It took only seconds to determine no one was home. The house felt strange, not just empty, but alone somehow. He found the note in the kitchen and headed for the phone, ignoring his trepidation at speaking to Emma's family members.

"Hello," a woman said a few moments later. Andrew assumed it was Emma's sister-in-law Janet. "Blair residence."

"Hi. This is Andrew Davidson. I just got in and found a note saying Emma's staying with you. Can I speak with her, please?"

The woman on the other end of the line was silent for a long time. "She's sleeping, Andrew. Can I take a message?"

Now it was Andrew's turn to pause. "Is she all right?"

"She will be," Janet said in clipped tones. "I'll let her know you called." She hung up before he had a chance to say anything else.

Sunday morning he called again. A man he could only assume was Emma's brother Tally answered this time. Andrew hadn't ever spoken to this brother before. "Good morning,"

Andrew began. "I'm trying to get a hold of Emma."

"She can't come to the phone," Tally said. "I'll tell her you called." He hung up before Andrew had a chance to protest.

Andrew hung up the phone and started walking through the house. Something wasn't right, but he couldn't put his finger on it. He opened the cupboards. They were fully stocked, but the fridge was nearly empty—something he'd never seen since Emma had moved in. Most of Catherine's clothing, as well as much of Emma's, was missing, and it made him wonder how long she'd been staying with Janet. A dark thought occurred to him, and he wondered if she had found out what he'd done and left. He closed his eyes as a new disgust filled his heart. Was the reason she'd been out of contact with him the same reason he'd been avoiding her? The idea made him sick.

His flight left at eight o'clock Sunday night, and he tried calling Janet's house one last time. This time no one answered. He penned a note of his own and left it on the counter before locking up the house.

Lacey usually checked on things at the house, but since Janet had met a friend for lunch in Salt Lake today she was the one who stopped at the house. She brought the note back with her. Emma read it after Janet left the room.

> *Emma,*
>
> *I won't be back for a few more weeks. I've got some projects to finish up, but when I do, we need to talk. I'm sorry I haven't kept in contact, but please know I've thought about you often. I hope you'll be back home when I return.*
>
> *Andrew*

It was almost sweet, but it didn't matter. Emma had managed to avoid him once, and with any luck she'd be able to do it again. At the same time, she knew she needed to think about how and when to tell him. Time was running out.

A few hours later, Janet knocked on the door again.

"Lacey's here," she said excitedly, her eyes dancing. Emma sat up and swung her feet over the edge of the bed as Janet disappeared. She had to rest for a few moments to let the wave of nausea pass. Lacey suddenly appeared with Catherine in her arms. Emma choked down a sob at seeing her daughter for the first time in months and held out her arms. Her hair was longer, and she wore clothes Emma didn't recognize. Was this really her baby? She looked so grown up.

Catherine squealed and lunged from Lacey as soon as she was close enough, causing Emma to fall back on the bed. Thank goodness the TPN line had been removed earlier in the week. Otherwise it could have been disastrous. Emma held her close as tears coursed down her cheeks. "Oh, baby girl," she cooed softly, holding her as tight as she possibly could, as if by holding her tightly enough she'd never have to let her go again. Catherine only put up with it for a few more seconds, however, before she pulled away and began to investigate the room.

"Oh, don't touch that," Emma said, pulling Catherine from the bedside table before she could get a hold of the open prescription bottle. As she pulled her away, Catherine grabbed the fresh mug of grape Kool-Aid and tugged it onto the bed, drenching both of them with the cold, purple liquid. Emma gasped and Catherine started to cry. Lacey immediately interceded and picked Catherine up.

"No, no," Emma said, reaching for her. "It's okay."

"I'll bring her back," Lacey said quickly as she left the room. "She just needs to get cleaned up." Emma fell back onto the bed, ignoring the irritation she felt at being so dependent on others. Then she closed her eyes as she reminded herself that Catherine was home. She smiled and took a breath of strength. She was halfway through the pregnancy, and Cate was back. She needed to count her blessings, not her tribulations.

CHAPTER 39

*B*y the time Andrew made it onto a Salt Lake-bound plane, nearly a month had passed. He wanted to come sooner, but work wouldn't allow it, and he'd needed the extra time to build up his courage. He was going to tell Emma. He had to. It was obvious to him that his distance had hurt her, that she was angry, and he couldn't blame her. Knowing he was about to give her even more reason to be hurt and angry tied him in knots, but he couldn't live with this anymore. He'd always considered himself a man of honor and integrity, and going back on that once had been bad enough. Going back on it twice by not telling Emma what he'd done was eating him alive. He tried not to think too much about what her reaction might be, not wanting to scare himself out of making his confession. All he had to rely on was that telling her the truth was the right thing and keeping it from her wasn't. But he felt sick just thinking of what lay ahead.

When he landed in Salt Lake, he drove straight home to see if Emma was there. She wasn't, so he called her brother's house again.

No one answered, so he left a message. After half an hour,

he jumped on the Internet and found Tally Blair's address. If he waited much longer, he'd lose his nerve.

"Emma," Janet called through the closed door of the bathroom, "are you sure you don't need help?"

"I'm fine—I'll be fine in a few minutes," Emma called back, her attempts at making her voice sound strong failing. She was on the floor in the bathroom waiting until she was sure she was okay. "Did he call again?"

"No, just that once," Janet replied.

Emma nodded and was glad Janet hadn't answered Andrew's call. At the same time, she knew she couldn't put it off much longer. She just couldn't imagine how that scene would play out. After two weeks of feeling better, the vomiting had returned. This time it turned out to really be the flu. Joining with her already unstable condition, it had come on with a vengeance, and she'd lost the few pounds she'd managed to gain over the last few weeks. Dr. Evans had said he would give her two more days to get over it, and then she would have to be put on a feeding tube. She tried to eat something every hour. Sometimes she was lucky, but more often than not she would throw it back up. This time there had been blood too. The doctor had warned her about esophageal tears and that as soon as they started, she would be hospitalized. She was trying to downplay it, telling herself that it wasn't much blood. If she could go the rest of the day without vomiting, surely it would be fine. With that resolve, along with the fact that her nausea had abated, she pulled herself to her feet and then put a hand to her stomach. It felt tight and awkward, probably from having been bent over the toilet for so long. Hearing that Andrew had called didn't help a bit—the stress of it had made everything worse.

The baby kicked and she smiled. The ultrasounds confirmed that the baby was growing well. With the amount of calories she was keeping down every day, it amazed her that either one of them were even alive.

She opened the bathroom door, gave Janet what she hoped was an encouraging smile, and went back to her new spot on the living room couch. It was nice not to be relegated to her bedroom, and although she was still worthless, at least she could help play with the kids a little bit. Right now they were outside though, so she just laid down and closed her eyes. A glance at the clock told her she had forty minutes before she had to eat again. She tried not to think about it. A new wave of nausea hit her, and she quickly leaned over the bucket again. With a grunt of frustration, she got up and hurried to the bathroom, taking her bucket with her. *Why can't this just go away?* On her way to the bathroom, the doorbell rang.

After dumping the contents of the bowl in the toilet, she washed her hands. Looking up, she caught her reflection and stared at the gaunt face in the mirror. She resisted the nearly overwhelming desire to feel sorry for herself. She knew it would only make her more upset, and that usually led to crying, which led to getting sick again, which was the cause of all her self-pity. She turned away and left the bathroom, wondering if she should go back downstairs. Surely it wasn't any fun for Janet and the kids to hear her throwing up and see her running back and forth to the bathroom every twenty minutes.

She heard Janet's voice talking to someone at the front door as she turned the corner and headed for the living room. *Great, a neighbor probably stopped in.* That made the decision for her that she ought to go downstairs. People were usually shocked when they saw her, and she hated the stares. She'd just grab her blanket off the couch and make a hasty retreat. The voices stopped when she entered the living room, and as she leaned down to grab her blanket she glanced up at the visitor. Then she froze—and stared at Andrew for a few moments. Janet looked back and forth between the two of them.

"What is going on?" Andrew said very slowly, his face

showing anger and shock. Emma simply looked down at her protruding belly and closed her eyes, steadying herself by grabbing the couch. The room began to spin, and Janet appeared at her side to keep her from falling. Emma had tried not to imagine this moment at all and now found herself unprepared for the intensity of it.

"She's been terribly sick today, Andrew. Come talk to her later, not now."

Andrew stood there for a few moments before turning and disappearing down the porch steps. Janet helped Emma lie down on the couch as Emma started to cry.

He knew—she had to explain! "I need to talk to him, Janet. Please get him before he leaves."

"Okay," Janet said, heading out the front door.

She returned just a few seconds later. "I didn't catch him in time," she said. Emma grabbed her stomach, feeling the tightness and the need to throw up at the same time. She leaned over the bucket as Andrew's face swam before her.

He knows. Now what?

CHAPTER 40

Three hours later, Mark was on the phone in his L.A. office when the door of his office burst open. He startled and only had a split second to register the unannounced visitor as Andrew before the other man's fist hit him squarely in the jaw. The force sent Mark sprawling backwards. The chair fell loudly and Mark hit the wall. When Andrew came around the desk, Mark looked at him with absolute terror, his mind moving a million miles an hour trying to figure out what was happening. Andrew swore at him a few times before pulling Mark to his feet and preparing for the next blow.

"Something you want to tell me?" Andrew hissed at him. But without giving him time to answer, he landed another punch in Mark's face. Mark once again fell to the floor, but this time he scrambled to his feet and hurried to put some distance between himself and his assailant. Gingerly, he put a hand to his face and pulled it back to reveal that the wetness he felt on his face really was his own blood. When he looked up again, Andrew was coming toward him, and he quickly moved away. When Andrew finally stopped, so did Mark, although he didn't take his eyes off of him this time.

Nearly a dozen people were cramming their heads through the doorway, watching the drama, but Mark hardly noticed. He was only interested in the one man standing across the desk from him. Andrew had asked him something, but he couldn't remember what it was.

"So tell me, Mark," Andrew spat, "was it worth it?"

Mark creased his brow. "What are you talking about?"

"The last thing you want to talk to *me* about, that's for sure," Andrew said as he began coming around the desk again. Mark hurried to keep the safety zone between them. "Did the fact that she was my wife cross your mind even once?"

Again Mark gave him a confused look. "Andrew, I don't—"

"Did you plan it out beforehand? Or did you just meet her in the hallway and let things happen naturally? Maybe it happened in my own house, in the next room even."

Mark was silent for a moment. "Are we talking about Emma?"

"Yes, Mark, we're talking about Emma," Andrew said loudly. "My wife and the mother of *your* child."

The heads in the doorway let out a collective gasp, and Mark's eyebrows shot up. But he didn't speak. "There is nothing I want more, at this moment, than to tear you apart," Andrew breathed. He leaped around the desk and almost caught Mark, but he got out of the way just in time.

"Emma's pregnant?" Mark asked. Andrew just narrowed his eyes—Mark took that for a "yes." "Andrew, it isn't what you think," Mark quickly added.

"I just left her in Salt Lake, Mark. I might be stupid enough to let you sleep with my wife right under my nose, but I'm not so dumb that I didn't notice she's pregnant." Again Andrew lunged forward, and again Mark managed to stay just out of reach.

"Will you please calm down for a minute!" Mark suddenly bellowed from one side of his desk. The heads at the door looked at him and almost immediately turned to look at Andrew, who had stopped his attack but was still glaring at his opponent. "Are you sure she's pregnant?" Mark asked.

Andrew put his hand out about a foot from his own stomach. "About this much. Yeah, she's pregnant. Were you two trying to hide it from me? Did you think I wouldn't notice?"

Mark sighed and cursed under his breath. The heads in the doorway caught his attention, and he went toward the door. Andrew moved toward him, and Mark decided to keep the desk between them rather than dispose of the audience. "Did you ask her if it was me?"

"Do I really need to?" Andrew answered sarcastically. "I warned her not to get too close to you."

"But you didn't talk to her about it, did you? You didn't ask her what happened?"

"No, I left so I could come *kill* you."

"It's not mine, Andrew, and I haven't spoken to her since that ski weekend," Mark finally said.

Andrew smiled, but it looked more like a wolf baring his teeth. "Now, how did I know you would say that?" And with that he dove again. Mark wasn't fast enough this time and was thrown to the floor, grateful he had a large office and didn't encounter any bookshelves on his way down. Before he had time to think about what to do next, Andrew was straddling his chest with his arm pulled back, ready to strike.

"It's yours, Andrew," Mark squeaked as he clenched his eyes shut and waited for the blow. After a few moments, he dared open his eyes to find that Andrew hadn't moved. He seemed frozen in place but ready to hit him at any moment.

"That is almost funny," he said, although there was not a trace of humor in his voice. "You *know* that isn't true."

"It is," Mark said with a little more confidence, still waiting for the fist to fly. "She was the girl you were with that night."

Andrew stared at him but didn't speak. Mark swallowed and hurried to explain. "You gave that blonde in the bar Emma's room number. Emma took you back to yours."

"No, she didn't," Andrew said in a somewhat calmer, almost hesitant voice. "Emma wouldn't have—"

"But you think she'd sleep with me?" Mark cut in. Andrew finally lowered his hand. "When I went back to your room that morning, it was Emma there, not the woman from the bar. She was embarrassed to have me find her there and didn't understand why you had left and why I was there. I told her the truth." Andrew shook his head again, but Mark could see fear in his eyes. He felt the confidence seep back into his mind and relished being able to share the secret he'd been obsessing about for so long. "She was devastated that you didn't know it was her and made me promise not to tell you. I've called her dozens of times since then to see if she's okay, but she never returns my calls. If I'd known she was pregnant, I'd have stormed *your* office."

Andrew thought back to his memories of that night, specifically the fact that he had truly thought it was Emma. He shook his head again. *It couldn't have happened the way Mark said. It wasn't Emma! It couldn't have been.* "Why wouldn't she want me to know it was her?" Andrew finally asked as he moved to the side and allowed Mark to sit up.

"Isn't it obvious?" Mark said carefully as he backed away. "You were so drunk you didn't even know who she was—but she knew very well what she was doing, who she was with. It meant something to her—and nothing to you."

Andrew sat back on his heels. *It couldn't have been her,* he thought in one last desperate attempt not to face the truth. But his mind was adding details he hadn't wanted to pay attention to when he thought it had been someone else. He recalled the scent of her shampoo, kisses that seemed so familiar, and suddenly her voice filtered through his mind: *"I think I'm falling in love with you, Andrew Davidson."* Andrew groaned and dropped his head, falling to the side and staring at the floor he was now sitting on. "I can't believe this," he whispered and finally looked up at Mark.

Mark stared at him for a few moments. "Do I get to hit you now?"

CHAPTER 41

*A*ndrew went to his apartment and from his liquor cabinet retrieved a bottle of whiskey that hadn't been touched for nearly six months. For what seemed like hours, he sat on his couch and stared at the bottle. Having been convinced that it *had* been Emma that night made everything fall into place. Never in his life had he had a one-night-stand—never. The fact that he had been married to Emma and then fallen into a trap he had avoided all those years had just not made sense. He had rationalized that he'd been so drunk he had pretended it was her. It sickened him for many reasons, but that was the conclusion he had drawn. When he had awakened that morning and heard the shower, he hadn't even considered that it could have been her. It seemed impossible that she would spend the night with him.

Yet she had. And *she* hadn't been drunk; she had known *exactly* what she was doing. He knew that for Emma to have made the choice to stay with him that night was no trite decision.

He pictured how she must have looked when Mark told her the truth, and he got a lump in his throat. And to top off all the shock and shame of it, she was pregnant. He remembered what she'd told him about getting sick with her pregnancies, of how horrible it had been, and his heart sank even lower. She'd looked awful when he'd seen her this afternoon—and he was responsible for that too. His eyes went back to the amber bottle. Quickly, he picked it up and took it into the kitchen before he lost his strength to resist. Since that night he had been afraid to drink, afraid of his inability to make good decisions when he drank too much. But now it was more than that. If he hadn't been drinking that night, who knew where he and Emma would be now.

In the kitchen, he opened the bottle and poured it down the sink. The rest of his wet bar followed, and when the last bottle was empty, he took a deep breath and asked himself what he was going to do now.

A knock from across the room startled him. He walked to the door and opened it slowly. He hadn't buzzed anyone in, and anyone coming or going from his apartment complex had to be let in. Two young men in shirts and ties stood smiling in the doorway. The building didn't allow solicitors or uninvited guests, but he waited for them to speak before informing them that they better get out before he called the manager.

"Hello," the shorter of the two men said. He was young, twenty years old or so, and Andrew doubted he needed to shave yet. "We're here for an appointment with Mr. Edgars."

"Mr. Edgars is in three-sixty-two," Andrew said. "This is three-sixty-five."

The men looked down at a blue card one was holding. When the short one looked back up at Andrew, he was still smiling.

"I'm sorry to have bothered you, sir," he said evenly. "I guess we read the number wrong."

Andrew nodded and had begun to shut the door when his eyes caught the name tag each young man had on the breast pocket of his shirt. "Wait," Andrew called quickly, opening the door and stepping over the threshold. They both turned to look at him. He pointed to their name tags and stepped closer so he could read them. Just as he had thought; they were the same words he'd seen at the house in Salt Lake—he couldn't remember where. On some paper of Emma's maybe. "The Church of Jesus Christ of Latter-day Saints," he read aloud. He looked up to meet their eyes. "Is that the Mormon church?"

Both men's faces lit up. "Yes. Are you familiar with our church?"

"A little bit," he said.

"We have an appointment with Mr. Edgars," the taller man said. "But when we're finished, we could come back and speak with you about it, if you'd like."

The night in Salt Lake when he'd been so offended by the teacher-guy came to mind, and he stiffened. He had no desire to sit through that again. "Okay," he said, shocking himself. He didn't want to talk to these men. In his experience, there was little to like about Emma's church. Why would he want to hear more about it?

"We should be finished around eight o'clock," the shorter one said.

Andrew just nodded, still disbelieving his own behavior.

The hour of waiting seemed to stretch forever, and he nearly wore through the Oriental rug as he paced back and forth, arguing with himself. When they knocked, he froze and contemplated not answering the door. Surely it was best to keep them on the other side. They knocked again, and Andrew shook his head in frustration. As he opened the door, he decided he would talk to them for fifteen minutes just to be polite and then tell them he wasn't interested.

Almost forty minutes later, Andrew leaned forward. "So God and Jesus just visited this guy, out of the blue?"

"No," the shorter one, Elder Randal, said. Andrew had quickly determined he was the more knowledgeable of the two. "Joseph had been pondering what religion to join for many years. He was very familiar with the New Testament, and so he prayed, with a pure and burning faith, believing his prayer would be answered, just as the Bible promises."

"And do you guys get visited by angels when you pray?"

"No," Elder Randal said with a chuckle. "Joseph's vision was the beginning of a great miracle, the ushering in of a fullness that had been taken from the earth for many centuries. A restoration of that magnitude required something great, something majestic, and that was what it was."

Andrew leaned forward and spoke a little softer, as if soliciting them to tell the truth. "Do you really believe that?" He'd asked Emma the same question, and he could still remember the feeling he got when she explained that she did. It was kind of creepy but in a good way.

Elder Randal smiled and nodded. "I believe it with all my heart. Joseph Smith was a prophet of God, the first prophet of this dispensation. Through him all the keys and glory of Christ's gospel were restored to this earth. And because of him, we, the sons and daughters of God, are entitled to eternal families, life without end, and lives of peace and joy. I know who God is. I know that He knows me and wants me to be happy. This is Christ's church, and I know it is true."

Andrew sat frozen. He felt as if he'd forgotten to breathe. He probably had. That creepy feeling was back—but creepy wasn't the right word. His head was tingling, and all the questions he had been ready to beat these guys up with were forgotten. The two men just looked at him, as if they knew exactly what he was thinking. He looked at the other man. "And you believe it too?"

Elder Iverson took a breath, and with less eloquence but just as much intensity, he also explained what he believed, and why he believed it.

Again Andrew was stunned. He'd never felt anything like this. They didn't speak for nearly a minute after Elder Iverson stopped talking. Andrew put his elbows on his knees and his hands under his chin as he stared at the floor and reviewed the things he'd just been told. He'd never been a religious man— never given much thought to God. And he'd always been an honest man anyway. He believed in respect, integrity, and living up to his obligations.

So what are you doing here? a voice said.

He looked up at the two men. "What did you say?"

The men looked at each other, confused.

If you are a man of integrity, who fulfills his responsibilities, why aren't you with your wife and child?

Andrew gasped and stared at the two men, knowing they hadn't spoken. He looked around the room quickly, fearful of the strange things happening to him.

"Mr. Davidson?" Elder Randal asked with concern. "Are you okay?"

Andrew looked back at them, speechless. "I . . . I thought I heard something . . . someone."

The two men were now very still, and after a few moments Elder Randal spoke. "Could we kneel in prayer, Mr. Davidson?" he asked.

The room seemed to get smaller, warmer, full of an energy Andrew didn't recognize. Andrew nodded and followed their lead as they knelt on the floor facing one another.

Elder Randal's voice wasn't loud and forceful—it was small, humble, and soft, almost like a child's voice. "Dear Heavenly Father," he began. After expressions of gratitude, he asked that the Spirit might lead Andrew to the answers he sought, that his heart would be open, and that he might thirst for the truth. "Bless him with Thy Spirit, that he might know the road he should take. Help him to trust in Thee, and in us, that he might grow in ways he's never dreamed, that he might know of Thy glory and of Thy love. In the name of Jesus Christ, Amen."

When Andrew looked up, he felt dazed and unable to comprehend the feelings in his heart.

"We'd like to come back," Elder Randal said in a quiet voice. "Would seven o'clock Sunday evening work for you?"

Andrew nodded and took the blue book Elder Iverson handed him. "This is a copy of The Book of Mormon.

It's another testament of Christ, similar to the Bible. We've marked some passages. Will you commit to read them before our next visit?"

"Yes," Andrew said with an odd eagerness. "I can do that."

Elder Randal stuck out his hand. "We'll look forward to seeing you."

Andrew showed them out and collapsed on the couch, the events and emotions of the evening still swirling around him. He didn't know what to make of it. He wasn't sure he wanted to pursue it. The newness was frightening, and on one hand it didn't make sense—yet on the other hand it was as if he'd always known this but had forgotten it until now. He closed his eyes and shook his head as a thought came to mind. *It's either true, and this Spirit the two men talked about is responsible for all my feelings, or I'm losing my mind.*

He wasn't sure which one of the two options he preferred.

That night he dreamed about his mother. He'd had other dreams, but there was something about this one that stuck with him. In the dream, he answered the door to find the same two men, but with his mom standing behind them. She was young and radiant, much like she was in that picture he still hadn't found. She looked him in the eye and said, "Listen, for both of us."

Andrew woke up with a start and had the oddest feeling, almost as if she were there with him. And he got the distinct impression that life was only going to get weirder from here on out.

CHAPTER 42

*J*anet arrived home around nine o'clock. She tossed her keys on the table and bent down to catch Josh, who was running at her full speed. She picked him up with effort, due to her large belly, and hugged him tightly, holding him a little longer than usual. When she looked up, Tally was watching her. She went to him and kissed him lightly on the lips.

"So?" Tally asked with concern.

"Let's get the kids to bed." She looked down at Catherine, who was eating dry Cheerios out of a bowl, and her heart ached. Catherine had just come back, but she and her mom were separated again. After Andrew had left that afternoon, Emma had thrown up over and over again. She was so sick that she almost hadn't noticed the contractions. But they didn't go unnoticed for long. Janet called a neighbor to watch the kids and rushed Emma to the hospital. Tally came home as soon as he could and took over babysitting, waiting for a report.

Half an hour after coming home, Janet fixed hot chocolate for both of them before collapsing on the couch.

"So?" Tally repeated, taking a long sip of his cocoa and regarding his wife over the rim of the mug.

"They stopped labor, but she's dilated to a two."

Tally groaned. "How far along is she? Twenty-eight weeks?"

"Twenty-seven," Janet clarified. "They're going to keep her in the hospital until the baby's born—preterm labor on top of everything else makes her too fragile to come home again."

"Twenty-seven weeks," Tally said in shock. "That's too early."

"They're encouraged that they were able to stop the labor as easily as they did, and they'll watch her closely. She's also on Zofran IV, making it much more likely that she'll avoid any vomiting attacks as severe as this one."

"Is that what started it then?"

"That's what they think," Janet confirmed. "The shock of seeing Andrew seemed to have set her off. But she's in a good place. She'll have around-the-clock care and, as horrible as this is to say, I won't be run so ragged. Having both her and Catherine has been a real challenge."

Tally put down his mug and slowly took hers from her hand. He leaned forward, causing her to lie back on the couch. When he had her adequately confined, he ran his thumb along her cheek. "Have I told you lately how much I love you?"

"Yes," Janet said softly, staring into his eyes and remembering all the reasons she loved him too. "You told me this morning."

"Did I tell you how much I appreciate all you've done for Emma? I could never have supported her the way you have."

"I've been where she is, or almost, anyway." Emma's struggle had been a constant reminder of when Josh's dad had turned his back on both of them, just after Janet had learned she was pregnant. It was hard to watch Emma struggling and impossible not to be empathetic of her situation.

"You're a remarkable woman," Tally said, kissing her lightly and resting his head on her chest as he traced his fingers along her belly. She wished Emma had made better choices so that she wasn't facing this alone. She had her brothers and sisters-in-law, but when it came right down to it, she was alone. Janet knew what that felt like, but she also knew that the only person who could remedy the situation was Emma, and she didn't seem to understand her choices well enough to fix them.

CHAPTER 43

*S*unday evening the Mormon missionaries returned to Andrew's apartment for their second discussion. Andrew had read the assigned verses, but he stopped there. Tonight he was thirsty for more, just as Elder Randal had prayed he would be. But as they taught the plan of salvation, his doubts returned. They finished and asked if he had any questions. He wasn't sure where to start.

"What if you're wrong?" he asked after a long silence. "What if there is no plan of salvation? What if no angels really came to Joseph Smith? What if all this time you've believed in something that isn't true?" He paused long enough for them to interrupt him if they wanted to. They were content to listen for the moment. "So, you don't drink, don't smoke, don't . . . do other things. You go to church every week. You do everything you're told to do, and then you find out you're wrong. Do you ever wonder about that?"

"I think everyone wonders about that sometimes," Elder Iverson said. He had given the discussion and was much more talkative this time around. "But that's why we have prayer, so that we can each know individually."

Andrew's expression must have communicated his doubt because Elder Iverson seemed compelled to explain further.

"Incidentally, even if this weren't the only true church, if Joseph Smith had somehow made it all up, I'm grateful to have the support and motivation to live a clean life. I'm the only member of the Church in my family, Mr. Davidson, and I've lived the other side through my parents, siblings, and friends. I don't envy their lives. My life changed when I prayed to know if this really is the true church. And with it, my future changed too."

Andrew paused. That sounded familiar. "Like what?" he asked. "What about your future really changed?"

"Family, for one thing," Elder Iverson said with a dry chuckle. "My mom's been married three times, and I don't know where my real dad is. My stepfathers were the most worthless pieces of trash I've ever met." Elder Randal cleared his throat as if to protest the direction this conversation was taking, but Andrew waved him to be quiet and let Elder Iverson continue. "I wanted to be a stockbroker and make millions. I was going to have three houses on three continents and live my life any way I wanted to."

"And that all changed?"

"Now I'm going to get my MBA," he said with an excited grin. "I met a girl a few months before I left on my mission. She's so awesome. She's not waiting, necessarily, but so far she still writes, and I can totally see my life with a girl like that. I'm going to go into banking so I can be home at night with my wife and kids. The world I saw as my oyster, really is one now—with pearls I'd never noticed before. I'm looking forward to being a good husband and father, to changing the generations of ignorance I came from. Those are things I never expected four years ago."

Andrew sat up and put his hands behind his head as he let out a breath. "I don't know what to think," he said. "I've never even thought about these things. I don't know if I want to think about them anymore."

"Why?" Elder Randal asked. "Why don't you?"

"Because I love my life," Andrew said before stopping himself. Did he love his life? He loved his lifestyle—well, that wasn't entirely true. He loved nice things and the fact that he could afford to buy them. He loved being successful, and he loved what he did. Did he love being alone most of the time? No, and his dislike of it had been growing of late. Did he love spending holidays by himself? No, he never had. Did he love knowing that if he stayed on his current path he would die alone, with some business associates to say "poor man" at his funeral, and no one to leave his money to? Maybe he *was* missing things that he'd never noticed were missing.

"You guys want to hear a story?" he said after gathering his thoughts for a minute. They nodded. "It's a little sordid," he warned. "It's got sex, drinking, betrayal—all the juicy stuff."

"So does the Bible," Elder Iverson said with a grin. Elder Randal didn't seem as excited, but Andrew continued anyway.

He started at the beginning—his life before he'd known about the trust. Then he explained the trust, his brilliant idea to marry Emma and make a cool two and half million. Within a few more minutes, he'd introduced them to Emma, to her life, and how she grew in his regard. Then came the fateful ski weekend, and finally his discovery just three days earlier that Emma was pregnant with his child, and desperately ill because of it.

"What would you do if you were me?" he asked. "I've never considered having kids, Emma hates me, and now . . ." He paused as the thought of his own child threatened to overwhelm him with alien emotions he didn't understand. "I *will* be a father. And I don't know what to do. Part of me thinks I should stay here, let Emma do it her way, and keep my life as it is. I've never been around kids, and I didn't have a dad, so I don't have a clue how to be one. I . . . *feel* that I should be the man I wish my father had been—but I still don't know where to start. It's like a war going on in my head. And then you guys knocked at my door, and now I'm more confused than ever."

The two men were silent. Andrew reminded himself that they were just kids. What was he doing asking them for advice? He was about to apologize for dumping his life on them when Elder Iverson spoke.

"If I were you, Mr. Davidson," he said softly, "I would make sure that I wouldn't regret whatever decision I made."

"How?" Andrew prodded. "I've always had amazing instincts in business, but this leaves me dry."

"Pick up your Book of Mormon. Let's look some things up," Elder Randal said. They first turned to Alma 5:46. The scripture spoke of knowing for oneself, through prayer and fasting. Then they turned to Mormon 9:37 where it spoke of receiving answers from God if we have faith. Lastly they turned to James 1:5 in Elder Iverson's Bible, and the elders explained that this was the scripture that led Joseph Smith to pray in the grove. "If any of you lack wisdom, let him ask of God, that giveth to all men liberally, and upbraideth not; and it shall be given him."

Andrew took a deep breath. "This sounds as weird to me as skydiving into a huge vat of pudding."

They laughed, but then Elder Randal spoke again. "If you're willing to fast and pray with faith that God will answer you, you will know what you should do."

Andrew nodded slowly, feeling a great comfort in those words. He wanted to know—desperately. According to every-thing they had just read, if he did what they said, he could have that knowledge. "Will you pray again, before you go?"

"Why don't you say the prayer this time?"

That night Andrew dreamed of his mother again. They were walking on parallel sidewalks a few feet apart from each other and chatting about his childhood and how much she enjoyed being his mother. Then their sidewalks started moving farther apart from each other, until they were yelling back and forth. "Andrew," she finally yelled, "This isn't work-ing—we're too far apart to make any sense of one another."

He woke up with a start again and knew that he needed to move back to Salt Lake. Like the dream, he and Emma were too far apart to make sense of one another. How or why he knew that made no sense at all, but it was a fact. Now the trick was figuring out how to do it.

CHAPTER 44

*T*uesday afternoon Andrew sat in his office making notes, checking files, and returning calls. His secretary buzzed in and said Jeff Freeman was here. Andrew took a deep breath and told her to let him in. Jeff Freeman was a developer, like Andrew, although his company wasn't nearly as large.

They spent a few minutes catching up on each other's business before Andrew got down to the reason he'd called the meeting. "Jeff, I'm in a bit of a spot, and I'm hoping you can help me."

Jeff spread his hands, showing he was open to anything, although his expression betrayed his curiosity. Andrew continued. "I had my secretary do some research to find construction companies that had offices in L.A. as well as in Salt Lake. Your name was on the list."

Jeff looked a little confused, but he nodded. "Yes, we have this office and the Salt Lake office as well."

"How did that happen?"

"Well," Jeff began, "we originated in Salt Lake, but my brother-in-law had a great piece of land here in L.A., and we decided to get our foot in the door by developing that land into an office complex."

Andrew nodded and motioned for Jeff to continue.

"By the time we finished, about four years ago, the area was overbuilt, and we had to sell it for a lot less than we had hoped. We didn't get the solid start we'd been hoping for here, but we're on our way up, and in a few more years I think we'll have made up for the loss."

Andrew nodded. "I remember that year. I had a few casualties myself. How's the Salt Lake office?"

"Doing pretty well," he said with a smile. "It's been a bit of a struggle keeping both offices productive and cash flowing, but we do a lot of work for the Church, which is good business in Utah and getting better in California all the time—"

Andrew leaned forward in his seat. "The Mormon church?"

"Sorry, yes, the Mormon church. In Utah we refer to it as 'the Church,' and everyone knows what we're talking about."

Andrew nodded, his interest growing by the second. "That's great," he said slowly. He paused thoughtfully, staring at his desk for a few moments as he tried to decide how far to proceed. This was only supposed to be a preliminary meeting.

"If you don't mind my asking, Mr. Davidson," Jeff said, "why the interest in my company?"

Andrew folded his arms on the desk and leaned forward slightly. "My wife is in Salt Lake, and she prefers it there rather than here."

"Can't say as I blame her for that," he replied. "I'm from Provo. My wife's from here—she won too."

Andrew smiled and continued. "Living apart isn't working out, and I'm trying to formulate a way I can move to Salt Lake full time." Jeff lifted his eyebrows while Andrew paused for a few moments. "What would you think of combining our interests, sharing our strengths, and growing both places together?"

Jeff was silent, shock written all over his freshly shaved

face. "A partnership?"

"Yeah," Andrew said, surprised with his own eagerness. "I would go to Salt Lake, continue to strengthen what you already have, and you would run our combined business here."

The room went dead silent as Jeff absorbed what he'd just been offered. "My business isn't nearly as strong an interest as yours," Jeff said, still reeling from the shock. "And . . . I have a hard time seeing what's in it for you. You could start your own company in Salt Lake without a problem."

"Here's the catch," Andrew added quickly. "I need to leave here as soon as possible, and I need someone I can trust to leave in charge of my interests here. I don't want to start a new company in a new town. I can't give it that kind of time right now. I'm willing to make the sacrifices I need to in order to put my ducks in a row, so to speak, as quickly as possible." Jeff still looked doubtful. Andrew decided to show all his cards. "I've only been married ten months, and my wife's having a difficult pregnancy." As he spoke, he had no doubt this was the right thing for him to do.

He'd prayed by himself for the first time after the missionaries left on Sunday. Monday he began his first fast the way they taught him to. They had agreed to fast with him. It had been awful, but before having dinner with the missionaries last night to break the fast, he'd prayed again. By this morning, his decision was made. He was still anxious and overwhelmed, but the missionary's words echoed back to him continually, *Make sure you don't regret the decision you make.* If he turned his back on Emma, he'd regret it forever.

And then there was his child. *His* child deserved to have a father.

"I've been in L.A. throughout the whole pregnancy, and I'm just starting to understand how close I am to losing them both. It will take a lot of work on your part. I'll continue to help out and do what I can, but I need to be in Salt Lake."

Jeff was silent. Finally he leaned forward. "Are you serious?"

Andrew knew full well what this offering was to someone in Jeff's position. He would go from an average contractor to a triple-digit professional almost overnight. If Andrew hadn't stayed up until the early morning the night before reviewing all of Jeff's information, he'd have never handled it quite like this. But Jeff Freeman's credentials were impressive, and his integrity was without question. Meeting with him now, and having the opportunity to take his own measure of this man, only solidified what he had already believed. His heart told him that Jeff was a man who could be trusted.

"I'm very serious," Andrew said strongly.

"I need to talk to my wife about it," Jeff said, his voice quickening with excitement. "Can we meet tomorrow?"

"Whatever we need to do."

Jeff stood, they shook hands, and Andrew watched him hurry out of the room. He questioned himself, more out of habit than anything, but he truly felt this was the way to go. He got back to work. There was a lot to get done, and he had no time to waste.

The next morning Jeff was ushered into the office. They shook hands, and Andrew smiled at the other man's eagerness. Within ten minutes, they were reviewing details, and Andrew's secretary was on the phone with Andrew's lawyer, getting the contracts started.

CHAPTER 45

$\mathcal{T}$he following Wednesday morning, just a week from the day he and Jeff had shaken hands and started their merger, Andrew caught a plane for Salt Lake. His apartment had been put up for sale, the contracts had been signed, and the foreman of each project he was overseeing had been introduced to Jeff Freeman at a company dinner the night before. The L.A. office would continue as Davidson Development, because of its reputation. The Salt Lake company would retain the title of Freeman Construction for the same reason.

As Andrew settled into his window seat in first class, he thought of where he was going—to Emma. It had been almost two weeks since he'd learned of the baby, and his mouth went dry every time he thought about facing her. But it had to be done. He'd turned his life upside down to do what was right, and he continued to have faith that it would not be in vain.

Faith. Two weeks ago I didn't know the meaning of the word. Now I'm living by its precepts. Weird.

That evening he unpacked his suitcases and put them in the closet. A moving company was bringing his things from L.A. sometime next week. The one thing he'd brought with him other than personal items was a small silver frame he'd finally found. He took it downstairs and placed it on the mantle in the living room. Then he stepped back and admired the photograph. Once again he marveled at the love he could see in his mother's eyes and the pure adulation that shone in his own. Tears welled in his eyes for just a moment, but he wasn't sure what to do about the nostalgia, so he distracted himself by wandering through the house. He absently tried to find something to do, hating how empty the house felt—when he heard the garage open. He was in the basement and quickly went to the stairs. As he reached the top, he heard the door that led from the garage to the kitchen open. He strode briskly toward the door that separated the kitchen from the dining room, thinking with a smile that Emma had come home. He was less than a foot from the door when it swung open, slamming into the side of his head. He heard a woman scream as he fell back and crashed into the wall. The room spun as he slid slowly to the ground with his face in his hands. For several seconds, he was disoriented, and when he could finally focus his eyes and see clearly, he looked up to see Janet standing in the doorway, her hands cupped over her mouth in shock. Slowly she dropped her hands.

"I am so sorry," she said. Then she looked toward the kitchen. "I'll get some ice."

She disappeared for a moment, and Andrew heard sounds from the kitchen as he gingerly touched the growing contusion on his left temple. She returned a few minutes later and handed him a baggie filled with ice and wrapped in a dish towel. "What are you doing here?" she asked a few moments later.

"Me?" Andrew asked with surprise. "It's my house. What are you doing here? And where's Emma? Is she with you?"

Janet's face darkened, and she looked away, as if suddenly annoyed with the whole situation. "Hardly," she said with a snort. She then left the room, leaving Andrew to wonder what he'd said to upset her. She returned a minute later with a stack of mail in her hand—the same mail he recalled seeing scattered across the living room floor where it had fallen through the mail slot. "We've been coming for the mail once a week for months," Janet explained. "Emma can't read the mail, much less come and get it herself."

"What do you mean she can't read the mail?" Andrew asked in confusion, ignoring the throbbing in his head.

"She's been very sick. She can't read, watch TV, or stand half the time. She's been living with Tally and me."

Andrew looked at the ground, filled with guilt.

"Now she's in the hospital," Janet said.

Andrew looked up quickly. *The hospital!*

Janet continued. "The day you showed up she went into preterm labor. They stopped it, but she'll stay in the hospital until the baby's born."

Andrew was dumbfounded. "How long will that be?"

Janet shrugged. "It could be tomorrow, but hopefully she'll make it another month—then the baby will have a better chance." She was silent for a few seconds. "Please do us all a favor, Andrew," she finally said. "Leave her alone. She married you—you'll get your money soon—but please just stay away. This is hard enough as it is. She doesn't need you to make it harder."

"Make it harder?" he said in shock. "It's my baby, she's my wife, and you want me to leave her alone?" He was so confused. Weren't Mormons all about family? Wasn't that part of why he was interested in the Church? Janet was going against everything he thought he understood.

"Don't start wearing the father crown when it works for you, Andrew," Janet countered. "Fatherhood is an all or nothing responsibility. She's accepted your rejection and will take care of it herself. Just don't—"

"Rejection?" Andrew said, finally getting to his feet. Janet was a tall woman, but he was still able to look down at her. "How can I reject what I don't know exists? Maybe she's had six months to figure out what she wants to do, but I've had two weeks. Don't think for a moment I'm going to let you or anyone else tell me how I'm supposed to handle this situation." He was fuming. Janet stood there looking at him, a mixture of anger and confusion on her face.

"Two weeks?" she asked.

"Yes, two weeks," Andrew repeated. "That day at your house."

"But . . . she said you didn't want it."

"What?" Andrew said slowly and with forced calmness.

"She said that you didn't want any part of the situation, and that's why you stayed away so long."

Andrew just blinked until finally closing his eyes and letting out a painful sigh. He considered telling Janet the whole truth, wondering just how much she knew. But almost as quickly, he decided against it. Anger filled his chest, and he wanted to drive to the hospital and let Emma have it for misleading everyone. But he also knew that she was the one who'd shouldered everything for so long, and he *had* said many times that he had no desire for a family. Could he blame her for taking him so literally?

When he looked up, he saw that Janet was watching him. "I didn't know," he said. "But I'm here now, and I want to do the right thing."

Janet nodded, her attitude still distrustful. "I'm on my way home. Can I call you after I've talked to my husband?"

Andrew nodded. He didn't care who she talked to, but he needed some time to think this through. She smiled slightly and then hurried back through the garage door. He imagined the hatred her family likely felt for him and shook his head. *What now?* He wondered what Emma really thought of him. Was there any hope he could redeem himself? Or had too much happened too late for him to even have a chance?

"Are you happy, Mom?" he muttered as he got ready for bed. He could have sworn someone said *yes*.

CHAPTER 46

$\mathcal{A}$ ndrew watched Emma's chest rise and fall as she slept. She looked so small, like a child, and he wondered how much weight she had lost. It had been almost ten minutes since he had slipped into the room, and he was grateful that he'd had the time to get used to her appearance. It was hard to believe this was the same vibrant, energetic woman he'd taken skiing all those months ago. She looked so much like his mother had during her final months, and the thought made his stomach tighten. He had to keep reminding himself that *she* wasn't going to die—but he wasn't sure he believed it.

A few hours after Janet had left last night, Chris and Tally had shown up on his doorstep. During the forty minutes or so that they talked in the living room, their attitudes didn't soften much. They didn't try to be friendly. All they wanted were answers. He breezed over the details of the night at the ski resort and wondered how long it would take to be put out of his misery if they decided to kill him. Their expressions had remained frozen while he explained what had happened, as if their having believed something different for so long made it impossible for them to believe anything else.

Now he was here, wondering what to say when she woke up and wondering how she would react to his sudden appearance. It was a few more minutes before she shifted in her sleep and turned to face him for the first time. In contrast to the childlike appearance of her body, her face looked old in the dim light of the room. His eyes drifted to her rounded belly, and he swallowed. Tally had told him the baby was a boy. A son. But it was still hard to believe. Looking back at her face, he questioned how the baby could be healthy when she looked so ill. Her eyes fluttered open briefly, and his heart rate accelerated. A few moments later, her eyes opened all the way, and she squinted at him. She wasn't wearing her glasses, and he wondered if she recognized him.

"It's me," he said softly, although it sounded very loud in the small room.

She closed her eyes, and he watched her expression fall as if she'd been dreading this for a long time. It did nothing to ease his worries. She said nothing, forcing him to continue. "We need to talk about things," he began. "I'm not sure—"

"Just go away, Andrew," she said in a small voice.

"I'm not going away," he countered, his heart sinking in his chest. "I want to be here, be a part of this."

"Part of what?" she said angrily, although her voice was still quiet. "Your part is done."

Andrew leaned forward, a knot forming in his throat. "Emma, I am so sorry about that night. I—"

"Please go away," she said, her voice now pleading. "Go back to California. I'm not going to come after you for anything. You don't need to be noble. Forget you ever knew me. Just move on."

"I don't want to forget," Andrew said in desperation. "I want to be here, for you, for him—for me."

Emma watched him for a few moments. Then she snorted as if just figuring something out. "You'll still get your money," she said coldly. "I'm not going to file for divorce or anything, not until the trust is paid. I need that money more than ever."

For the first time since his mother died, Andrew felt tears in his eyes. She was shutting him out, unwilling to give him a chance. A deep regret filled his chest as he considered for the first time what he would do if she was really unwilling to let him back into her life. "Don't do this, Emma," he whispered. "Please give me a chance to make it up to you."

Emma lifted her hands to her face. Miscellaneous tubes were stuck in her arms, and he was reminded that she was fighting for not only her life, but the life of their child. He reached out and touched her arm. She pulled away. Finally she removed her hands, and tears streamed down her face. "You can make it up to me by leaving, right now, and not coming back," she said evenly. "Nothing you do now can make up for what happened then. You're wasting your time." As the last word was spoken, she lurched forward slightly, and then almost immediately she did it again. She clamped one hand over her mouth as she began feeling around the covers with her other hand. Andrew pulled back in confusion until she extracted a small kidney-shaped tub from under her blanket. Andrew swallowed and looked away as she threw up. When he turned back, she was leaning forward, breathing deeply. "Get out of here," she said in a scratchy voice. Andrew hesitated until she looked up at him, her cheeks flushed and her eyes angry. "Leave," she nearly screamed. She started throwing up again, and he felt he had no choice but to go, at least for now.

After leaving her room, Andrew sat in the parking lot for a long time, trying to decide what to do next. His mind was blank. When she said she didn't want to see him, she'd meant it. The lump in his throat got bigger, and he rested his head on the steering wheel. "What else can I do?" he asked no one in particular. How could he make things right? It was several minutes before he started the car and drove toward his new office—without any answers.

Andrew spent the rest of the day and evening familiarizing himself with the new office. Jeff flew in around noon, and they traveled to the different project sites. That night they hosted a dinner for all the Salt Lake employees. When the evening ended, Andrew felt encouraged and ready to dive into this undertaking.

If only he was as sure about Emma. Each time he thought of her, his stomach sank further.

CHAPTER 47

The next morning Andrew went back to the hospital on his way to the office. He hadn't received any divine inspiration; he hadn't even dreamed of his mother last night. He just felt sure that if he could prove to Emma how dedicated he was, she would soften toward him. The elevator doors opened, and he made his way down the hall. Breakfast smells still lingered, and he made a mental note to grab something to eat on his way to work. When he reached her room, he saw a sign on the door. "Restricted Visitation. Please check in at the nurse's station."

"There's a note on my wife's door about restricted visitation," he said to the plump nurse at the nurses' station a few moments later.

"Mrs. Davidson?" the nurse asked with an uncomfortable nod as she looked toward Emma's door. "The doctor gave the orders last night." The nurse shifted in her seat. "She had a really bad day yesterday."

"What happened?" Andrew asked anxiously.

The nurse seemed to hesitate. "She had a severe bout of vomiting and has a small esophageal tear. She's been put on a feeding tube again, and her meds were increased."

"Can I see her?" Andrew asked as he felt the color drain from his face. "I'm her husband."

"I know," she said. "I worked yesterday. I'm the one that had to call the doctor just after you left."

Andrew froze at the not-so-subtle implication. The nurse continued. "Your wife is in a very fragile state, Mr. Davidson, and she can't handle much stress right now. The doctor has asked that no one be allowed to visit her without one of the nursing staff present."

"Can you come with me then?" Andrew asked anxiously. He felt sick to his stomach and wanted to assure himself that she was okay, as well as get another opportunity to explain himself.

"And you're not allowed at all."

Andrew's jaw tightened. "She's my wife," he said quietly, sadly.

"I'm sorry, Mr. Davidson," she said with sympathy. "But the health of your baby is our top concern right now. If you'd like to talk to the doctor, he'll be in around six o'clock tonight to check on her. I'm sure he'd be happy to speak to you about it."

Andrew was waiting for the doctor by a quarter to six. The stone in his stomach had accompanied him all day, and he'd cut short a project management meeting in order to ensure he wouldn't miss his opportunity to speak with Emma's physician. The doctor was kind but frank as he explained the orders he'd given. "I'm the father," Andrew reminded him. "How can she refuse to let me participate?"

"When the baby is born, you can participate, Mr. Davidson. But your visits are not good for your wife right now, and this is not the time to solve whatever marital problems you're having. If anything changes, I'll let you know. Until then, Mrs. Davidson has agreed that the nurses can keep you informed of her condition whenever you like. But until the baby is born, you need to keep your distance."

The stone was now a lead weight in his stomach. He lay in his bed that night and stared at the ceiling, trying to make sense of how his life had been turned so completely upside down. He'd avoided marriage and family all his life. When his mother died, he'd determined never to suffer that way again. He was an investor, and if he'd learned anything over the years, it was not to invest more than he was willing to lose. And yet here he was, so heavily invested that he wasn't sure how to continue if Emma wrote him off for good.

CHAPTER 48

November

"Maternity," the nurse said into the phone. "This is Carrie. Can I help you?"

"Hi, Carrie. It's Andrew Davidson. How's Emma?" Carrie smiled sadly to herself. "Same as yesterday," she informed him. "But she's officially thirty-two weeks today."

"Oh, that's great," Andrew said with a brief laugh. "We've been waiting for this."

"They did an ultrasound yesterday afternoon, and he's not quite three pounds yet. But everything else is perfect. Since Emma's now finished all the Betamethazone shots, we can expect that even if he's born tomorrow, he'll be able to breathe on his own."

"Wow," Andrew said, smiling to himself. "That's wonderful." He was silent for a few moments. "Did you guys get the flowers I sent yesterday?"

"Yes," Carrie said, looking at the large bouquet of yellow roses sitting on the counter. "We put Emma's in her room. The daisies are always her favorite. And you know what?" she said, leaning forward as if to keep eavesdroppers from listening in, "I think she knows they're from you."

"Really?"

"Well, she's never asked who sends them, not once in almost a month. It's as if she knows but doesn't want it said out loud. And she never asks us to take them away. Hopefully that's a good sign."

"I think it is," Andrew said. "And how are your wedding plans coming along?"

Carrie brightened. "Perfectly. Three weeks and counting."

"Where are you getting married?"

"The St. George temple," she said. "Bart's from southern Utah."

"I haven't seen that temple," Andrew said, "but I'm sure it's beautiful."

"It is," Carrie agreed.

"Well, I better get back to work. Call me if anything changes, will you?"

"Of course," she said, smiling. "Have a nice day." She hung up the phone and shook her head. She would never understand some people. She looked toward Emma's door and wondered how such a nice woman could treat her husband so horribly.

"Andrew Davidson?" the other nurse at the station asked with an arched eyebrow.

"Of course," Carrie said with a nod. "Nine o'clock every morning. I just can't understand why she won't see him. It seems so unfair."

The other nurse nodded. "When you have your first fight, you'll understand a little better. The fact is you just never know what happens in other people's relationships." She paused for just a moment. "Come to think of it, you don't always know what happens in your own relationships." She shrugged. "Hopefully when the baby's born, they'll be able to work it out."

CHAPTER 49

*A*ndrew got home around eight o'clock—earlier than usual. He pulled a TV dinner from the freezer and put it in the microwave. In the four weeks he'd been in Salt Lake, he'd taken every opportunity to repair or establish what relationships he could. Besides sending flowers to the hospital every week and calling every day, he'd convinced Janet to let him take Catherine one evening a week. They went to McDonald's every time, since he had quickly realized that taking a two-year-old anywhere else was just asking for trouble. Janet had invited him over for Sunday dinner his second week in town, and that was followed by Jazz games with Tally and Chris. They had stopped regarding him as a demon and had come to accept him almost as a brother-in-law. If Emma would just give in and let him be the husband he wanted so desperately to be, things would be perfect. But she still refused to see him and sent messages with her family that he should go back to L.A. Her dismissal was painful, but he refused to give up hope. Or maybe it was faith. The missionaries called it both.

A knock at the door came at precisely the same moment

the microwave announced his delectable dinner of beef stroganoff and julienne beans was ready. He left the dinner and went to the door. The missionaries weren't coming until tomorrow. He didn't know who else it could be.

The young man on the doorstep looked vaguely familiar, but Andrew couldn't guess who he was. "May I help you?"

The younger man shifted his weight nervously. "Uh, you probably don't remember me, Mr. Davidson. My name is Eric Peterson. I met you and your wife last January when Brother Epperson and I came to your home."

Ah, yes. The home teachers. Andrew tried not to let his feelings show; he hadn't forgotten that night. "I remember you," he said easily. Because of that experience, Andrew had requested that no ward missionaries be involved in his continued investigation of the Church. He liked talking to the full-time missionaries but was anxious about members of the ward and didn't want them involved—at least not yet.

"I've seen your lights on the last few weeks, and then I saw you pull in tonight." He paused, looking nervous and uneasy. He looked at his shoes as he continued. "I feel really bad about that night we came over. I just didn't know what to do when he started going off on you."

"Don't worry about it," Andrew said with a forgiving smile. "It wasn't your fault."

"He shouldn't have said those things, not like that. I could have stopped him. I'm sorry I didn't."

Andrew opened the door a little wider. "Would you like to come in?" he asked. "I'm about to sit down to dinner."

"Oh, uh sure." He came in, and Andrew offered him a TV dinner. Eric shrugged, and so Andrew popped another one into the microwave. Over dinner Andrew learned that Eric had just received his mission call to Hartford Connecticut, Spanish speaking. Andrew eventually told him that he was taking the discussions, and Eric raised his eyebrows. "You are?"

"The missionaries are coming over tomorrow to teach the fifth discussion."

"Wow," Eric said in awe. "Are you going to get baptized?"

"I'm not sure yet," he admitted. "Right now I'm trying to learn everything I can about it. But I'm not ready to commit to baptism yet."

"Why not?" he asked in youthful innocence.

Andrew was silent. "I just want to make sure I'm doing it for the right reasons."

Eric was chewing a mouthful of pepper steak. He swallowed a few moments later. "Are there wrong reasons to be baptized?"

The subject turned to other things shortly thereafter, but Eric's question echoed in Andrew's brain all night. He decided that there were definitely wrong reasons to be baptized. For instance it would be wrong if he joined in hopes of impressing Emma or her family. But he hadn't told any of them he was investigating, so it wasn't even an issue yet.

Eric had asked if he could attend the fifth discussion with Andrew "to see how the missionaries taught it." Andrew agreed, and so the missionaries taught them both the following night. Andrew liked Eric, liked the energetic youthfulness in his face, and determined he would make a very good missionary. The discussion was about living a Christlike life, and Andrew listened intently. Living a selfless life, paying tithing and fast offerings made sense. Being obedient and following God's commandments were both relatively easy to accept as well, especially when he looked at having a strong family as the trade off. But at the end of the discussion, the missionaries asked the fateful question. They'd asked the same question after the previous two discussions. This time, however, they phrased it a little differently.

"Why do you think Christ was baptized?"

Andrew had no answer. Surely Christ didn't need to be baptized—he had no sins to wash away. "I'm not sure," he finally admitted. "Unless it was to show everyone else how to do it."

"Kind of," one of the missionaries said. "It was, in part, to set an example, but along with that it was to obey the commandment. God commanded that all His children should be baptized, including His only begotten Son." He paused for a few seconds. "Andrew, we'd like to invite you to be baptized too. To take upon yourself the name of Christ and be numbered as one of His followers. Are you prepared to take that step?"

Time seemed suspended as Andrew reviewed all he'd learned. Until that first meeting with the missionaries in L.A., he'd never spent much time thinking about God or heaven. And yet, as he was taught the gospel he had gone from feeling it was unbelievable to wondering if he'd known it all before. The more he learned, the more connected to all of it he felt. The more connected he felt, the more he longed for the fullness of the gospel in his life. He knew from what they'd taught him that when he was baptized he'd have the gift of the Holy Ghost, like a full-time life consultant. He yearned for that. Yet he was still hesitant. If he was simply remembering what he'd known and somehow forgotten, how could he have lived thirty years without it?

He looked up to find all three of them still staring at him. "Yes," he heard himself say. The room was silent, and then they all smiled, shook hands, and slapped him on the back. They made an appointment for the sixth discussion and set a time for Andrew to have an interview with their zone leader. After they left, he changed into his swimsuit and headed downstairs for the pool. He climbed the steps to the diving board and walked to the edge. Below him the water reflected the light in swirling ribbons that moved along the pool's surface. The water created a lens, and from his position he could see each individual tile that made up the bottom of the pool.

Right now, at this moment, everything seemed that clear. The gospel offered him everything he never knew he wanted. He thought of the ability to walk away from his mistakes and start again, start fresh. Emma came to mind, accompanied by the familiar ache that always attached itself to thoughts of her. But he had made peace with that too. He'd created this situation, and although he couldn't make her love him, she couldn't keep him from their son. He took a deep breath, lifted his arms over his head, and dove into the still water. The pool swallowed him up, and he propelled himself toward the other side. When he broke the surface, he gulped for air and rolled onto his back, smiling at the ceiling. He was going to have a son! And his son would be raised with all the things he had missed. What a blessing—what a gift!

He did laps for nearly an hour, relishing the burning in his muscles as he pushed himself to the limit of his endurance. When he finished, he pulled himself onto the edge of the pool and toweled off. He padded up the stairs to his room and turned on the shower, allowing it to heat up while he brushed his teeth. He wondered if he'd dream about his mom again; she seemed to always come after he met with the missionaries. He wondered what she thought of his baptism—and then he paused. He was acting as if she were alive. The strangest feeling came over him, and he finally admitted that she was. He laughed out loud at the thought and wondered if it was really her appearing to him at night, and not just his own dreams. It seemed highly plausible, given the peculiar ideas and beliefs he'd come to embrace. If he tried hard enough, could he ask her questions? Hmm.

The phone rang, and he hurried to rinse out his mouth before moving quickly to the phone on the bedside table.

"Hello?" he said, looking at the clock. It was almost midnight.

"Mr. Davidson?"

"This is he."

"This is Amy from labor and delivery. The nurses from the maternity wing said I was to call you." His hand gripped the telephone tighter. "Your wife was just admitted to our floor. She apparently had another vomiting attack that started labor. We've given her medication to try and stop the labor, but it isn't working as well as we'd like. You should probably come down."

"I'll be there in ten minutes." He hung up the phone, turned off the shower, and ran to the closet for his clothes. From the hallway closet by the front door, he retrieved a small suitcase that held all the newly purchased items Lacey had told him to take to the hospital when the moment arrived. He threw it onto the passenger seat as he slid behind the wheel of his car and pulled out of the driveway. His heart was pounding and his head was tingling. *This is it!*

CHAPTER 50

$\mathcal{L}$acey was already there when Andrew arrived. There was no stopping the labor, she explained just before she entered the delivery room. She told him to wait in the hall, and he regrettably agreed. He wanted to be there, but then again maybe he didn't. He didn't know anything about childbirth, and he wasn't sure he wanted to experience it firsthand. A nurse brought him a chair, and he waited, paced, and fidgeted for almost two and a half hours. Every time someone came out of the room, he asked how she was, if he could do anything for her, and if the baby was all right. Each time they assured him everything was going just fine. He wished someone was here to wait with him, to reassure him that this was normal. He'd never felt so alone, and yet he felt comfort too, and deep down he believed that things were going to be okay.

In answer to his prayers, Tally and Janet arrived around 2 A.M., after getting a neighbor to come over and stay with their kids. While they waited, Tally explained what it was like when his daughter had been born. Andrew sucked up the information like a sponge and ached to be in the room with Emma.

Finally, after what seemed like an eternity, three nurses

and the attending pediatrician wheeled a small incubator from the delivery room. Andrew sat frozen until one of the nurses told him to follow them. It was several minutes before he was given an unobstructed view of his son, and when he did, tears came to his eyes, and his heart felt as if it had stopped beating all together. He didn't even look like a baby. His head looked huge compared to his thin body. His face was swollen, and his whole body was covered in fine hair. He had an IV in his head, in his arm, and another in his foot, as well as monitor wires taped to various places on his tiny chest. A miniature blood pressure cuff, the size of Andrew's thumb, was around one ankle, while a plastic apparatus that was hooked to a ventilator was taped around his mouth. "Is he . . . okay?" Andrew whispered as he sat heavily on a chair and stared through the Plexiglas.

"He's fine, Mr. Davidson," the doctor said. "He weighed in at three pounds and three ounces." The doctor continued telling Andrew things he didn't really understand about gestation and medications. What he did understand was that a lot of people were going to give their best to make sure his son got all the help he needed. *This is my son!* It was amazing, and despite the conditions, Andrew had no doubt that this was the purpose for which his life was meant.

Janet joined him a few minutes later.

"How's Emma?" he asked, still staring at this little alien person that was a part of him.

"Good," Janet said, staring fearfully at the incubator as she spoke. "She's in the recovery room."

"What's his name?" the nurse interrupted. She held a marker in one hand and a name card in the other. All the spaces were filled in except the name. He looked at Janet.

"Why don't you go ask her?"

"Me?" Andrew said in surprise. "Does she want to see me?"

"Probably not," Janet conceded. "But the two of you have a son now, and he needs a name."

A few minutes later, he took a breath and parted a curtain. Tally and Lacey were with Emma but excused themselves. Emma didn't seem to understand why they were leaving until Tally moved out of the way, revealing Andrew's presence. Tally patted Andrew on the shoulder as he passed. "Congratulations," he said before he disappeared behind the curtain.

Emma looked away as Andrew approached the bed. "How are you feeling?"

"You shouldn't be here," she said evenly.

"Thank you, Emma," he said softly as the emotions finally surfaced. She turned to face him. He wiped at his eyes. When he spoke, it was in a shaky whisper, and he had to pause and gather his thoughts. There was so much he wanted to say. "I just want you to know how sorry I am that it started the way it did, that you had to suffer so much to get him here." Emma's own eyes filled with tears. "Thank you," he said again.

She didn't say anything and looked away. An awkward silence hung in the air until Andrew spoke again. "What's his name?" he asked. "They need it for his crib . . . thing."

"Why can't you just go away and leave me alone?" she finally asked, fidgeting with the blanket, her moment of emotion past.

"Because we have a son," Andrew said as evenly as he could. They both knew she couldn't shut him out anymore—at least not completely. But he had hoped she would be more accepting of his involvement. "I'm not leaving," he continued. "I joined with a Salt Lake company and sold my apartment in L.A. I'm staying here, Emma, and one of these days you're going to have to accept that I will be a part of his life, and somehow you'll have to find a way to make peace with what happened, to forgive me, and to move on. For all of us." He paused for a breath before continuing. "What's his name?"

"Michael," she whispered, still not looking at him. "Michael . . . Andrew Davidson."

A lump formed in Andrew's throat, and all he could do was nod. Had she always planned it that way, or had she decided to include his name just now? He carefully placed his hand over hers and gave it a slight squeeze. Then he slipped away.

CHAPTER 51

The next two days found Andrew either at Michael's incubator or in the parking lot talking on his cell phone in an attempt to keep the office rolling along. He'd only tried to visit Emma once, but she'd immediately asked him to leave, and he hadn't gotten over the rejection enough to try again. On the third day, he was on his way back to the Newborn Intensive Care Unit—NICU, or Nick-U as the staff and parents came to refer to it. He was walking past a nurse pushing a wheelchair when he happened to glance down.

"Emma," he said in surprise. They stared at each other for a few moments. He looked at the nurse. "May I?" he asked. "I'm her husband." The nurse looked at Emma. She nodded, although reluctantly, as if she knew she couldn't say no. Andrew thanked the nurse and began pushing Emma's wheelchair down the hall. "You must be feeling better," Andrew said, ignoring the tension between them.

"Finally," she said. "It takes awhile for my body to get back to normal."

"Have you seen him yet?"

Emma nodded. "But I haven't spent much time with him,

and they wouldn't let me touch him." The timid excitement in her voice made him smile. When they arrived at the NICU, they went through the laborious hand-washing procedure, and he helped her put a hospital gown over the gown she already wore. Then he pushed her toward the first incubator on the right side of the room. When he slowed the wheelchair to a stop, he pulled up a chair next to her.

"He can hold your finger," Andrew said as he unfastened the circular door on the side of the incubator and swung it open. He slipped his hand inside and pressed his finger against a tiny palm. Michael curled his little hand around Andrew's finger, not even close to gripping it entirely. Andrew looked at Emma and smiled. "He's got a good grip," he said, "for a three-day-old, premature baby."

Emma smiled as Andrew extracted his hand. She followed his example and took a quick breath as Michael grabbed her finger. She stared at her son for several seconds, a look of amazement on her face. A few minutes later, a nurse asked if she wanted to hold him.

"I can hold him with all those wires and tubes?" she asked. The nurse assured her that she could, although it took a few minutes to get Michael ready for the "outing." Emma closed her eyes briefly as the baby was laid in her arms. Then she opened her eyes and seemed to take in every detail. "He's so small," she whispered to no one in particular. "I can hardly feel him."

Andrew smiled and watched her closely. With Michael's arrival, it seemed so possible that they could work things out, and yet if he thought about it long enough, it still seemed so far away. "Are you my little man?" Emma cooed, gingerly touching his fuzzy little head. "Are you going to grow big and strong?"

A lump formed in Andrew's throat as he watched them. A few minutes passed before the nurse said she had to put him back. He could only be outside the heated incubator for a few minutes at a time before his temperature began to drop. Andrew wheeled Emma back to her room.

"Can we talk for a few minutes?" Andrew asked.

Emma sighed. "I guess I can't avoid it forever."

Andrew took that as a yes.

A nurse helped Emma into bed, took her vital signs, and gave her a pain pill. Once she was settled and the nurse had left, Andrew sat in the chair beside her bed.

"I want to start by telling you how—"

"I don't want to talk about that night," Emma interrupted.

Andrew hesitated. He wanted to explain himself. "I think you'll feel a lot better if we do."

Emma shook her head. "No," she said strongly. "I've accepted that you're here, that you want to be a part of Michael's life, so let's just deal with what's ahead, not what's in the past."

"Michael's not the only reason I'm here."

"I know that," she said with a nod. "I was trying to figure it out, and then I remembered the clause in the trust about living together, and that must have been the deciding vote." She spoke so casually, as if there was no question that his actions were driven by greed. "I don't blame you. I don't want to chance it either. So you're here, and you've decided you're willing to give fatherhood a shot. Fine. I'll go back to the house, we'll finish this, get the money, and go our separate ways."

"I don't want to finish this," Andrew said after a moment of silence, leaning forward. "I don't want to go our separate ways, ever. I want to . . . to try to be a family, all of us."

Emma shook her head. "No, you don't," she said with irritation. "You're feeling heroic, Andrew, but don't lose sight of reality just because circumstances changed. I'm glad you want to be in his life, but you never wanted me, Andrew. I know that, and I'm not going to punish you for it anymore. I'll be discharged tomorrow, and I'll go to the house."

Andrew was staring at the floor, wishing he could somehow make her understand that he *did* want her, that it wasn't only honor that had brought him here. "Please, Emma," he whispered. "Please let me try this again, the right way. Let me prove to you how I feel about you. Let me try to—"

"Do you love me, Andrew?" she interrupted. He looked at her and saw the hardness in her eyes. "Can you look me in the eye and tell me that you love me?"

He said nothing and had to look away. "I want to—"

"To what? Love me?" she interrupted. "What you want, Andrew, is to make everything all better. Don't fool yourself into thinking it's more than that. We have a son, and he needs as much of both of us as we can give him. But we are very different. Too different. I don't want you to have to try and love me, Andrew, and I'm not going to play games anymore. I'm going to see this trust thing through, and then we're done—for good."

His frustration had grown with every word. She was right about a lot of things. They were different, and he didn't know if he could love her the way a husband should love his wife—he wasn't even sure what that kind of love is. But he did feel a great love and respect for her, and he believed that they had a chemistry with potential to turn into something great—if she would give it a chance.

But he couldn't do it by himself. He looked into her face again. She had closed her eyes, and her face reflected her exhaustion. This wasn't the time, he decided. At least she'd agreed to come back to the house, and that would give them some time together. He lifted his head. "Okay," he finally said as he stood. "I've got to get to work this afternoon, but I'll be back tonight. I'll take you home tomorrow."

Emma nodded, seemingly unaware of his irritation. "Janet said she'll keep Cate until Monday. By then I'll be up and around much better."

Andrew left the room, taking with him all the things he'd wanted to say. *She* didn't want to solve the problems between them. *She'd* lied to her family about his intentions, but *he* was still the bad guy, unable to redeem himself. Maybe it wasn't all going to work out. Maybe there really wasn't any hope. *But there's still Michael*, he reminded himself. *If nothing else, there's Michael.*

CHAPTER 52

*N*ow, the breast pump has been checked out, so you can take it with you, but be sure to pump every two hours to keep your milk. Put the milk in the sterilized bottles and bring them to the hospital so the NICU can give it to your baby." Emma nodded as the nurse continued with instructions. Andrew sat in a chair in the corner. He'd been there for twenty minutes, and she had yet to make eye contact with him. *Why can't he just go away?* she wondered for the zillionth time. How was she supposed to ignore her feelings for him if he was always around? On top of the tension of just having him here, he'd been sitting there for all the breast-feeding info as well as some hygiene instructions that embarrassed her horribly. She hadn't looked at him, so she didn't know if he felt the same way. When the nurse finished, she smiled. "Do you have any other questions?"

She had so many questions. Mostly questions like how could they send her away from her baby? How would Michael know who she was if she could only see him twice a day? A lump started to form in her throat. "No," she said quietly, knowing the nurse couldn't give her any peace.

The nurse nodded and headed for the door. "You're welcome to stay in the NICU as long as you like, but you need your rest, Mrs. Davidson. Don't forget to take care of yourself." She looked pointedly at Andrew, and he nodded, as if assuring her that he'd take care of Emma himself. Emma looked away. Having Andrew around was salt in an open wound.

She walked to the NICU herself, washed her hands, and took a deep breath as she pushed the button to open the door. Andrew was still washing his hands when she entered without him. She walked to Michael's incubator and stared at his little body. A nurse approached her from behind and asked if she'd like to hold him.

Emma nodded. "My nurse was telling me about skin to skin," she said almost shyly. "Can I do that?"

"Sure," the nurse said eagerly. "It's so good for the baby to feel your heartbeat, and it keeps him warmer so he can stay out longer."

The nurse pulled a curtain around the incubator to ensure privacy before instructing Emma to unbutton her shirt. Then she placed the tiny body against Emma's chest. Michael opened his eyes slightly, and Emma focused on the feel of her son's downy skin against her own. He wasn't able to attempt breast-feeding yet—he was too small and very weak. But in a few days, they would try to bottle feed him. Later she could try to nurse, although with the battle her body had been fighting, there was no guarantee she'd have the resources available to produce enough milk. They estimated he'd be in the NICU for at least a month, possibly as long as six weeks. He was on a feeding schedule of every three hours: two o'clock, five o'clock, eight o'clock, and eleven o'clock—A.M. and P.M. She was welcome to come for any of the feedings, but they preferred that she choose specific times so the nurses would know she was coming. It seemed unnatural to set appointments to see her own baby, and she hated the thought of being separated from him.

She looked up when the curtain parted and pulled at the

edges of the blanket to ensure she was covered. Andrew hesitated. "Can I come in?" he asked.

She almost said yes, but after taking a few seconds to consider it, she shook her head. "I'd like to be alone." She saw the hurt in his eyes, but he nodded his understanding and let the curtain close. She heard his footsteps as he walked away and berated herself for her pettiness. Then she remembered Mark's startled face when he'd opened the door to Andrew's room that morning. She wasn't being petty. She was protecting herself, and no one could blame her for that.

Ten minutes later, the nurse said it was time to put Michael back. Emma reluctantly gave him to the nurse. He'd never cried. They said he would when he got bigger. She longed to hear him cry. The curtain was pulled back, and she saw Andrew, sitting off to the side looking uncomfortable. He stood and walked around to the other side of the incubator without meeting Emma's eyes. She watched him open the side door and put his hand inside.

They'd been told that because of underdeveloped nerves in the skin, preemie babies don't like to be stroked. Instead they prefer a warm hand on their head or leg. She watched Andrew take Michael's tiny foot in his large hand and gently close his fist. He bent down and said something to his son that she couldn't hear, and her heart ached just a little. Andrew loved Michael. Perhaps his reasons for coming here were purely financial, but he had fallen in love with his baby. She finally looked away as visions of divorce court, custody battles, and child support overwhelmed her. It was the inevitable ending. She tried not to think about it.

Andrew was at her side a few minutes later. They both stood there, staring at the tubes and wires. Finally Andrew cleared his throat. "Are you ready?"

Emma nodded, the lump in her throat growing by the second. She turned away and started out the door. Andrew followed. She made it to the car before the tears came.

"Are you okay?" Andrew asked a few moments later when

the tears had turned to sobs.

"Of course I'm not okay," she returned with more anger than was necessary. But it came easier to her than any other emotion. "I just left my baby with strangers." She turned and looked out the window, feeling as if her heart were being ripped from her chest. Andrew said nothing while she kept crying.

When they pulled up to the house, Andrew came around and opened her door. She walked heavily up the sidewalk, exhaustion descending with every step. Andrew grabbed her bag from the back seat and hurried to the front door in time to open it for her. When she stepped across the threshold, she took a deep breath, inhaling the spirit of this house. She'd missed it. She'd missed the peace of it, the independence she'd felt here. If only her arms weren't empty, everything would be perfect. *Almost perfect*, she corrected as Andrew came up behind her. She could smell his cologne and took another deep breath.

"I fixed up the master bedroom for you," he said as she moved aside to let him pass.

"I'm fine in my own room."

Andrew was shaking his head long before she finished speaking. "You deserve to have a bigger room and your own bathroom. I already traded our stuff around and got your things from Tally and Janet. I took a guest room downstairs so that you'll have your privacy."

"It's your house, Andrew. You don't need to take the guest room."

"It's *our* house," he replied. "And it's best this way. I'm fine with it."

Emma let out a breath while admitting to herself that she didn't have the energy to argue with him. Andrew was watching her and seemed to read her mind. "I'll put your bags in your room." He went upstairs, and she watched him go, wishing she could find even a shred of hope within herself that maybe—just maybe—there was a chance for them. But she'd searched and searched a million times, and the answer was always the same. She and Andrew were just too different.

A few minutes later, she sat gingerly on the bed—Andrew's bed—and lay down. Her body was worn out, exhausted by seven months of illness, depression, and medications to fight both. Now, she'd reached the goal that had kept her going this whole time, only to come home alone. She curled up on her side and hugged a pillow to her face as she started to cry again.

She wanted Michael.

CHAPTER 53

When she woke up, the digital clock said it was almost four o'clock in the afternoon. She hurried to get out of bed, even though she had plenty of time to get ready before the five o'clock visit. Her muscles ached, and the bed called to her, but she wasn't going to sleep any longer. In the kitchen, she found a note from Andrew saying he'd gone into the office for a few hours but would be back to get her at four thirty. Next to the note was her prescription that he'd gotten filled for her. She let out a breath. Getting through the next five months of their marriage was going to be the ultimate test for her. *It would be extremely helpful if Andrew would stop being so nice.*

She swallowed a pain pill just as the doorbell rang. *Who would come without calling first?* It took her longer than usual to get to the door. She was still moving slowly. The woman on the doorstep was Gloria, her former Cub Scout partner and the visiting teacher she'd worked so hard to ignore. Gloria was a little shorter than Emma, with long blond hair pulled up in a ponytail. She wore a little makeup, jeans, and a form-fitting T-shirt. In her arms, she held a cookie sheet filled with a variety of casserole dishes. Emma remembered the meals she'd received when Catherine was born, and for some reason wished she hadn't answered the door. She hadn't made her peace with the Mormons yet.

"Hi, Emma," she said when Emma opened the door.

"Hi," Emma answered slowly, still guarded. She didn't want to be rude, but she didn't want to give any false impression that she was a soul in need of saving. Gloria continued without giving her the chance to respond. "I made Lacey promise me she would call when you needed a meal, so here I am."

"You didn't have to."

"It was no problem," she said quickly. "I just made double what we were having. Can I put it in the kitchen?"

"Um, sure." Emma stepped aside and let her enter.

Gloria immediately began looking around the foyer and into the living room. "What a beautiful place," she said in awe. Emma thanked her and led the way to the kitchen. Gloria continued to praise as they went. She placed the cookie sheet on the counter and turned to Emma again. "Most of it isn't cooked, in case you're going to the hospital before dinner time, but I wrote the instructions right here." She pulled out a small index card and continued to point out what each pan held. Chicken cordon bleu, mixed veggies, twice-baked potatoes, rolls, and peach cobbler. Emma's mouth began to water, which surprised her since it had been months since she'd felt hungry.

"You really didn't need to go all out."

"Well, I didn't. I bought the chicken frozen, and the rest isn't too complex. I'm glad to do what I can." She smiled sweetly before continuing. "How are you feeling? You look good."

Emma doubted that she looked good. She weighed a hundred pounds, her eyes were sunken, and her face was pale— but she appreciated Gloria's attempts. "Skipping the last two months of pregnancy and only gaining three pounds has its up side. I'm still really tired though."

Gloria nodded her understanding. "And the baby—how's he doing?"

"Pretty good," Emma said, sadness creeping into her voice.

"They say everything's going just the way it should."

"Except that he's there and you're here," Gloria added. "I had to leave my little boy too."

"You did?" Emma asked, suddenly more interested in the conversation.

"He was four weeks early, and he weighed five and a half pounds, so he looked like a giant compared to all those little babies. I'd been in a car accident that started labor, and then he got an infection during delivery."

"How horrible," Emma commiserated.

"It was horrible," Gloria agreed, looking away as if remembering just how horrible it had been. She looked back at Emma and forced a smile. "He came home after about two weeks and hasn't had any problems since. But going home without him was the hardest thing I ever did—well, up to that point in my life anyway."

Tears started to prick at Emma's eyes, and she looked away. An uncomfortable silence hung in the air between them. It had been a long time since she'd really felt connected to anyone and not been treated like a baby. But those thoughts also reminded her of what a jerk she'd been in her experiences with Gloria. Finally she regained her composure and looked up. "Thanks for dinner," she said with sincerity. "That will be a big help."

"I put my number and address on the index card, so you can call me if you need anything else. I'll try to stop by in a few days and pick up the pans." Gloria started toward the door and Emma followed, noticing how Gloria continued to take in the details. When she noticed Emma watching her, she smiled shyly. "We bought a fixer-upper a few streets down from here. It still needs a lot of work, so I love looking at other houses and getting ideas."

Emma thanked her again just as she heard the kitchen door open. Andrew was home. She immediately stood straighter and felt her easy manner fade away.

"I'm a few minutes late," he said. Seeing Gloria for the first time, he smiled. "Hi, I'm Andrew Davidson." He strode over and shook her hand.

"Gloria Drewry," she said. "I live a few streets over."

"Oh, nice to meet you." He looked at Emma as if expecting her to say something, but she avoided his eyes and smiled at Gloria instead.

"We're going to the hospital," Emma said.

"Of course." Gloria said. At the door, she turned toward Emma. "Call me if you need anything."

"I will," Emma assured her. When she shut the door, she turned around and headed for the kitchen. "Should we go?" she said as she passed Andrew.

"Um, yeah," he said, a trace of confusion in his voice. In the car, he spoke again. "She seems nice," he said.

"She is nice. She brought us dinner."

"Oh, wow," he said with surprise.

"It's a Mormon thing," she explained, realizing she was talking too much. When Andrew asked more questions, she just gave yes and no answers until he quit trying. They stayed at the hospital for almost an hour, but Emma held Michael against her chest again and wouldn't let Andrew in, so it was awkward.

"I think we should go to the hospital at alternating times as soon as I can drive myself, which will only be a few more days," Emma suggested as they pulled out of the parking lot. "That way Michael will have more visits with us."

"It's kind of nice to go together though," Andrew offered.

She shrugged. "I'll be attempting to breast-feed soon, and it doesn't make sense for you to just sit outside the curtain all the time."

"I don't mind so much," he said. She knew he was lying. He hated waiting outside the curtain.

"I think it's better if we don't go together," she said. The not-for-negotiation tone in her voice seemed to get through to him.

"If that's what you want," he said in surrender.

She nodded, staring out the window in order to avoid looking at him. "It's what I want," she said. They didn't speak about it anymore, and she knew that she'd made the point that they were parents, not partners.

CHAPTER 54

$\mathcal{A}$ ndrew finished his morning laps and took a shower. He could hear the TV as he approached the kitchen door. He swung it open and headed for the fridge. "Good morning," he said.

"Good morning," Emma returned evenly. It had been almost two weeks since she'd come home from the hospital. Michael now weighed four pounds two ounces and was growing every day. His little body was better proportioned, and the IVs and ventilator had been removed. He still had the feeding tube, monitors, and oxygen through his nose, but he was getting stronger and doing well. At home they'd fallen into an arrangement that, although not quite comfortable, was livable.

Andrew went to the eight o'clock feeding every morning and then went to work. Emma took Catherine to day care for four hours each day—long enough to visit Michael at eleven o'clock and get a few hours of rest in the afternoon. Andrew would then take a late lunch and see Michael for the two o'clock visit. The two of them hadn't gone together since Emma had regained her ability to drive.

After the first week, Andrew had offered to watch Catherine while Emma went to the evening eight o'clock visit, and she'd surprised him by allowing it. It was one of the few things she allowed him to help her with, and he enjoyed the time with Catherine. He even put her to bed most nights.

He'd tried to reestablish the friendly relationship they'd once enjoyed, but Emma was a pro at keeping him at arm's length. When they did get an opportunity to talk, Emma acted disinterested, and he finally took the hint and kept his distance.

Today, however, he hoped that she would let down the walls for a little while. He fixed himself a cup of Postum—a caffeine-free breakfast drink that was supposed to taste like coffee. It didn't taste a thing like coffee, but it was better than herbal teas, and he just couldn't seem to get going without something hot to sip in the mornings. Cate wandered into the kitchen and handed him a stuffed animal. He crouched down to her level and praised the toy. Her face lit up, and she ran back to the TV room to get another treasure. He took a breath and walked around the counter separating him from the sitting room. It was like crossing the demilitarized zone and entering enemy territory.

"What are your plans tomorrow?" he asked casually, hoping the excitement in his voice wasn't obvious. If she sensed it, he knew she'd shut off. It was just the way she worked lately.

"Same old, same old," she said. "I'll go to the hospital at eleven, come home and wait until I go again at eight." She looked up at him suspiciously. "Are you still able to watch Cate for me?"

He usually watched her during the Saturday visits, but Cate wasn't the problem. "Would it work for you to go at two, instead of eleven?"

She turned on the couch and looked at him warily. "You go at two."

He took a breath, hoping to calm his nervousness as he ran his finger along the rim of his mug.

"I . . . I'm getting baptized."

Emma lowered her chin and opened her eyes wide. "Baptized?"

Andrew nodded and smiled nervously. "I finished the discussions last week and passed all my interviews." He couldn't help smiling wider as he spoke.

"You're getting baptized?" Emma repeated dryly, her eyes narrowed. "Why?"

Andrew met her eyes and realized from the look on her face that she thought he was doing it because of her, or for her. He hurried to explain. "These missionaries ended up at my apartment in L.A. a couple of months ago and . . . well, they gave me a Book of Mormon. I . . . I read it and I've been praying. Life looks different to me now, and I want to give Michael the best of everything. The gospel is near the top of that list." He stopped speaking, and she just continued to stare at him. "I'd like you to come to my baptism tomorrow at eleven thirty."

Emma looked past his shoulder, and the silence seemed to stretch for a very long time. "I have to go to the hospital," she said, turning back to face the TV.

Andrew stared at the back of her head as anger began to rise in his chest. He strode around to the front of the couch to face her. "This is a very important day for me, Emma," he said with forced calmness. "I would really appreciate it if you and Cate would come."

She let out a breath and looked up at him. "They will be expecting me at the hospital."

"So tell them you'll be there at two instead of eleven."

She folded her arms. "No."

"No?" he repeated, no longer hiding his irritation. "I would think that you of all people would want to support me in this."

The "Emma fire" he remembered from days gone by burned in her eyes, and he wondered why she was suddenly *this* angry.

"So you're getting baptized to impress me?" she asked.

Andrew took a deep breath and spoke slowly. "I am the father of your son, and I'm taking a major step in my life that will affect his future a great deal. I would think you'd be happy for me."

Emma stood up and looked at him strongly, her eyes full of anger. "You want me to be happy for you?" she said sarcastically. "Fine, I'm happy for you, but I won't miss the opportunity to see my son."

"Fine," he whispered as he went back into the kitchen, not wanting her to see how deeply she had hurt him. He went downstairs and fell on his knees next to the bed. Emma was the only person he wanted there, and she didn't care that he'd changed his whole life, his whole belief system. He started to pray for the ability to get past her rejection and remember that, with or without her, this would still be one of the biggest moments in his life.

Emma tried to watch TV, but she couldn't concentrate. She didn't know what to think of Andrew's baptism. If he was doing it to impress her, why hadn't he said anything about taking the discussions? She shook her head. She didn't want to think about it. Why should she care anyway? She hadn't been to church for months and was beginning to think she wasn't cut out to be a Mormon at all. It seemed like the Church didn't work for her. *If Andrew thinks he has what it takes, fine.*

She started cleaning the kitchen, uncomfortable and anxious as she kept reviewing the situation. Finally she picked up the phone and dialed Lacey's number. She hadn't been in touch with the family much lately. Her mom had called several times, upset that she couldn't come and support her daughter, but it couldn't be helped. The *Church* came first. But Emma didn't mind so much. She enjoyed being independent again. But now, once again, she was having to ask for help—oh, how she hated it. Lacey picked up on the second ring.

"Hi, Lacey, it's me," she said, cradling the phone against her shoulder. "Is there any way you could watch Cate while I go to the hospital tomorrow morning?"

"Um, sure," she said with hesitation. "But I thought Andrew watched her for you."

"Well, not this time," she said briskly. "He's getting *baptized*. Can you believe that?"

Lacey was silent for several seconds. "Andrew's getting baptized?"

"Yeah, go figure."

"Aren't you going?"

"I have a four-pound baby who needs me, and I'm not going to skip seeing him just to indulge some whim of spiritual fancy."

Lacey was silent again. "I can't believe he's getting baptized. He's never said anything about it."

Emma didn't like the support for Andrew she was sensing over the phone. "Anyway, he's going to be a little busy. Are you sure you can watch her?"

"Oh, sure," Lacey said. "Bring her over."

Andrew's prayer was interrupted by the ringing of his cell phone. He lifted his head, pulled the phone from his pocket, and put it to his ear before realizing he hadn't closed his prayer. "Just a minute," he said quickly before putting the phone on the bed and finishing his prayer. He hoped it still counted. He picked up the phone, realizing he didn't recognize the number. "This is Andrew," he said, walking toward the closet to retrieve the suit he would wear to work today.

"Andrew, it's Chris."

"Oh, hi, Chris," he said. "How are you?"

"I'm fine," he said. "Lacey was just talking to Emma, and she said you're getting baptized tomorrow. Is that true?"

"Yeah," Andrew said hesitantly. "I am."

"You've been taking the discussions?"

"Yeah."

"Why didn't you tell us?" Chris asked.

"I didn't want to do this for anyone but myself," Andrew answered truthfully. "And judging from Emma's reaction, that was probably a really good decision."

Chris was silent for a few moments. "I can't speak for Emma, but we would like to support you in this. Can we come?"

"Emma probably won't like it if you do," he said. However, until Emma's rejection, he hadn't realized how badly he wanted someone there.

"It isn't Emma's decision," Chris replied. "It's ours, and we'd like to be a part of this."

Andrew gave him the time and address of the stake center before hanging up and proceeding to get ready. His heart was lighter, his head was clearer, and the excitement Emma had temporarily extinguished was returning. He was getting baptized tomorrow. He was joining the kingdom of God. He still wasn't certain he knew what all that meant, but he knew it was the right thing to do—Emma or no Emma.

Andrew left for work quietly, not bothering to say good bye, and Emma pretended she didn't care. An hour or so later, Emma loaded up Cate and took her to day care. After dropping her off, she got back into the car and saw the tray of clean dishes on the seat. Gloria had told her to call when she needed the pans picked up, but Emma had put them in her car a few days before, planning to drop them off. Maybe she'd do it today after she went to the hospital.

She held Michael for nearly forty minutes, loving every minute of it. He wouldn't attempt to nurse, but he took a bottle for a couple of minutes before falling asleep against her. These moments were the best of her day. She even dreamed about them at night. Everything else melted away when this little boy was in her arms. It never seemed long enough.

On the way home, she decided to drop off the pans at Gloria's. She found the address and headed for the door. It was a nice home, but she could see a few projects in progress that testified that it was still in need of work. She rang the doorbell and smiled when Gloria opened the door. Gloria was holding the phone to her ear and put up one finger indicating that she would be just a minute. She ushered Emma inside. Emma shifted her weight uncomfortably as she waited for Gloria to finish. She was considering just putting the pans in the kitchen when Gloria said good-bye and hung up the phone.

"I'm sorry," she said. "It was my mom."

"Ah," Emma said with understanding.

Gloria smiled and looked at the pans Emma had put on the coffee table. "I am so sorry. I kept meaning to stop by and get those. How's everything going?"

"Good," Emma said. "Michael's almost four and a half pounds and took a bottle for a couple minutes this morning."

"That's great. Any idea how long until he comes home?"

"Three weeks at least," Emma said evenly.

"That's not very long," Gloria encouraged.

"Not long at all," Emma agreed as she looked around the room. She could feel Gloria watching her and wondered why she didn't leave now.

"Is everything okay?"

"It's fine," Emma said. Her tone was unconvincing even to herself.

There was silence for a few minutes. "How's Andrew? Did he go with you today?"

"No," Emma said, looking at the floor. For some reason, she felt pressed to explain further. "We're having some problems."

Gloria nodded as if she'd already guessed that. "I'm sorry."

Emma shrugged. "It's never been good, so it's not like I've got anything to mourn."

"There's always something to mourn when relationships struggle." There was a pause before she spoke again. "We saw him at church last week, but I didn't get a chance to say hello."

Emma resisted rolling her eyes. Andrew and the Church were sore subjects, and she could feel the bitterness rise at the reminder. "Yeah, he's in a church phase right now."

"Is he a member then?"

"Funny you should ask," Emma said as she shook her head. "He's getting baptized tomorrow."

Gloria's eyes went wide. "You're kidding!"

"But he just told me about it today. Shows how close we are."

Gloria stood up. "That's wonderful!" she said with excitement.

"Is it?" Emma asked boldly, wondering why she was being so open. She figured she just had to let it out somewhere. "I don't think he has a clue what he's getting into."

"Do any of us? Baptism is a hard concept to grasp, but the mere fact that he's taking such a big step is remarkable."

Emma turned toward the door, weary of the conversation. Trying to get anyone who was already active in the Church to understand where she was coming from seemed futile. "Well, it's his decision."

"Maybe it will help things between the two of you."

"No," Emma said strongly, stopping at the door. "It's way past that now."

"Oh," Gloria responded. "That's too bad."

Emma just shrugged. "Thanks again for the dinner. It was great."

Gloria smiled. "No problem. Let me know if I can do anything else for you."

Emma drove home and thought about Andrew's baptism again. Part of her wanted to go, but she couldn't fathom why.

She felt as if she'd succeeded in talking herself out of her feelings for Andrew. There were plenty of reasons to write him off, and even though they argued and fought most of the time, she still looked forward to seeing him. He still permeated her dreams at night, and the longing she felt for him hadn't gone away. It made her so angry! She couldn't continue her life the way she wanted to if she was still hung up on him. Because of all that, she knew she wouldn't go tomorrow. Supporting him went against everything she was trying to do.

CHAPTER 55

The next morning Andrew sat in the front row of chairs facing the baptismal font. One of the elders was giving a talk on the Holy Ghost while the other one was sitting beside Andrew, dressed in white just like he was. He had butterflies in his stomach and kept tapping his feet without realizing it. Before he knew it, he was descending the steps of the font. The water was barely past his waist. The elder baptizing him placed his hands just as they'd practiced. Janet, Tally, Lacey, and Chris were all watching him, while their children and Catherine crowded around the edge of the font. He took a deep breath as the elder began the ordinance. His heart was beating so fast he could hardly hear the words being said. The elder finished, helped him plug his nose, and lowered him into the water. When he came up, he wanted to laugh out loud. He'd done it! He looked around at the faces of those who had come to support him and swallowed his disappointment that Emma wasn't there. He would not let her ruin this day.

After the baptism, he took everyone to lunch. No one talked about Emma's absence, and for that he was grateful. He didn't want to discuss it. But he was thrilled to have

Catherine there. She kept feeding him her French fries, and he kept eating them far past the point of wanting them.

He didn't feel that different from his prebaptism days, but he knew there were changes—important ones—and nothing could bring him down from the cloud he was on. After going to the two o'clock feeding and holding his son for almost an hour, he was told to put him back. With great reluctance, he lifted the side of the incubator and carefully placed Michael inside. It took a minute to fix his position and straighten out the wires, but Michael slept right through it. Andrew pictured blessing him in church the way he'd seen another baby blessed a couple of weeks ago and felt a lump in his throat. There was still so much to learn. But he felt so good that it didn't matter too much. Lacey took Cate home, not wanting to advertise that she'd gone against Emma's wishes, and Andrew went shopping for nursery room furniture and baby clothes. He wondered why he'd always believed having children somehow decreased a man's masculinity. He'd never felt better about being a man. It was almost eight o'clock when he got home. Emma was waiting for him. She didn't say anything as she left for the hospital. Andrew went to find Catherine. He could hear the TV in the kitchen sitting room, and sure enough Catherine was in front of it. That was just about the only thing Emma did with her daughter these days. They immediately started playing, chasing one another up and down the stairs.

Jake called a few minutes later, wondering why he hadn't heard from Emma or Catherine in a few weeks. Andrew had never spoken to Jake but decided that now was as good a time as ever. He filled Jake in on everything that had happened and Jake expressed his concern. Catherine garbled at her dad for awhile, and then Andrew ended the call. He couldn't help but wonder if his relationship with his own son would end up that way—phone calls every few weeks and occasional visits when Emma felt like it. The idea burned, so he pushed it away. He didn't need to dwell on that yet. He still had hopes that things would end up differently.

After putting Catherine to bed a short time later, Andrew laid a card on the dining room table. He'd purchased it earlier that day and hoped Emma would find it. Then he went downstairs to work out before he went to bed.

It was almost nine thirty when Emma got home. The house was quiet, although she could see that lights were on in the basement. She hoped Andrew wouldn't hear her and come up, as he sometimes did. But then again she felt pretty confident that he was so mad and hurt that he didn't want to see her either. She looked in the fridge for something to eat, but since she hadn't been cooking there wasn't much in there, and what was in there didn't look appealing. On her way toward her room, she saw the card. For a few seconds, she stared at it. Then she picked it up and undid the seal. There were daisies on the front. She opened it slowly. There was no printed message, just a handwritten note.

> *I missed you today, but I think I understand. Thanks for all you do.*
>
> *Love, Andrew*

"Love, Andrew," she whispered to herself. *That's what started this whole situation in the first place.* She left the card on the table and went to bed, alone and lonely through no one's fault but her own.

CHAPTER 56

*T*he next day was Sunday, and even if Emma had wanted to go to church, she wouldn't have gone with Andrew— so skipping it was easy. Chris and Lacey didn't go to church until one o'clock, and they had offered to watch Catherine while Emma went to the hospital, since Andrew would be at church. She hated driving all the way to Bountiful and back, but she couldn't take Catherine to the hospital, and she didn't know anyone else. So Bountiful it was. Andrew came home about two, just as she was putting Catherine down for a nap. When she came back downstairs, he was waiting in the living room, his scriptures open in his lap. She resisted rolling her eyes at what looked to her to be a showy display of his righteousness.

"Hey," he said in an animated voice.

"Hi," she said evenly, not stopping. He quickly stood and followed her. She cringed inside and wished he'd leave her alone. Being nasty and rude was the only defense she had, and yet she felt horrible for acting that way. If he'd just leave her alone, they would both be so much better off.

"I wanted to ask you about something," he asked with excitement in his voice.

She didn't say anything but continued into the kitchen and started putting dishes in the dishwasher. He wasn't deterred and leaned against the counter. "I'd like to have a dinner party next week some time, and I wanted to know what you thought of the idea."

"I think it's lousy," she said without looking up. He was silent for a moment as if he couldn't believe she'd reacted that way. *Did he honestly think I was going to say anything different?*

"Why?"

"Because we happen to have a very sick baby in the hospital. I don't know about you, but I don't feel like having a party while he lays in a big plastic box all by himself."

"That's just it," Andrew continued. "Once he comes home, we'll need to keep him inside and away from people for several months. We won't have the chance to do much socializing. So I thought we could do something this week, have Chris and Tally and some people in the ward over, so we can get a chance to meet them."

"Maybe I don't want to meet people in the ward. I'm only going to be here a few more months anyway."

Andrew was silent again. "Emma," he finally said. She continued with the dishes. "Look at me."

She turned slowly and looked at him, even though she didn't want to. He took a few steps forward but stopped when her expression hardened.

"I thought you might like something to keep you busy. I thought maybe it would help. I don't know what else to do, Emma. I really want things to be better between us. But I'm running out of ideas."

"You want things to be better?" she repeated with sarcasm as the anger began to roll within her. It was time to let him know exactly where she stood; in fact she probably should have done it weeks ago. "Nothing will make things okay between us. So stop already. Live your life however you want to—start dating if you want. I don't care anymore. But leave me out of it."

"This is silly," Andrew said. "All I want is for us to make peace somehow. I'm surprised you don't want the same thing. I mean, is your life so great that you're not willing to even try to make it better? I—"

"My life sucks," Emma interrupted loudly. A heavy silence hung in the air for a few moments. Andrew recoiled at the anger in her voice. "My life is miserable, thanks to you. You want peace? The only peace I will ever have is when I am no longer your wife, when I can walk out of this house a free woman. Don't give me your petty offerings, Andrew, and don't waste your time trying to make things better. It isn't going to happen." She threw the sponge in the sink and stormed out of the room. She was halfway up the stairs before he caught up to her. He grabbed her arm, stopping her progress and spinning her to face him.

"Your life sucks?" he repeated angrily. "You have two great kids, you don't have to work, you live in a beautiful house, have all your expenses paid—and your life sucks? You're not a prisoner here, Emma, and if you're miserable, then that's your fault. I think we have a chance to be something more than we are, but if we can't have a decent conversation, I don't know how much longer we can live in the same house."

"Four months," she hissed back at him. "That's how much longer we can live in the same house. I'm sorry you've wasted so much time hoping for the impossible, because we will never be more than what we are."

"Do you really believe that?" he asked strongly. "There was a time when we obviously cared for each other very much. Have things changed so much?"

"You took advantage of me. That changed things." As soon as she said it, she clamped her mouth shut and wished she'd have thought before she'd spoken. She knew right where this was headed.

"*I* took advantage of *you?*" he asked, raising his eyebrows. "Are you sure about that?" Her eyes narrowed, and he let go of her arm. She hurried up the rest of the stairs, her face red with embarrassment. But she couldn't face that possibility. Andrew was the bad guy here! It was his fault—not hers.

"Only one of us knew what we were doing that night, remember?" he called after her. Tears started falling down her cheeks as she entered her room. With a powerful kick, she slammed the door shut. Then she covered her face and cried into her hands.

Andrew shook his head as he sat heavily on the stairs and raised his hands to his face.

Why had he done that? He'd been baptized only twenty-four hours ago, and already he'd insulted his wife. Maybe the dinner had been a dumb idea, but he was just trying to help, trying to find some normalcy again. Sudden emotion caught him off guard, and before he knew it he was sobbing. Why was this happening to him? He'd hoped for so much, worked so hard to do the right thing, and it had all fallen apart. Despite all the changes he'd made, Emma hated him, and there didn't seem to be anything he could do about it. If there was only some way he could make it better. At this point he'd do anything. Her hurt and anger was ripping him apart.

That night his mother came into his dreams again, and she wasn't happy. She scolded him like he was a four-year-old, and he took it like a man. "Andrew, what did I tell you when you caught all those ants and kept them in a jar?"

"That I should let them go," he answered.

"I said that if the ants came back, you could keep them, but if they didn't, they never belonged to you in the first place."

"None of them came back, Mom."

"That's because they weren't yours."

He'd woken up then and punched the pillow in frustration. He hated these bits and pieces. Why couldn't she just say what she meant? But the meaning wasn't lost on him. He turned his face to the pillow and cried again.

CHAPTER 57

*T*uesday morning, Emma stood at the counter, leaning on her elbows as she thumbed through a magazine. She and Catherine would leave for day care as soon as *Barney* was over. She was getting tired of the trek to day care, the hospital, home, and day care again. And yet she was increasingly anxious about the day that Michael would be ready to come home. Emma glanced at the clock. She heard the door from the garage open and felt herself tense as Andrew entered the kitchen. He'd left for work hours ago. What was he doing back? She flipped another page, irritatingly aware of his every movement as he made himself some toast. They had succeeded in completely ignoring each other since their fight on Sunday. She hoped it would stay that way. She couldn't handle much of anything right now—especially not him. She heard the toast pop and his knife slide across the rough surface as he spread the butter. He turned toward the door leading to the dinning room and then paused. *Here we go*, Emma said to herself. *Why can't he just ignore me like I ignore him?*

"Emma, could I talk to you in the dinning room, please?"

She was tempted to say, *no, I'm busy.* Instead she said,

"Sure." Whatever it was he wanted to discuss, she might as well get it over with. Following him into the dining room, she pulled out the chair opposite of the one he chose and sat down, carefully avoiding his eyes as she waited for him to start.

"I've been thinking about what you said to me the other day," he began. "I've thought about it a lot, and I came up with a solution."

"There is no solution, Andrew. We've already determined that."

"That's not quite true," Andrew replied as he pushed a piece of paper toward her. She looked at him briefly as she turned the paper around and started reading. A few seconds later she looked up.

"Is this some kind of joke?" she asked with irritation.

Andrew shook his head. "Keep reading."

She continued reading for a few more moments. Then she looked up again. "You want a divorce?"

"No, *you* want a divorce, but I'm willing to give it to you."

"Now?"

"Now."

Emma pushed away from the table and stood up. "Oh, please," she said dramatically. "Do you really expect me to believe you're going to turn your back on two and a half million dollars?"

"Yeah, I do."

"You think I'll be so impressed with your *noble* offering that I'll give in and make everything all better." She laughed dryly and pushed the paper back toward him. "I'm not some game for you to play anymore, Andrew." She turned toward the kitchen.

Andrew slammed his fist on the table, causing the flower arrangement in the center to teeter. Emma spun toward him and then pulled back at the anger in his face.

"You do *not* know me, Emma," he said angrily. "You have never tried to know who I am or how I feel about anything. I never *played* you, and I never meant to hurt you, even though

I know I did. What I'm trying to do now is the right thing. And yet, over and over again, you throw it back in my face." He paused long enough to take a breath. "I'm not being noble, Emma. I just can't stand this anymore, and I'll do anything to stop the misery for both of us." He pointed to the paper. "This is a letter of intent I'm ready to send to the trust attorneys, informing them that we've begun divorce proceedings and that I'm unable to meet the requirements of the trust."

"Like I said before," Emma countered, "I don't buy it. You're trying to pull something."

Andrew clenched his jaw. "You know what your problem is, Emma?" he began, speaking slowly as if calculating every word. "You blame everyone but yourself for your unhappiness. Jake didn't love you enough, your family doesn't understand you, I've ruined your life, and I fear one day Cate and Michael will just be holding you back—when all this time it's been you. You make yourself hard to love, Emma, and then you blame everyone else for it. I don't need the money, and at this point I'd pay twice that amount for some peace in my life."

"What a lovely explanation," Emma spat, not admitting to the sting of his words. "But I need my portion more than ever, so—"

"I'm still going to pay you the money," he interrupted. "I bought this house with my mother's life insurance. I'm going to sell it and split the profits with you. I'm also prepared to pay your monthly expenses, if you'll agree to stay home with the kids and not work. In exchange, I want joint custody and an agreement that we will do all we can to be friends. We should give Michael that much at least."

Emma was stunned and had run out of words. Was he serious? They stood there looking at each other for nearly a minute.

"What do I have to do?" she finally asked, looking back at the paper. She wasn't convinced of his sincerity and refused to give an inch.

"Sign this," he said, pushing the paper toward her again.

"Then call a lawyer and file the papers."

"Why don't you file the papers?"

"Because I'm not the one who wants the divorce."

"It's your idea."

Andrew took a deep breath as he placed both hands on the table, his elbows locked. "Emma," he said in almost a whisper, looking at the top of the table. "My idea was to be a family—at least try it out. But you've made it abundantly clear that you have no intention of letting it work. You told me you wanted out of this marriage more than anything in the world, and I believe you. So let's get on with it. I'll get an apartment until the house sells. You can stay here."

"In four months, you turn thirty," she reminded him.

"In four months, I'll be out of my mind," he returned. "I can't stand it. I'm not willing to live this way anymore. It isn't good for any of us, and I won't have Michael come home to so much tension."

Emma looked at him closely. "You *are* serious," she said with just a touch of awe.

"Yes," he said with a sigh.

She folded her arms across her chest, stalling while she tried to figure out what to do. "What if I don't want a divorce either?"

"Then you're going to have to change your attitude," he said, looking up at her again, just a glint of hope in his eyes. "Whether you believe it or not, you're a special person to me, and I simply can't look at you and see such bitterness anymore. I've made mistakes. Plenty of them. But I can't take this any longer. Maybe if we part ways now, we can find a way to be civil to one another in the future. However, if we can make peace somehow, I would love to discuss that option."

She didn't know what to say, but she couldn't dismiss the possibility that he was only making this grand overture in order to soften her toward him. She couldn't soften. If she gave in even a little, she'd crumble. She knew she would. The only way to stand being around him was to hate him. "Do you have a pen?" she asked casually.

The disappointment in his eyes was intense, but she didn't falter. He handed her a pen and watched as she signed and dated the paper. Then she stood and stalked back into the kitchen. She stopped in the middle of the floor, once the door had closed behind her, and raised both hands to her face. *What is wrong with me?*

She thought of what he had said on Sunday about her blaming everyone except herself, and she shook her head. That wasn't true. She blamed herself for everything. Anger and distance were the only ways she knew to protect herself from further pain and disappointment. If she didn't care so much, she couldn't hurt so much. And she was willing to cost him over two million dollars to make that point. It made no sense, and yet it made perfect sense at the same time. Her shoulders began to shake as she wondered if she would ever understand how things got this ugly.

CHAPTER 58

$\mathcal{S}$he didn't see Andrew for two days. She heard him come and go and yelled to him when she was leaving for the evening hospital visit, but he just answered back without making an appearance. Catherine was always asleep by the time she got home, and Andrew was in the basement. She felt increasingly bad for signing the letter of intent to divorce but continued to tell herself that it was for the best. She was pulled so tight, she feared that one wrong move would cause her to implode. And Andrew was one of the biggest stress factors—at least that's what she told herself.

Instead of getting her strength back, as she'd expected would happen once Michael was born, she felt increasingly tired. Every day it was harder to get out of bed than it had been the day before, and although Catherine kept her going it was increasingly difficult for Emma to care for her. Thursday morning she dropped Catherine off at day care and went to the hospital as usual. Michael had been moved from the critical care area just two days before, and it was predicted that he'd be moved to the "home bound" area in about two more weeks. When she got to the NICU, she went about the routine of changing his tiny diaper, switching the pulse ox monitor to his other ankle, and carefully taking him out of the incubator. He was sound asleep, so she wrapped him in blankets and rocked him while she waited for the nurse to bring a bottle. She'd been pumping breast milk at home and had brought the bottles in an insulated container.

When the nurse arrived, she didn't have a bottle; instead she had the breast milk in a syringe, the way it was prepared when he was being fed through the feeding tube still threaded through his nose. "No bottle?" Emma asked as the nurse hooked up the syringe.

"The doctor gave orders last night to discontinue the bottle feedings."

"Why?" Emma asked, somewhat alarmed.

"Something to do with his heart rate. She'll be talking to you about it today." The nurse left quickly, moving on to the next baby. Emma looked at the heart monitor above Michael's crib. It seemed normal to her.

"Mrs. Davidson." Emma glanced up and watched as Michael's doctor sat down across from her. "I wanted to fill you in on something we're paying special attention to." She flipped open Michael's chart and turned it so Emma could see inside. There were two strips of paper with long triangular lines, and she recognized them as heart patterns similar to those continually displayed on the monitor. "This is a pattern taken just a few days ago," the doctor explained, pointing to the top sheet. She then pointed to the lower sheet. "This is a strip we ran last night."

Emma compared the two papers, noting that the bottom one had a varying pattern. "What does it mean?" she asked, still staring at the different strips.

"Michael is experiencing an irregularity in his heartbeat. Last night we discontinued bottle feedings, thinking perhaps that was causing the problem. But as of this morning, it seems to be worsening." She flipped the paper and there was another strip. This time Emma could see a stark difference between it and the first strip taken a few days ago. "We're watching him closely and hope to see it repair itself. Sometimes pree-mies have a hard time with the electrical impulses that con-trol heartbeat. It's probably nothing, but we wanted you to be aware of it."

"But it isn't serious?"

"No, it's fine. Just irregular. We're watching him closely, and we'll keep you updated."

"Thanks," Emma said, looking back at Michael's tiny face. The doctor moved on to her next patient. Emma looked back at the monitor and watched the lines jump up and down. *They said it wasn't serious,* she told herself, trying to dismiss the unease she felt. She looked back at the tube that took her breast milk to her baby's stomach and the other tube that brought oxygen to his lungs and took a deep breath. *I have enough to worry about without overreacting about this.*

Still the unease stayed with her. It was just one more thing to sap her energy, and she wondered if she would ever fully recover. When she pulled up to the house, a U-haul was parked in the driveway. Andrew came out the front door a few moments later. He was carrying a box labeled "Study." They stopped in front of one another on the sidewalk. "I found an apartment," he said. She nodded, wondering if she should tell him about Michael or not.

"Some guys from work offered to help me move out," he continued as he stepped around her. "I'm not too far away, and I'd like to keep watching Cate in the evenings, if it's okay with you."

"That would be a big help," she said softly, not moving. His feet continued behind her, and she wondered why she was feeling so lonely all of a sudden. She was still standing there when he came back. He didn't stop but just walked around her again and ran lightly up the steps before disappearing in the front door. He didn't seem angry anymore. In fact he seemed relieved to be moving out. She started walking again. Who could blame him?

CHAPTER 59

*O*ver the next two days Michael's condition didn't improve, and Monday morning Emma arrived to find his spot in the NICU empty. She turned around frantically, looking for the closest nurse.

"Michael Davidson," she said quickly as soon as she had someone's attention. "Where is he?"

"Over here," the nurse said as she placed a calming hand on Emma's arm. Emma followed her to the right side of the large room—the critical care area reserved for the very new and very sick babies. Her heart sank when she stopped in front of his incubator. "I'll get his doctor," the nurse said.

Emma just stared. There was an IV in his head again, the tape crisscrossing his tiny skull, and another in his leg. Her whole body went numb as she tried to make sense of the change in his appearance between now and last night when she'd been here. The doctor soon approached and explained that they had determined the cause of Michael's irregular heartbeat. Michael had contracted an infection, and they were attempting to treat it with antibiotics and anti-inflammatory medication.

"What kind of infection?" Emma asked tonelessly, still staring at all the tubes and wires.

"It happens sometimes," the doctor replied somewhat evasively. "It's called staphylococcus. We call it staph. When it gets into the bloodstream, it can be dangerous."

"How dangerous?"

"It can cause infections within the body and sometimes causes heart damage."

Emma looked up. "Heart damage?" She looked back at Michael.

"As you know, we've been waiting for the problem to correct itself, but it's gotten steadily worse. This morning we did a series of tests and finally determined the cause. We're hopeful the antibiotics will do the trick, but we've scheduled more tests this afternoon to see if any of his heart valves have been damaged. If so, we'll have to replace the damaged valves."

Replace a heart valve on a five-pound baby? The blood seemed to drain from her whole body. She couldn't absorb this. "Can I hold him?" she asked, her voice breaking.

"I'm sorry," the doctor said. "He's quarantined."

Emma didn't know how she got home or how long it took. She drove around for what seemed like hours, until finally picking up Catherine and heading home. She fixed cereal for Catherine's dinner and tried to take a nap, but she couldn't sleep. She kept picturing doctors with scalpels surrounding Michael. She'd seen Andrew only briefly over the weekend when he came to the house to watch Catherine. They didn't speak to each other except for the bland obligatory courtesies they exchanged. Ironically, she missed him now that she didn't have to try and avoid him. She'd never felt so lonely in all her life. Around five o'clock, she heard the garage door open.

Andrew let himself in and found Emma sitting on the couch with her legs curled underneath her, watching *Finding*

Nemo with Cate. She didn't acknowledge his presence but didn't object to it either. He came and sat next to her but remained silent for a few moments.

When he went to see Michael for his usual two o'clock visit, he'd been told what he later learned Emma already knew. He'd gone back to the office but found it difficult to concentrate. The arguments and the impending divorce seemed very small and insignificant all of a sudden. The fact was that Emma was the one person who knew exactly how he was feeling. "Are you okay?" he finally asked.

She stared ahead for a moment and then shook her head as her chin began to tremble. After a few seconds, she raised her hands to her face and began to cry. A lump formed in his own throat, and it surprised him that when he reached toward her, she turned to him. He scooted closer, and soon she was crying into his shoulder. He rubbed her back and closed his eyes. He wanted to bask in this closeness—something he'd longed for—but his own fear and worry made it difficult to feel the victory. However, he was deeply grateful that she would turn to him for comfort, and that in the process he could find comfort himself. She cried for a very long time, eventually laying her head in his lap. He stroked her hair and said nothing. There was nothing to say. The movie ended, which caused Catherine to pay attention to them for the first time. She leaned over to look into her mother's face, concern written all over her little features. "Mommy sad?" she asked. Emma reached out a hand and caressed her daughter's face.

"Yes, Mommy's sad," she whispered. Andrew had to choke back a sob of his own. Catherine looked up at him, as if unsure how to handle this information. He reached out a hand and helped her climb up next to him on the couch. They sat that way for a few minutes. Andrew had one hand around Cate's shoulder while the other rested on Emma's back. They all seemed absorbed in their own thoughts until the phone rang. At first he considered just ignoring it, but after the second ring he eased out of the comfort zone. When he hung up, he turned to see Emma watching him fearfully—she'd heard his end of the conversation.

"The hospital wants to meet with us tomorrow afternoon at four."

Emma's eyes went wide for a moment before she closed them and made a little gasping noise in her throat. Andrew hurried back to her and wrapped her in his arms, but she didn't cry anymore. She just lay against his shoulder, staring at nothing. After several minutes, he pulled back to look at her. She wouldn't meet his eyes. "Why don't you go lie down," he said. "I'll get Cate to bed."

Once Catherine was taken care of, he went to Emma's room and tapped on the door. She didn't say anything, and he decided that was an invitation. She was under the covers but fully clothed, turned away from him. He didn't want to say the wrong thing and set her off, and yet his heart was so full and his fear was so real he didn't know if he had the ability to pick and choose which words to use.

Finally he settled for sharing his own feelings, rather than trying to explain hers, and sat on the edge of the bed. "I can't believe this happened," he whispered, as if talking to himself. He spread his hands out over his lap, pinky fingers touching, and just stared at them. His hands held this way were almost the exact length of his son. *How could they possibly do such an intricate procedure on a tiny baby?*

When Emma spoke, he turned his head toward her. "God hates me," she said.

"No, He doesn't," Andrew countered. "He doesn't hate you."

He watched the back of her head as she nodded. "I was taught all my life what was right and wrong, but as soon as I could choose for myself, I chose anything but His way. I broke the law of chastity— I lied to my family about why I had to marry Jake. I never went to church after I got married, and then I got a divorce, taking Cate's dad away from her. Then I married you, making a mockery of the whole institution of marriage, and took the first opportunity I had to act on the impulses I knew needed to be ignored. I've broken all the rules, all the promises I made to Him, and now He's punishing me."

Andrew was silent for a long time. He had been a member of the Church for almost nine days. How was he supposed to know how to respond to this? But truth burned inside him, even if the knowledge or scriptural passages were unknown to him. "God loves you, Emma," he said softly. "More than we can know. What's happening to Michael isn't God's doing, and it isn't our fault. It's circumstance. The missionaries told me that when Christ atoned for us, He paid for our suffering, whether it was sin-induced or not, and He's the one that can help us now, if we let Him."

She said nothing, and he looked at the floor, afraid he'd offended her with his lecture. "You really believe that, don't you?" she finally said, still turned away.

"I really do," he answered.

"I wish I believed the way you do," she said in humility. "But every time I try, something happens that destroys whatever faith I gained. Then I just stop."

"I think those times are when you have to do better than ever. You have to pray more, read the scriptures with greater desire, and do all the things you know are right, so that your trials don't overcome you—at least that's what the missionaries said I should do."

"Are you doing it?" she asked. "Are you praying and reading and all the other stuff you're supposed to do?"

"Yeah," he said. "I'm hungry for it."

Again there was silence. "I've never had that hunger, Andrew." She paused as the emotion got the better of her, and her voice broke. "Even when I've tried to live a good life, do all the things I'm supposed to do, I've never had that hunger like you do, like my family does. I'm not sure I ever will."

Andrew had no more advice, nothing left to say, but he was reminded of what the missionaries had told him. Everyone has different experiences, different strengths, and different weaknesses. He didn't know why it was easy for him to accept and believe and desire the gospel when he'd lived most of his life without even caring. It made little sense that Emma, surrounded by that same truth all her life, would struggle to believe it or even want it in her life. But he did know that anything worth having in life was worth fighting for. "If you want it, even just want to want it, and you ask for it, He'll give it to you, Emma. I know He will."

She didn't respond, but he hoped his words had found a place within her heart. A few more minutes passed, and then she scooted over in the bed, away from him. He interpreted the gesture as a signal for him to leave, but when he stood, she spoke again. "Don't go," she whispered softly, cautiously. He turned toward her, but she was still turned away from him. After hesitating a few more moments, he sat back on the bed, removed his shoes and socks and unbuttoned the dress shirt he'd worn to work, leaving his pants and undershirt on. Then, without a word, he turned off the light and climbed into bed beside her.

For a few moments, he lay there, straight as a board, afraid of touching her, but finally he couldn't resist. He turned toward her, molding his body behind hers. He found her hand and laced his fingers through hers, basking in the closeness, the contact, and the comfort he found at her acceptance. He'd mailed the letter of intent to Mr. Austin already. He would receive it in another day or so, and the trust would be canceled. He assumed Emma had already contacted an attorney. The marriage was basically over, but being with her, touching her, knowing she wanted him to comfort her, was more fulfilling than any intimacy he had ever known. He didn't tell himself how nice it would be for life to be like this forever. He didn't ask himself what were the implications. He just closed his eyes and prayed silently that the Spirit would be with her—that she would find peace and that Michael would be okay.

CHAPTER 60

$\mathcal{A}$ndrew woke up the next morning with a start, not recalling how he had gotten here. When he looked to the side and saw Emma lying next to him, his memories returned, and he let out a breath of relief. Catherine's voice from the other room caught his attention next, and he reluctantly got out of bed.

It was almost eight o'clock when Emma found them in the kitchen sitting room. He looked up when she entered. "We already had Cheerios," he told her as he studied her face for her current mood. Was she angry? Embarrassed? Repentant? He couldn't tell.

"Are you going to work?" she asked, running her finger along the edge of the counter.

"I have to," Andrew replied. "Can I pick you up at three thirty?"

She nodded before turning around. She began to clean the kitchen. Her mood was still very much like last night—shocked and overwhelmed. He hoped she'd at least had a good night's sleep. He had little doubt she'd needed it.

At four fifteen the tension was becoming unbearable. He'd

picked Emma up right on time, but they'd been waiting for what seemed like hours. They'd checked in at the NICU early enough to stare at Michael for a few minutes before being ushered into a small conference room where they were told that the neonatal surgeon would join them. Andrew decided there should be a rule about making parents wait for meetings like this. When the surgeon finally entered, they all shook hands and sat down again.

For the next ten minutes, he explained the operation by pointing to a large diagram of the heart, reminding them that Michael's heart was the size of a walnut. Tests had revealed that the aortic valve had been damaged by the infection. The operation would be tricky because of Michael's size, but the pediatric cardiologist had a good track record of success. The good news, he said, was that they had treated the infection successfully, and it would not create further damage. Andrew nodded throughout the explanation and asked questions when necessary. Emma said nothing.

There was risk of secondary infection, rejection of the artificial valve, as well as the possibility of finding greater damage once they opened his tiny chest. Michael would have to see a cardiologist for the rest of his life and would need subsequent operations as he grew older. The doctor produced consent forms, which outlined each risk in excruciating detail. Emma closed her eyes as the surgeon explained the possible side effects of the anesthesia and the slight chance that Michael wouldn't make it through the surgery at all. But if the surgery wasn't performed, they could count on his further decline and eventual death. This was really their only option. Still Andrew felt like he was signing away his own soul when they finally signed the consent forms. The operation would begin at nine o'clock that evening, after all the remaining preparations had been made.

At Michael's incubator, Emma kissed her fingers and pressed them against the plastic, letting them linger there as she watched him. His tiny chest rose and fell rhythmically, and now and then he'd kick or clench his fist. But for the most part, he was completely still, his energy no longer lending itself to alertness but instead focused on keeping him alive. Finally she turned away as if not wanting him to see her cry, and they returned to the car.

The events of the last twenty-four hours seemed so surreal, almost dreamlike, and Andrew had to keep asking himself if it was really happening. "Why don't we pick up Cate and call your family to see if they can watch her tonight. We can order some pizza for dinner."

Emma nodded and retrieved Catherine when they pulled up to the day care center. When they got home, Cate ran for her toys while Emma sat on the couch, still lost in her own world. Andrew was worried about her but unsure of what he could possibly do about it. He pushed the blinking light on the answering machine in his study as he pulled out the phone book and looked up the number for Pizza Hut.

"Emma, Andrew? This is Tally. Just wanted to call and let you know Janet had our baby this afternoon, around two. It's a little girl. Seven pounds ten ounces. We're naming her Tiffany Julia, and we'll call her T.J. She's cute as a button. I'll call you later."

He walked out of the room with the phone book in hand. "Did you hear that?" he said with a smile, hoping the news would lighten Emma's mood.

Emma was wiping at her eyes. "Can you watch Cate for a while?" she asked. "I'd like to go for a walk."

"Uh, sure. Are you okay?"

"I'm fine, Andrew," she said. "I just need to collect my thoughts."

He nodded as she walked toward the door. It was mid-November and freezing outside, but she pulled the collar of her coat up, wrapped a scarf around her neck, and stuffed her hands in her pockets. *It will probably only be a few minutes,* he decided as he punched the number into the phone. If she needed a little time to collect her thoughts, he'd give it to her. They had a long night ahead.

The pizza came just as snow started to fall. Andrew ate a couple of slices, let Catherine eat a piece in her high chair, and changed his clothes—glad he'd thought to pack a bag when he'd stopped at the apartment that morning. The clock said it was six o'clock. Emma had been gone for an hour, and he started to worry. He'd already called and talked to Lacey, but since she was already watching Janet's and Tally's kids, he didn't ask her to watch Catherine as well. Instead, he called Emma's visiting teacher, whose number was on the fridge. Gloria said she'd be happy to watch Catherine for the night. Andrew waited until seven thirty, his worry for Emma growing by the minute, and finally loaded up Catherine and an overnight bag.

"Where's Emma?" Gloria asked after placing Catherine on her hip a few minutes later.

"I'm not sure," he said, unable to hide his worry. "She went for a walk and hasn't come back yet. I'm going to drive around and look for her."

Gloria creased her eyebrows. "How long ago did she leave?"

"Two hours."

"In this weather?"

Andrew nodded, echoing her concern. "I should have done something sooner, but . . . any ideas where she might be?"

Gloria shook her head. They lived in a residential neighborhood, so there were no stores or places of attraction that Emma might wander through. Andrew turned to leave. "Andrew," she called, "maybe it's none of my business, but has Emma's doctor said anything about postpartum depression?"

Andrew turned to face her fully just as Bryan, Gloria's husband, walked up behind her. "She dropped off my dishes a couple of weeks ago, and I wondered if maybe she wasn't dealing with things very well. She seemed very . . . distant."

"I've never met Emma's doctor," Andrew said. "I don't

know anything about it."

"You might want to talk to someone about it, just to be sure."

Andrew turned toward his car and thought of how Emma had been lately, how withdrawn and listless she'd become, and wondered if maybe Gloria was right. A greater urgency to find her quickened his pace. "Let us know if you need reinforcements," Bryan called from behind him.

"I will. Thanks for taking Cate."

He climbed back into the Jeep and began a slow drive through the streets of their neighborhood, hoping he'd find Emma soon. They were supposed to be at the hospital in an hour.

CHAPTER 61

*T*he Foothill Fourth Ward choir practice was over. Marlene Summerhays said good-bye to the last of the singers before gathering the sheets of music from the choir seats. Once they were neatly stacked, she put them in her "I Love to Sing" book bag and cautiously made her way down the steps at the front of the chapel. She'd had knee replacement surgery just two years ago and had to use caution when dealing with stairs. As she headed up the aisle she saw a young woman sitting in one of the back rows, leaning against the wall. Family members sometimes came to choir practice and watched, but everyone had gone home already. Marlene glanced at the clock on the wall and saw it was nearly eight thirty. She doubted there were other activities planned this late in the evening.

"Choir practice is over, young lady," she said sweetly when she approached the bench. "They'll be coming to lock up the ward house soon."

"I'll only be a few more minutes."

Marlene continued up the aisle but then stopped and came back down. Something didn't seem quite right. She sat on the end of the pew and followed the direction of the woman's gaze.

She seemed to be staring at the stained glass window that filled the opposite wall of the chapel. It was a depiction of the Father and Son appearing to Joseph Smith. "It's beautiful, isn't it," Marlene said.

"You don't see windows like this in ward houses very often," the young woman said.

"I guess not," Marlene said, looking at the window again. "It's probably quite expensive these days."

The woman nodded but continued to stare. For several minutes, Marlene sat with her, casting sidelong glances at her companion. The woman looked worn out, tired, and . . . hopeless. Marlene wondered if she was ill. "Are you all right, dear?" she finally asked.

"Everyone keeps asking me that."

"Then you must have a lot of people who care about you."

She hesitated before answering. "My husband told me I'm hard to love," she explained, still staring at the window.

"But he didn't say he didn't love you," Marlene answered. "Sometimes the hardest things in life are the ones most worth doing."

The woman said nothing for several minutes. When she spoke again, she was staring into her lap. "I told him I want a divorce."

"Why did you do that?"

"I'm not sure."

Marlene was beginning to have serious concerns about this woman. "It's a woman's prerogative to change her mind," she said lightly.

The woman looked at her then for the first time. "Even over something like that?"

"Especially over something like that."

"I'm not sure I love him anymore."

"If you loved him once, you can love him again."

"We have a son. He's very sick." Her voice had grown soft again, and she was once more staring at her hands in her lap.

"All the more reason to stick it out."

Another silence lapsed between them. "What's your name, honey?" Marlene asked.

"Emma."

"Emma what?"

"Davidson."

"Would it be okay if I called your husband for you?"

She didn't say anything more, so Marlene stood and made her way to the foyer phone where she called her neighbor. Together they searched the stake directory, finally finding an Emma Davidson in the fourteenth ward. Marlene wrote down the number and called, but no one answered. Next she called the Relief Society president, who gave her the number of Emma's visiting teacher, who gave her Brother Davidson's cell phone number. Brother Davidson answered immediately, and Marlene explained the situation.

"Oh, thank God," he breathed. "I've been looking for her everywhere."

"She doesn't seem well," Marlene explained. "But I'm not sure what's wrong."

"Right now," he said, "everything's wrong. I'll be there in a few minutes."

Andrew hurried into the chapel and then slowed his step. He made his way to the pew in front of her. Emma wouldn't look at him, and he thought she looked very small and very tired. The lady who had called him slipped out, leaving them alone.

"I'm sorry, Andrew," Emma said quietly.

"It's okay," he said, his irritation evaporating. "Did you get your thoughts collected?"

"Sort of," she said with a nod. She looked up suddenly, panic in her eyes. "What time is it?"

"I already called the hospital and told them we'd be late. They said they would go ahead without us, but I'd like to show you something before we go up there."

She looked up at him. He reached a hand toward her and smiled when she took it. Hand in hand, he led her to the Jeep and started driving toward downtown Salt Lake. The snow was still falling when they pulled up to Temple Square. "Have you been here before?"

She shook her head and stepped out of the car. It was closing time, and when they reached the outer doors of the visitor's center, a woman was just locking up.

"Can we please get in there?" Andrew pleaded.

"We're closed," she said. "I'm sorry, come back tomorrow."

"We really, really need to get in there tonight. Just for a few minutes."

She hesitated a moment but finally opened the door. "Five minutes," she said.

"Thank you." Andrew pulled Emma behind him until they reached a spiral ramp that led to the second floor. There was a mural of outer space painted along the wall and ceiling, curving around until it disappeared around itself. Andrew let go of her hand. "Go up there."

"Alone?"

"I'll come up in a minute, but I want you to see it by yourself first."

Emma slowly began climbing the ramp, looking at the beautiful depiction as she went. She was reminded of the phrase "worlds without end." A peace fell upon her as she slowly rose, until she turned the corner. Her eyes traveled up the huge expanse of brilliant white marble as she continued walking. Soon she stood facing the massive sculpture of Christ. She'd seen it in pictures but hadn't realized how truly magnificent it was. She took a few steps back so she could see the entire edifice and a loud voice began to speak, momentarily startling her. "I am Jesus Christ, the creator of this world and all things. . . ."

Unprepared for the wave of emotion that washed over her as she listened to the words. Then she bowed her head and pressed her hands to her face. "Come unto me. . . I am He who died for you. . . I will make your burdens light." Could he?

Could he really lighten her burdens that seemed beyond lifting? Who was she to him?

"For you are my little ones."

Tears began to stream down her cheeks, and she moved forward so that she could see the imprints on His hands and the spear mark in His side. Her eyes traveled back to His face, and Andrew's words from the other night came back to her. *He atoned for our suffering, sin-induced or not.* She closed her eyes then and slowly sank to her knees.

Emma had been taught that all He asked was a broken heart and a contrite spirit. Until now she hadn't been sure what that meant. Now she felt she understood. She was broken inside, and her spirit felt as if it had been in mourning for a very long time. Somewhere in her life she'd lost hope—lost hold of all the good things she'd been taught to surround her-self with. Last night she'd told Andrew she didn't know if she would ever feel the hunger he claimed to possess. He had said that if she wanted it—even wanted to want it—she could have it. Hot tears continued to fall, and she could feel her heart soften. The prayer of her heart was without words, but the feelings seemed to be enough. For perhaps the first time in her adult life, she felt as if her prayer was heard, and she was reminded that she was not alone. There were people all around her, asking that she let them help her.

As she opened her eyes and gazed at the statue once more, she hoped it wasn't too late to fix what she'd been working so hard to destroy.

She thought of Andrew, and as she did, she could feel his presence. She turned slightly, still on her knees, and saw him sitting on one of the benches behind her. She wondered how long he'd been there. "Andrew?" she whispered, surprised at the change in her voice. It sounded alive like it hadn't for a long time. She watched him stand and walk toward her. As he sank to his knees beside her, she looked into his eyes and tried to think of what to say.

Almost a minute passed while she searched. He just looked at her, his expression soft. She thought back to the day in the pool, the look in his eyes. She thought she'd seen a void, a hunger, and she noticed it wasn't there anymore. She wondered if he saw the same thing in her eyes now. She opened her mouth several times to speak, but the words wouldn't come.

Finally he smiled and nodded his head. "I know exactly what you mean."

CHAPTER 62

*I*t was nearly two the next morning when the doctor came out to say that the surgery had gone perfectly. Through-out the preceding hours, they had taken turns praying and pacing—apparently it had paid off. It would be another thirty minutes before they could see Michael, but the surgeon had every expectation that he would be as good as new in a few weeks. Emma and Andrew watched him leave and then turned, embracing one another to share their relief that he was all right.

Emma pulled away, and Andrew noticed how much softer her countenance had become. She had a contented smile on her face as she tucked her hair behind her ear and turned toward the doorway. "I wish we could see him now," she said with longing.

"Emma," Andrew said with his heart in his throat. He'd been trying to find an opportunity to talk to her all night, but their anxiety had been too intense. Now, however, he worried that if he didn't take advantage of this time they had together, and the newness of their trust and friendship, he might lose his chance altogether.

She turned to look at him.

"I thought it was you that night at the ski resort."

Hardness crossed her features, and she shook her head. "Andrew, please." She turned away, and he took a few steps to close the gap between them and placed his hand on her arm.

"I did," he said, continuing before she could stop him. "When I woke up that morning, someone was in my shower, and I only remembered bits and pieces of what had happened. I panicked at what I thought I had done, since I was *sure* it couldn't have been you. I couldn't imagine that you would have spent the night with me. But I had thought it was you—or that I'd fantasized it was, and that made me even sicker."

Emma stared at the floor, but at least she was listening. He hurried to finish. "I remembered saying your name. I remembered feeling your lips on mine and thinking they were familiar—but I reasoned that it was impossible. For all those months, I beat myself up over what I'd done, over the betrayal—and yet at night I dreamed of you. I lived those moments over and over. But it only seemed to further convince me of what a twisted man I was. I've never had a one-night stand, Emma. I truly believed it was you, and being with you was something I wanted very much—but not like that. I've thought many times where we could have been had that night not happened. I think we could have found a great deal of happiness together by now."

She turned her face and met his eye for the first time, and although he saw the doubt there, he also saw a spark of hope. "When I realized you were pregnant, I flew to L.A. intent on killing Mark for—"

"Mark?" Emma said in confusion, her eyebrows nearly touching.

"I thought that . . . he and you . . ."

Emma looked away, offended by the insinuation. "You didn't think I would *possibly* sleep with you, my husband, but you thought I'd sleep with Mark?"

"I know, it's crazy," Andrew explained. "But I *knew* I hadn't been with you, and he was the only other person I could think of—if it makes you feel any better, he was as offended by my assumption as you are right now."

She shook her head, but she met his eyes again and seemed hungry for more proof, more evidence that what he was saying was true. "Once he told me the truth, everything made so much sense. I understood why it was you invading my dreams and not some stranger. I realized why you hadn't called me and how devastating it must have been to you, and I remembered one more thing that until then I thought had been a pure figment of my fractured recollection." He watched her to make sure he had her full attention, and then he let his hand slide down her arm and take her fingers in his grip. "I remembered you saying that you were falling in love with me."

Emma's cheeks colored, and she dropped his hand and tried to walk away, but he grabbed both her arms and made her face him. "I'm not trying to hold you to that, Emma, and I know that I deserve your distrust." The emotion rose into his face, and for all his efforts to keep it down he couldn't. He lowered his voice, hoping it wouldn't shake, and continued. "But please believe me when I tell you how sorry I am. I haven't had a single drink since that night, and I've thought about you every day since it happened, trying to work up the courage to face you again and not knowing what to say. But I am so sorry. The last thing I have *ever* wanted was to hurt you, and I want the chance to make up for the pain I've already caused."

Tears had slowly risen in Emma's eyes as he spoke, and he prayed that she would open her heart to what he'd told her. "Andrew, I just . . ."

"Just what?" he prodded when she didn't finish.

"I just don't know where to go from here. I'm not sure what I want or what I have left to give."

"Me neither," Andrew agreed. "But you said once that you believed true love was something two people grew into through trials and sacrifice. I'm asking you to grow with me. If I could have my way, I would want to go through the rest of my life with you."

Her expression turned dubious, and he worried that perhaps he'd said too much. But he was speaking from his heart, and he needed to say what he felt. "I've never met anyone like you, Emma. I'm so impressed with the woman you are, with your strength and tenderness. You make me a better man, and you've given me motivation to change my life."

"Maybe you just see in me what you haven't had the chance to see because the women you've known before were so different. Maybe you'll change your mind."

"I don't think so," he whispered.

"But you don't know for sure."

Andrew took a breath. No, of course he didn't know for sure—but he had a very good feeling, and he wanted to go with it. He wanted her to have the same feeling, the same confidence, and he knew it was something she would have to discover for herself.

"Let's find out," Andrew said, giving her arms a little squeeze. "Let's find out together."

"Is this about the trust?"

Oh, she was impossible! "It has nothing to do with the trust. I already sent in the intent to withdraw. In fact, we should let the divorce go through and start all over again. Don't you see? I don't care about the money anymore. I care about you and Michael and the family we can become—that's *all* that matters. Please let us try. Let me prove to you how serious I am about making this work."

Emma looked at him, and he sincerely hoped that his eyes showed her how real those words were to him. "I think I'd like that," she finally said, and he felt like he'd been holding his breath. She reached up and placed her hand on his face. "You're a remarkable man, Andrew."

"All because of you."

That night Andrew dreamed of his mother once more. She told him right away that she wouldn't be back for a while.

"Why not?"

"Because we both have work to do."

"But if I'm asleep . . ."

"Andrew," she said, silencing his protests, "to everything there is a season, and our visits are over, for now. You're on the right path, you're going the right way, and I have other things to do. But don't lose sight of the changes you've made or the reasons you've made them. You have a gift, and you have a work to do. Go toward the temple—make your family strong. When you're ready, I'll be back."

He didn't wake up that time, not until morning. But when he did awake, he knew it was over. The reason she'd been coming was accomplished, and he could let her go—for now—knowing that it wouldn't be forever.

CHAPTER 63

Twenty-seven days later, Andrew held the door open while Emma fussed with the car seat. "You're letting in all the cold air," he said as he tried to shield the open door with his own body. It was mid-December, two weeks before Christmas, and Michael was finally coming home. He was still on oxygen and a heart monitor, but he was almost six pounds and doing too well to stay in the hospital any longer.

"Then shut the door," Emma chided, pulling her foot in so he wouldn't shut the door on it.

Good idea, he thought. He shut the door and hurried to the driver's side. He had butterflies at the thought that there would now be no nurses and doctors to take care of Michael—just them, Emma and Andrew Davidson. "Is he okay?" Andrew asked over his shoulder once he had fastened his seat belt.

Emma tucked a lock of hair behind her ear and looked up at him, her face glowing. "He's fine," she said. Andrew nodded and started the car, slowly driving through the parking lot. Once out in traffic, he got into the slow lane and drove carefully with both hands on the steering wheel.

"You could probably go the speed limit," Emma teased.

He ignored her. He wasn't taking any chances. When they got home, they both fussed over Michael until finally setting him in his crib—and then they just stared. "I can't believe he's home," Andrew breathed, placing his hand on Emma's shoulder.

She let out a contented sigh and turned to look at him. "I'm glad you're home too."

Andrew smiled and leaned down to plant a very light kiss on her forehead. He'd moved back into the guest room just last week.

Following Michael's surgery, Emma had gone to see her doctor—something she'd been avoiding. As it turned out, Gloria had been right. Emma was suffering from more than difficult circumstances. Weekly meetings with a counselor and a small white pill every morning had brought her out of the despair in which she'd been immersed, and with it came changes without number. She began to include Andrew in her life, inviting him to dinner and working hard to keep things good between them. Still, he'd been surprised when she asked him to move back. But he'd known better than to argue. Her bitterness may have passed, but that "Emma fire" was as strong as ever. The comfortable bantering friendship they'd once had was easier to resurrect than they had thought, and they became skilled at sparring once more—but without causing any damage.

Mr. Austin had called when he received the letter of intent. To say he was shocked that they would file for divorce just three and a half months before the payoff date was an understatement. At that time, Andrew was still living in his apartment, and he explained the situation honestly. Mr. Austin finally hung up, annoyed and irritated.

Andrew looked at Emma now and smiled. There was so much he wanted to say, so many things he wanted to discuss, but he didn't feel they were ready yet. What they had between them was still very fragile, and he knew that he had to treat it as such if he hoped to make it stronger.

She looked sheepishly at the ground. "Thank you for not giving up on me, Andrew," she said in a humble voice that made his heart swell. "I treated you horribly, and I'm sorry."

"I'm sorry too," he said, tucking her hair behind her ear. "But that's behind us now."

She looked up at him, hopeful skepticism in her eyes. "You think so?"

"I do."

"Did I mention I'm glad you're here?" she said after a moment.

"Yes, but I don't mind hearing it again."

EPILOGUE

I know it's in here somewhere," Andrew said, the frustration in his voice evident. Mark had met him at the offices of Austin, Longhorn, and Green, and they'd been reading through the trust information for almost an hour already, going through it fast at first and now more slowly so they wouldn't miss what they were looking for.

After things had settled between Emma and himself, Andrew had set about repairing his relationship with Mark. Lucky for him, Mark was a forgiving man, and Andrew was glad to have his best friend back.

Andrew had also gotten a call from Mr. Austin just two weeks ago informing him Emma had never followed through with her pursuit of the divorce; the Intent to Withdraw form had never been filed. This meant he still had two and a half million dollars coming to him. That should have been good news.

"Are you sure?" Mark said. "Maybe you made up the loophole."

Andrew shook his head as he continued to read down the page, following each line with his finger. "It's here," he said. "I know it is." What he didn't say was that he'd had a dream about it and seen it as clear as day. Mark wouldn't put much stock in Andrew's dreams, so Andrew had kept that bit of information to himself. Tally said that dreams were a spiritual gift, but Andrew still worried that it meant he was crazy. But he had found that by paying attention to the things that went on in his head at night, amazing things seemed to happen.

He looked up at the clock and let out a breath. He'd thought that he would turn right to it, but it was taking longer than he expected, and Mr. Austin said he would be locking up the office at eight o'clock. It was seven fifteen already.

"If I stood to inherit two and a half million dollars, I don't think I'd want a loophole," Mark said.

Andrew didn't respond at first. He understood Mark's perspective very well. He'd battled back and forth with that same idea. "I can't risk Emma ever thinking I'm in this for the money," he answered, still scanning. "And I don't want Michael to face the same conflicts I'm facing."

"Oh, yeah, I guess he'd be eligible just like you—what's he going to think of you screwing that up for him?"

Andrew gave Mark a sour look. "Hopefully he'll say thank you."

"I can't believe Emma's letting you do this," Mark continued.

"She's not thrilled," Andrew replied, turning yet another page. "In fact she threatened to divorce me—then realized that meant I wouldn't get the money anyway. But eventually she saw my perspective—unlike *some* people I could mention. It's not like I don't make a good living anyway."

Mark snorted and turned yet another page. The two men were silent for several minutes, and Andrew began wondering if perhaps his dream had been just that—a dream. Maybe he *had* made it up.

"I think I found it!"

Andrew looked up. "Really?"

"Yeah," Mark said, his eyes moving quickly across the

page. "It's real legal terminology, but basically it says that the only way to dissolve the trust is for an heir to take legal action within seven days of his thirtieth birthday and return all funds to the trust." He paused while reading ahead a little further.

"If any heir is willing to do this, all other heirs will split one half of the gross trust amount between them, with a ceiling of four hundred thousand dollars. Blah, blah, blah—that money will be placed in a separate trust that they will get full access to on their thirtieth birthday, without meeting the requirements of the original trust. But the Davidson Invested Trust will be dissolved. The heir that chooses to exercise this option will receive no payoff, and the money left in the Davidson Trust after the living heirs' portions have been secured will be donated to . . . the Humane Society of New Jersey?" Mark looked up. "This guy was truly whacked."

"What page are you on?"

"Uh . . . 125," Mark said as he read through the information again. Andrew flipped pages and read it himself. When he finished, he smiled—he'd done it! He'd found the way out.

"I can't believe you're happy about this," Mark said after watching him for a few more seconds.

"I'm ecstatic about this," Andrew said. He leaned back and punched his fist in the air as a sign of triumph. "Now neither of us will ever wonder why we're in this marriage—this is an answer to our prayers."

"Although without the trust you wouldn't even be together," Mark reminded him.

"I'm not so sure," Andrew said. "I have a feeling that Emma and I are just such stubborn souls that we needed something to kick us into being together. But I don't want to tempt my son with the same choice. It's caused too much heartache for me to wish it on someone else. Free agency should stay free, not looped into eligibility requirements. I want Michael to fall in love with his whole heart, not with his bank account in mind."

"Whatever," Mark said as he stood and stretched his arms

over his head. "If we hurry we can make it to the airport in time for your flight home."

"Great," Andrew said. "I'll just let Mr. Austin know this is my intent and that I'll be back the day after my thirtieth birthday to get this ball rolling."

Andrew didn't get home until nearly midnight, and he let himself in as quietly as possible. He checked on Michael, now oxygen free but still on a heart monitor at night. He would have ongoing issues with his heart for the rest of his life, but he was doing well and weighing in at ten pounds. Catherine insisted on sleeping in Michael's room. Andrew pulled the blanket up to her chin, smiling at the "I'm a big sister" night-gown she always slept in. Once assured the kids were safe and sound, he crept into the master bedroom.

Andrew and Emma had taken things slowly after he moved back in. Emma had gone back to school in the evenings, and they focused on their friendship first—as they should have in the beginning. Emma had made her peace with the Church, finally understanding that being righteous doesn't mean being perfect, and that she could take it at her own pace. Andrew made sure to let the choices she made in relation to the gospel be hers and hers alone. That freedom had led her back to the precepts she'd always known were true.

When Michael had officially turned three months old—just two weeks before—Emma surprised Andrew with a can-dlelight dinner after the kids were asleep. The time together led to a detailed discussion of their future, which led to Andrew moving out of the guest room once and for all. They would begin temple preparation courses in a few weeks, looking forward to the anniversary of Andrew's baptism, when they hoped to be sealed to their son.

Life was good.

"How did it go?" Emma whispered in the dark as he

shrugged off his jacket.

He made his way to the bed, glad she was awake. Sitting down, he looked at her face and brushed her hair behind her ear.

"Just as I expected," he said, bending down to kiss her on the mouth. "I'll need to go back next week to attend to the actual legalities, but at least I found it—I was beginning to wonder. How did things go here while I was gone?"

"It's never the same without you," she said. Her hand brushed against his, and he captured it, raising it to his lips.

"I love you, Emma," he said against the back of her hand.

"I know you do," she whispered back. "I just hope you don't resent me for this later."

"It was my choice. You tried to get me to keep it."

"You still can."

"Not with a clear conscience."

"You're a remarkable man, Andrew Davidson."

"And . . . ?"

She laughed at the ongoing joke they had between them. "And I love you too." He couldn't seem to hear that often enough.

Everything he'd never wanted was everything he'd been missing all along.

AUTHOR'S NOTE

About sixty thousand cases of Hyperemesis Gravidarum (HG) are reported annually, or less than 1 percent of pregnant women. That number, however, shows only those hospitalized and properly diagnosed. Conservative estimates put the nationwide price tag on HG hospitalizations at nearly two million dollars every year.

Though HG is directly related to pregnancy, its exact cause is not known. It is diagnosed through symptoms, the most common of which are

- Dehydration and production of keytones
- Malnutrition
- Metabolic imbalances
- Severe vomiting that interferes with daily life, often twenty to thirty times a day
- Loss of more than 5 percent of prepregnancy body weight, but usually 10 percent or more

There is no cure for HG, and only moderate symptom relief comes from antinausea medications, dehydration therapy, and intravenous nutrient renewal. HG sometimes subsides by the twenty-first week, but in 40 percent of women who have it, it lasts the entire pregnancy. Miscarriage is quite common, usually resulting from severe dehydration or persistent vomiting, which causes such severe muscle spasms that the embryo detaches from the uterine wall. HG also causes a heightened risk of premature labor.

Symptoms typically present themselves four to six weeks into the pregnancy. If unresolved during pregnancy, symptoms disappear twenty-four to seventy-two hours after delivery.

On the positive side, the effects on the baby are minimal if the pregnancy goes to term. The baby will still draw nutrients from the mother, and there seem to be no development disorders during pregnancy or after birth. Typically, HG worsens with each subsequent pregnancy—as did Emma's case in this novel.

Most textbooks state that HG is a psychological disorder rather than a physiological one, despite ongoing research proving otherwise. Researchers believe that HG is related to human chorionic gonadotropic (hCG), which is secreted by the fetus, and to increased thyroid levels. Research is still being done on these relationships.

Whether or not it is a psychological disorder, HG certainly has a psychological impact on the woman and her family. It is a debilitating disease that often leaves the sufferer depressed and despondent.

During my research for this book, I spoke with women whose doctors advised them to abort their pregnancies. One woman did so because she felt that she would die if she didn't. The effects of that choice—physical, spiritual, and emotional— have haunted her for many years. I learned of insurance companies that also try to persuade women in this situation to abort. Many women I spoke to had no idea that there was a name for their condition.

Though I have suffered from my own complications during pregnancy, I have not experienced HG firsthand. My heart goes out to those women who suffer so much during pregnancy. Emma's struggle with HG was a summation of many experiences—more severe than some but less severe than others.

For more information, visit the following resources:

www.hyperemesis.org

www.pregnancytoday.com

ABOUT THE AUTHOR

Josi Kilpack was born and raised in Salt Lake City and graduated from Olympus High School. Actively involved in church and community, she also enjoys reading, spending time with her family, traveling, and baking. She is the author of *Star Struck, Tempest Tossed, Surrounded by Strangers,* and *Earning Eternity,* all published by Cedar Fort.

Josi lives in Willard, Utah, with her husband, Lee, her four children, a cat, and three chickens. For more information about Josi and her books, go to www.josiskilpack.com.